D1630513

Sue

This book should be returned to any branch of the
Lancashire County Library on or before the date shown

08. SEP 08.

12. SEP 08.

16. MAR 09.

02. OCT 08.

19. JUN 09.

10. NOV 08

06. AUG 09.

11. DEC 08

02 OCT 09.

10. FEB 09.

Lancashire County Library
Bowran Street
Preston PR1 2UX

Lancashire
County Council

www.lancashire.gov.uk/libraries

Praise for Niobia Bryant

"[*Admission of Love* is] a well-crafted story with engaging secondary characters."

—*Affaire de Coeur*

"*Three Times a Lady* . . . this sneaky little romance heats up gradually, and then sizzles until done . . ."

—*Doubleday/Black Expression Book Club*

"*Heavenly Match* is a wonderfully romantic story with an air of mystery and suspense that draws the reader in, encouraging them to put aside everything and everyone until they have read the book in its entirety."

—*The RAWSISTAZ Reviewers*

"Sexy as sin describes [*Can't Get Next to You*] this provocative novel to a T."

—*Romantic Times*

"Run to the bookstore and pick up this delightful read. This reunion story is touching, warm, sensuous, and at times, sad. But just try to put [*Let's Do It Again*] down."

—*Romantic Times*

"Niobia Bryant has penned an awe-inspiring tale of finding true love no matter the consequence. Thoroughly enjoyed and highly recommended, *Heated* is sure to please."

—*The RAWSISTAZ Reviewers*

"[*Count on This* has] . . . sassy humor and sexy scenes . . ."

—*Romantic Times*

"In Bryant's first mainstream fiction offering, she does a great job of bringing forth characters that are feisty, diverse, and interesting . . . Bryant establishes well-developed characters. *Live and Learn* is a pleasurable reading experience."

—*Romantic Times*

Other Books by Niobia Bryant

ROMANCE
Admission of Love
Three Times a Lady
Heavenly Match
Can't Get Next to You
Let's Do It Again
Count on This
Heated
Hot Like Fire

WOMEN'S FICTION
Live and Learn
Show and Tell

ANTHOLOGIES
You Never Know (novella: "Could It Be?")

Show and Tell

Niobia Bryant

KENSINGTON PUBLISHING CORP.
http://www.kensingtonbooks.com

DAFINA BOOKS are published by

Kensington Publishing Corp.
850 Third Avenue
New York, NY 10022

Copyright © 2008 by Niobia Bryant

All Kensington titles, imprints, and distributed lines are available at special quantity discounts for bulk purchases for sales promotion, premiums, fund-raising, educational, or institutional use.

Special book excerpts or customized printings can also be created to fit specific needs. For details, write or phone the office of the Kensington Special Sales Manager: Attn. Special Sales Department. Kensington Publishing Corp., 850 Third Avenue, New York, NY 10022. Phone: 1-800-221-2647.

Dafina and the Dafina logo Reg. U.S. Pat. & TM Off.

ISBN-13: 978-0-7582-1722-6
ISBN-10: 0-7582-1722-6

First Printing: June 2008

10 9 8 7 6 5 4 3 2 1

Printed in the United States of America

For every little ghetto girl with big dreams.

Believe . . .

ACKNOWLEDGMENTS

Tony. Mama. Caleb. TJ.
Selena James. Robin E. Cook. Claudia Menza.
Kim Louise. Adrianne Byrd. Melanie Schuster.
Gloria Naylor. Tina McElroy Ansa. Octavia Butler.
Oprah. Idris Elba. Mary J Blige. Tyler Perry.
Martin Lawrence. Steve Harvey. Bernie Mac.
Niobia Bryant News Yahoo Group. My MySpace friends.
Black book clubs and bookstores.

And *most of all*, the readers.

For many different reasons I thank you all.

Part One

"Once Again, It's on"

Prologue

Ladies

2000

The four teenage girls walked through the double doors of University High's cafeteria like they owned the school. They knew without looking that all eyes were on them. Hating them and hating on them. They were used to it and maybe even thrived on it a bit. Popularity. Envy. High school fame.

Even as they settled at "their" table and began munching on the sandwiches they purchased from the store up the street—of course the cafeteria food was a no-no—people watched them. Wanted to be them. Wanted to be with them. But it was just the four.

Friends since freshman year, they weren't looking to enlarge their clique. It was them and only them. One for all and all for one. Even though they all were as different as night and day, they clicked. They had each other's backs. They knew their friendship would last past their high school years.

"Did y'all see the new Biggie video last night?" Keesha Lands asked, in the Tommy Hilfiger tank she wore with tight-fitting jeans. Her gold herringbone chain and bamboo earrings gleamed against her smooth dark skin and seemed to glisten in her cat-shaped eyes.

"Not me," Latoya James said, looking prim and proper as always in her white collared shirt and ankle-length navy blue skirt with her shoulder-length hair pulled back into a tight ponytail that seemed to make her caramel complexion stretch.

Danielle Johnson rolled her deep-set eyes heavenward as she applied pale pink lip gloss that perfectly matched her fair complexion and pretty features. "My new foster family let their sickening sons watch *Nickelodeon* last night," she said, putting the gloss into her Esprit purse before taking a bite of food. She made sure not to spill a drop on her dark denim dress.

"Well, I'm an only child and my parents ain't churchy, so you know I was right there in front of the TV," Monica Winters said, flipping her thick shoulder-length jet black hair over her shoulder as she flashed them a sassy smile on her cinnamon face. She did a little dance in her seat and winked at Keesha.

Keesha started rapping the words to "Juicy" and the girls all joined in with her. Even Latoya knew the words, although her parents ran a secular music-free zone. Ever since pulling the shy church girl into their fold, the girls were sure to bring Latoya up to speed on everything fun and fly.

They all laughed and gave each other high fives after they finished.

"Well, I've decided to call myself Dom," Keesha stated with confidence.

"Dom?" the other girls all asked in unison.

"Yup, Dom as in Dom Perignon," she explained with attitude. She pointed to Latoya. "You're Moët . . . Danielle, you're Cristal—"

"What about me?" Monica asked, feeling left out.

"I don't know any more champagnes," Keesha said with a helpless shrug. "But Biggie's always talking about Alizé. I heard it's a real sweet drink with liquor in it."

"Then that's me to a tee," Monica said with satisfaction.

The four girls all raised their cans of soda and toasted their new names.

Chapter One

Cristal

"Hello, this is Cristal again.
I have my mind on money and money on my mind."

2008

Okay. Let me explain how I feel in my man's arms—*if* it is at all explainable. I feel secure. Loved. Cherished. Pampered. Needed. Perhaps most important of all . . . I feel wanted. Growing up as a foster kid and not knowing if my parents were dead, alive, or indifferent, feeling wanted is important as hell to me.

I am Cristal, or Danielle Johnson, and my man is Mohammed Ahmed. He is tall, handsome, and strong with cocoa-scented dreads that reach to his waist. He is everything I ever needed and nothing that I ever wanted.

Just *try* to make me leave him.

"Danielle," he whispers in my ear with that sexy Jamaican lilt.

I shiver as he presses his warm naked body above mine. My legs spread with ease as I wrap them around his waist. His body and the bed sandwich me. The feel of his hard dick against my belly makes me anxious. Ready. Waiting.

As he bends his strong muscled back to lower his mouth—that delicious and skillful mouth—to my breast, he circles his tongue around my nipple. Clockwise. Counterclockwise. He uses his strong hips to prod the tip of his dick between my lips. We both gasp hotly.

He circles his hips, pressing his hardness against my walls. Clockwise. Counterclockwise.

Jesus.

These moments in his arms and his bed are worth it all. Worth every damn thing I gave up for him. For this. Each stroke delivers my point home.

The money.

Pop.

The fame.

Pop-pop.

The fancy houses and cars.

Pop-pop-pop.

The glamorous life.

Pop-pop-pop-pop.

Mrs. Sahad Linx.

Pop-pop-pop-pop-pop-pop-pop.

All of it. Gone.

We are in tune with one another. United. Joined. He knows he is making me cum and that makes his dick harder than jail time. And that makes me cum even harder until I am panting. Sweating. Clutching him with my pussy walls and my limbs as he strokes harder and faster inside of me.

"Yes," I cry out as he leans up a bit to look down at me with those silky brown eyes I love.

His sweat drips down onto my titties as each of his pumps makes them bounce up and down. "Dick good ain't it?" he asks roughly as his face gets intense. "Huh? Huh?"

"Yes, baby, yes," I whisper as I reach up to caress his handsome face with my quivering hands.

His head whips to the right to capture my fingers in his mouth. He sucks them deeply as he slows down his strokes to a lethal grind that brings the base of that dick against my clit.

Damn. Goddamn. Damn. Damn.

"Watch this, Miss Danielle," he says thickly around my fingers.

I already know what time it is.

His entire body freezes as he looks hotly down into my eyes. I feel the jolt of his dick against my clit as he fills me with his cum. He smiles as he licks my fingers like the freak that he is. Each pluck of my clit pushes me further over the edge until I am working my hips up and down off the bed to pull downward on *my* dick. His mouth forms a circle as he closes his eyes and pushes down deeper into me.

I reach up to snatch off the leather strap holding his hair and his dreads surround our heads like a curtain. "Who the best? Huh? Who?" I whisper up to him.

"Danielle . . . Danielle . . . Danielle," he chants as I drain that dick until it is empty.

With one final kiss to my lips, he rolls over onto his back and then pulls my weak body to his side. I gladly snuggle my face against his chest and take a deep breath of his scent like I can absorb it into me. With his free arm, he reaches over to turn off the lamp.

"Damn, that was good," he whispers into the darkness before he slaps my butt cheek playfully.

"I aim to please," I whisper back with a smile.

He laughs a little but soon his snores fill the air.

Damn, I love him.

"Good morning, Miss Danielle."

I open my eyes and stretch. There he is just as constant as time looking down at me as he lays on his side on the bed. Okay, I love him but I do not do morning breath. Okay? All right.

I pull the thin sheet up over my nose. "Good morning."

Mohammed just laughs at me before he flings back the covers and rolls out of bed. "You have time for breakfast?" he asks over his broad shoulder.

I hardly hear him. I am too busy letting my eyes skim over the hard details of his back and buttocks. "No, I did not bring a change of clothes," I finally answer once he turns fully to look at me.

Mohammed reaches down to open a drawer. "What do we have here?" he says mockingly. "An empty drawer. What should we fill it with? Any suggestions, Danielle?"

I give him a sarcastic smile. First a drawer and then some of the closet and then pack up all your things and move in. Nothing doing.

The last time I lived with a man he threw me out of his penthouse apartment. Well, he caught me cheating (ahem, *with* Mohammed) but that did not excuse the fact that if I had not kept my apartment for my friends, Dom and Moët, to live in, then my pretty high-yellow behind would have been homeless. To make matters worse, he kept mostly everything he ever bought me, even down to my lacy La Perla underwear.

No. I am nicely settled back in my beautiful apartment in The Top in Livingston. I have my best friends to help me keep up the hefty rent. Sure, I had to get used to the lack of quiet or privacy but it is *mine* and no one can throw me out.

Plus . . . Mohammed's house left *a lot* to be desired.

"One day, baby. One day," I promise as I roll out of bed.

I look at him and I know from the look on his face that he did not believe me. Truth. He is smart not to. I begin to climb back in the Gap charcoal gray turtleneck and pencil skirt I wore to our dinner date to IHOP last night. I wish I had a pair of sneakers to throw on instead of my suede high-heeled boots. As soon as I pull on my black leather trench, I walk over to where Mohammed is lounging across the foot of the bed watching a recap of some football game.

"Enjoy your day off," I tell him as I bend down to snuggle his cheek.

Mohammed is the repair man at The Top. My friends, Dom, Alizé, and Moët, still cannot believe I am with him. Not when my life used to be about men who helped keep me from my life of robbing Peter to pay Paul. Athletes. Celebrities. Wealthy businessmen. I had been on the hunt to be the ultimate celebrity wife. My ex-fiancé Sahad Linx is the CEO of Platinum Records. His money, his fame, and his lifestyle had almost been mine. I let it slip through my fingers like sand so that my hands were free to grab Mohammed.

He reaches across to lightly touch my face and I get chills. Fuck the money and the fame. I got love and lots of it.

"See you later?" he asks in that Jamaican accent that has the power to make me wet.

"Yes," I whisper against his lips.

Walking out of that bedroom and leaving my man in the bed

naked, willing, and with his dick rising is almost as hard as he is. I try not to judge his house as I grab my hobo from the kitchen table. I can fit half of Mohammed's entire three-bedroom house inside my living room. It is furnished just like the bachelor he is. Mismatched this. Tore-up that. Wal-Mart this. Target that. Mohammed likes to say his house has character. Whatever.

I look inside my Gucci purse (a purchase from my more glamorous days) for my keys and my hand rubs across my "bible." Forgetting the keys, I pick up the address book. Inside is each and every man I have ever dated or slept with. For each man there is a brief bio and a photo, if I had one. I used dollar signs to rate how free giving they were with their money, and stars to rate how good they were in bed. The more dollar signs and stars the better.

But this book isn't me anymore. Since I have been with Mohammed I have not made an entry. I have not called one number. I have good friends. A good man. A good life.

I am happy. I am.

Then why do I still have it?

Ignoring the answer to that million-dollar question, I shove the address book down deep in my bag. I finally close my fingers around the keys before I rush out of the house.

Chapter Two

Alizé

*"Whaddup y'all. It's your girl Alizé. Different day . . .
same old bullshit."*

I can do this. I have to do this. That's all there is to it. Fuck it.
I clear my throat as I double-check my appearance in the full-
length mirror. The navy pinstripe Gucci suit is a far cry from my
ghetto fabulous style but I can't stroll my ass into anyone's office in
booty shorts and gold high heels. There is a time and place for
everything. Trust. So this suit is made to instill power while still delivering style. I'm feeling pretty chic but my confidence level is at
an all-time low. Not because of anything physical. Shit, I'm cute as
hell and I know it. Just try having to face the man you love—ahem,
once loved—after he has married another woman. Face his ass.
Work with his ass. Try to pretend to his ass that I do not give a shit
that he married her just months after *I* turned down his offer to
make our platonic friendship something more. Just try.

I grab my Gucci briefcase. My goals to take corporate America by
storm ain't changed so I will just have to knuckle up, stroll into that
paid internship with my head held high and my heart protected. I already turned down the offer to intern at Braun, Weber last fall semester because I couldn't face Cameron Steele, who is the Vice
President of Mergers and Acquisitions for the large investment firm.
He's married now and living in New York. I'm fine with it. Time to
move the hell on. New year. New things. It's all about the MBA,
baby. Trust.

With one last wink at my reflection that is a big old front, I left my bedroom. While I'm in school—working hard to be able to make the money . . . one day—I still live with Mom. She is the epitome of a divorcée who'd rather be anything else. Unfortunately, my dad doesn't feel the same about reconciling as she does. *One day*, I hope to myself—and that's one day my mom will move on and not one day my dad will give in.

I walk to the head of the wooden staircase. I hate the nerves that clutch my guts just before I can take the first step.

Having my leg broken in half makes me anxious as hell. Anything that can lead to me breaking it again fucks with me real bad. My panic only lasts in those moments just before my foot hits the steps, but it's there each and every time. I shake away a flash of Rah's angry face looking down at me as I lay on the floor just before he raised his foot and stomped my leg, shattering it in two. That dumb motherfucker is in jail for what he did to me. Just like my ex-friend Dom's betraying ass is struggling to stay her project ass off of drugs.

Humph. *My* friend since high school slept with my man and then dimed me out to him about cheating. I walked into his apartment that night to find him fucking her nasty stripper ass and then he gone have the nerve to fight me. Ain't that some shit?

I feel anger rising like crazy.

I stop, close my eyes, and breathe as I count to one hundred slowly. It's a trick my therapist, Dr. Locke, taught me to overcome my anger. Shit, who wouldn't be mad about the betrayal of a friend, the betrayal of your man *with* your friend, losing the real man you love because your immature ass was too caught up in thug appeal to appreciate a stand-up man like Cameron, and never being able to quite dance like I used to because that fool broke my damn leg. I have plenty of reason to be mad as hell. Not being able to dance hurt me more deeply than Dom or Rah's no-good asses. I used to teach dance classes at Dana's Dance Studio but with the internship and classes I knew I wouldn't have time. Plus teaching and not dancing was hard for me.

Let it go, I tell myself. I try to think of Dr. Locke's calm voice telling me that my anger will only hurt me in the end. "Ninety-seven . . . ninety-eight . . . ninety-nine . . . one hundred," I finish calmly, grateful when the emotions bubbling up in me die down some.

I don't give a shit what anybody says. I'm a strong woman to put up with everything I dealt with in the last year. I overcame it all. And on top of it all, my ass is celibate. No dick for me. It has been months and trust, for me that is a *huge* deal. Dr. Locke says I should focus all of my energy on healing myself and that welcoming another relationship into my life at this time would be a setback. So, I have sworn off dicks and gladly welcomed masturbation into my life. Today is just another test of my clit. Another check of how much of a woman I really am. All of these months in therapy got me ready for this. I got this. I can do this. No, fuck that. I *will* do this.

My BlackBerry begins to vibrate in the pocket of my thin wool trench. I rush to pull it out. This is what good friends—*real* friends— are all about. They check on you when they know your ass is scared as hell. "Hey," I say in my little sing-song way.

"Are you okay?" Cristal asks in her mothering kinda way.

"Cris, what am I going to say when I see him?" I ask, not even trying to hold it back.

"I'm here too, Alizé."

I smile at the sound of Moët's voice on the line. Then I pause. These two bitches can be tricky when they want to. "Who *else* is on the line?" I ask with a voice that shows I ain't even playing.

They both sigh. "Dom is not on the phone, Alizé," Cristal says. "I am done trying to get you two back together. If you two do not care then I do not care anymore either."

"Good," I answer, even as I feel a little petty. Only a little.

"Are you sure you want to do this?" Cristal asks, changing the subject.

"Yes," I say with more confidence than I feel. "I am going to walk in there and be nothing but business all the way. In fact, if he doesn't want to talk anything but mergers and acquisitions then that is fine with me. In fact, that is perfect for me."

"You'll be fine. Just say a little prayer and make sure you call one of us as soon as you get a chance," Moët says in a positive way like only Moët can.

I shook my head even as I said, "Yes, I will."

Liar, liar, pants on fire.

"Alright, Ze, I have to go before I am late to work."

"I'll call y'all as soon as I can," I promise, before ending the call and sliding the BlackBerry back into the pocket of my coat.

With one last shake, I press my Donna Karan suede round-toe platform onto the first step. The rest are easy. Now if I can just convince myself of the same about seeing Cameron for the first time in months.

"Welcome back, Monica."

I look up from the company manual I'm skimming over to see *him* standing across the table from me. All of the air leaves my body. Suddenly the large conference room feels small as hell. My eyes eat him up. The tall muscular frame. His fine-ass square features. The way his suit fits his athletic frame. Here he is. The man that I loved and lost.

Breathe, Alizé, breathe. I rise and present him my hand in full professional mode. "Hello, Mr. Steele."

Cameron focuses his deep-set eyes on my outstretched hand. "Mr. Steele?" he asks with a sardonic tone before he enfolds my slender hand into a shake.

His touch reminds me of everything we never shared together. Everything my dumb ass pushed away. Our eyes lock. His hands feel so warm in mine. I feel so attracted to him. So pulled into him. But I have to remember that he's married now. This man belongs to someone else.

Not that I ain't never dealt with married men. Just not any that I had feelings for. Cameron Steele is—*was*—the first man I ever loved.

Thankfully, the conference doors open and the rest of the staff wander in. Cameron releases my hand with one last long look before claiming his spot at the head of the table. I only have moments to get myself together. I prayed no one notices that my nipples are rock hard. Sitting up in the meeting sweating like a crack fiend ain't a good thing.

I've never even kissed Cameron but throughout the entire meeting I have to make myself stay focused and stop daydreaming about him stripping me naked and fucking me doggy style in the middle of the conference table. Pulling my hair, slapping my ass, popping my pussy. . . .

I twirl my Mont Blanc pen in my hand as I cross my legs hoping to stop that steady throb of my clit. *Ba-doop. Ba-doop.* God, I am *so* horny and Cameron's married ass is looking so damn good. As I set the tip of my pen against my bottom lip, I wonder just what kind of lover he is. Gentle and sweet? Rough and ready? Deep and demanding?

What size dick does he have?

Does he eat pussy?

Would he talk nasty while pounding in this here pussy?

Is he a freak?

That day in my bedroom when he admitted that he loved me I should have at least given him some consolation pussy. I should've jacked my broke leg right on up to the sky and let him fuck away some of the pain of me turning him down. Now he is married to someone else.

I level my eyes on him as some random executive rambles off some report about something or other. Cameron is writing something on a notepad and just the strong, tight way he grips the pen makes me hot. It's not like me to not be focused on learning all I can but right now my celibacy and being within feet of Cameron has my mind *all* fucked up.

He looks up suddenly and catches my eyes on him. He looks away as if I am nothing but a stranger. No lie? My feelings are hurt.

I force myself to pay attention in the meeting. Getting my MBA is more important to me than sitting here sexdreaming about a married damn man. A married man that I still love.

I'm fucked.

I spent most of the day cooped up in another small office that is just an inch bigger than the closet they masqueraded as my office last summer. Delaney, Cameron's assistant, followed his instructions and made sure I had plenty of office manuals to read over. I saw

Cameron in passing a few times but he never once cracked his neck to look in my direction. Wifey must have his ass on a tight leash.

Or Cameron is the stand-up, reliable man that I know he is. I sucked air between my teeth. Man, you know what? I don't give a fuck how faithful his ass is. Shit, he ain't my damn man.

I pick up the phone and quickly dial Cristal's work number. Nothing like talking to her saddity ass to make me forget my troubles.

"Lowe, Ingram, and Banks."

"Hey girl. You busy?" I lean back in my swivel chair and then frown when the back of the chair hits the wall.

"Too busy to hear gossip? Never."

"Girl, how 'bout Mr. Cameron is ignoring my ass big time."

"No."

"Yes," I stress as I lean forward to pick up my Mont Blanc.

"Well, I hate to say it *but* I think it is definitely time for someone to say it."

I roll my eyes 'cause I already know where her ass is headed. "If you say it I will hang up on you. No lie."

Cristal makes a mocking noise. "When you had a chance to have Cameron you didn't want him. And I told you—"

I took great pleasure hanging up on her.

Yes, last year Cristal was the main one telling me to snatch Cameron up. At the time he was more her type than mine. Of course fate is a no-good bitch. Therapy helped me to realize that my parents' divorce—or rather my mother's reaction to the divorce—made me afraid to fall in love. My thug appeal was in direct contradiction to my ambition. It was real easy for me to keep my thuggish boyfriends from getting anywhere near my heart. I was afraid to fall in love. I was afraid to love Cameron.

And now it's too late.

Ain't life a no good, ragged-mouth, bald-headed bitch?

Knock-knock.

I look up to find Delaney peeking her head into my office. "Hi, Delaney," I greet her as I scribble a note in my planner to schedule an extra session with Dr. Locke.

16 *Niobia Bryant*

"Just checking up on you," she says, walking in to stand her plump frame before my desk. "I know reading can make you go crazy . . . *especially* in here."

"I'm cool."

"Everyone is real excited to have you back this semester."

My smile this time is a little more genuine.

"I'll have to remind Cameron to invite you to the wedding. We're all going."

I freeze. Say what? Say who? "The wedding? You . . . you're talking about Cameron's wedding?"

Delaney nodded, causing her bright red pageboy to swing back and forth past her round cheeks. "The first one was cancelled because Serena's mother was sick."

My heart is racing like crazy and I feel excitement fill me. I try not to show it as I casually flip through the manual. "When's the wedding?" I ask, sounding like I'm bored. Humph. Bored my ass.

"It's in April."

Five whole months away.

"I hope I get to go," I lie with a straight face. Fuck it.

"Well, I better get back to work." With one last wave, Delaney is gone.

I snatch up the phone and dial Cristal back.

"Lowe, Ingram, and Banks."

"Cristal, girl, guess what?" My excitement made me loud as hell on the phone.

The line went dead.

Now is not the time for payback. I dial her ass right back.

"Lowe, Ingram, and Banks."

"You feel better now?" I snap.

"Lots. Thank you very much."

"*Anyway*. Cameron didn't get married in December—"

"What!"

"They postponed the wedding." My damn hands are shaking.

"Oh-oh."

I nodded. "Oh-oh is right. Oh it . . . is . . . on. Trust."

Chapter Three

Dom

"I'm Dom, and I can't be nobody but Dom until the day I die. Fuck it."

I'm a junkie. Whether I'm snortin' a bag of dope or not I will always be a junkie. An addict. A dope fiend. A head.

Yeah, I did rehab. I laid on the couch and let some shrink help me figure out why I even started with drugs. I moved out of the projects. I got off the stripper pole. I cut all ties with Diane (my mother who didn't deserve to be called Mama) who was—is—an abusive, weed smokin', manipulative, money-hungry bitch. (Fuck it, that bitch done called me much worse.) I got an honest job that don't make shit. I have a better relationship with my daughter.

I been through a lot. I'm not makin' excuses, I'm just statin' fuckin' fact.

I've done a lot. Again no excuses. Fact.

My journal is full and it's funny 'cause I never thought my ass would ever read outside of school or flippin' through some fuckin' magazine or some shit, but here I am writin'. Tellin' my own stories. Healin' myself through a pen and pad. I even told my drug counselor that I might write a book one day but my life ain't over yet. Maybe when I'm old with gray hairs on my pussy I'll sit back and really recollect on everythin' I've done. Things I have to forgive or be forgiven for.

The death of my ex in a car wreck after we argued.

The way I started to fuck my kid's head up talkin' down to her the way Diane shit me up.

The bullshit I pulled on Alizé. Yeah, I was fucked up for fuckin' her man behind her back and tellin' his no good ass how she was cheatin' on him. Sometimes I still can hear the sound of her bone breakin' and her cry that gave me chills. Even though I helped the police catch Rah, Alizé still won't fuck with me. She ain't been to the apartment to visit since I moved in. I can't say that I blame her but I ain't kissin' her motherfuckin' ass either.

I still got Moët and Cristal and dem bitches help keep me straight.

Livin' in Livingston in that fancy apartment is different from my days in the projects. It helps keep me clean and away from them people who ain't want shit 'cept for me to get high with 'em. It's hard enough goin' to that area everyday to work here at the daycare center. I love Newark. I'm a fuckin' Brick City Baby 'til I die, but right now I ain't strong enough to move back. Not if I want to stay clean.

"Mama."

I look down at my little girl, Kimani. In her I see everythin' my ass wants to be. I want the way she feels about me to be different than the way I feel about Diane. So I will never smoke weed with her. I stopped cussin' at her little ass like she ain't shit but a stray dog. I stopped droppin' her off with anybody willin' to babysit. I stopped her from callin' me by my first name (that was Moët's idea).

I ain't tryin' to say I'm Mother of the year or some shit but I'm tryin.'

As she hugs my leg like I'm a fuckin' mix of Barney, Elmo, and Dora the Explorer I feel so much love for her. She looks just like me: slim, trim, dark, and beautiful.

"You ready to go?"

"Yup," she says.

I finish up cleanin' the area where I assist the afterschool teacher for the first graders. This shit is a long way from my days as Juicy up on the pole at Club XXXCite. Makin' mad loot for shakin' a little ass or workin' my ass off for damn near minimum wage? Being able to afford the best designer labels or having to learn to appreciate the value of Wal-Mart and stores like NY & Co and Gap? It used to be nothin' for me to drop two grand on a pair of shoes. Yes, I was livin' in the projects at that time but I strutted through that motherfucker dressed like I owned it. Oh, I miss that motherfuckin' money, don't get it twisted. But bein' on that stage was just a part of me tryin' to prove to myself that I was special. Pretty. Needed. All the shit Diane took from me with her hateful ass words.

As soon as Kimani and me step out the buildin' on Broad Street I rush her to my car—my same red Lexus that is kickin' my ass with the car and insurance payments. Just that small walk from the front door to my car door feels like I leavin' my damn self open to turn the corner and buy a bag of dope to sniff the fuck up.

Dope used to be my friend when I turned my back on my real friends.

My morals. My conscience. My life. My everythin'. All of it caught up in a bag of dope.

I drive until I'm in an area I don't know like the back of my hand. Where the drug dealers are hidin' in their houses to sling that shit and not on the street corners and in front of stores . . . waitin' for me. Out of sight. Out of mind. That's how I felt. Shit.

"Mama, where my daddy?" Kimani asks out the straight blue.

I damn near swerve into a car in the opposite lane. "Huh?"

"*My* friend Hiasha said her daddy was pickin' her up from school and *I* told her I didn't have a daddy and *she* asked me where he was and *I* said I don't know."

Shit, I don't fuckin' know either. But what do I say? Your daddy hauled ass as soon as I told that no good son-of-a-bitch I was pregnant. Last I heard he was livin' with some bitch in Hill Manor. He is a fuckin' drop shot just like my daddy, sperm donor, nut giver, man who gave my mother a wet ass . . . what the fuck ever.

I remember I asked Diane about my father the same way Kimani was questioning my ass. I remember that shit clearly. Humph, how can I forget it?

"Diane, where my daddy?"
She was laying on the couch in nothing but a T-shirt and a pair of thongs

smoking one of her funny smelling cigarettes. She turned her head to look at me sitting on the floor playing house with my dolls. "Somewhere with a glass dick in his mouth that's where."

She started to laugh until she choked. Thick smoke flew out of her mouth as she sat up suddenly.

I jumped up and came to stand by her. "Diane, you okay?" I ask, feeling concern as her eyes water. I touched her shoulder as my heart began to beat fast.

"Girl, get the hell off me and sit your stupid ass down somewhere," she snapped.

She pushed me roughly and I fell back on my behind . . .

Diane was an ignorant bitch and still is. I don't even know my father's name. Shit, after that I ain't never had the nerve to bring him up no more.

I shake off the tears I feel risin' up at the memory. Sad thing? Before my ass OD'd and went to rehab I was just as ignorant as Diane. I probably woulda told Kimani to shut the hell up or something. She wanted to know just like I wanted to know back then. Still, I don't know what to say.

I look at her and sure 'nough she waitin' for her answer.

"Your daddy and me broke up a long time ago and he moved away."

"So he won't pick me up from school ever?"

"Probably not."

Back in the day this was a get high moment. Roll a blunt. Sniff a bag. Anything to forget. Not to deal. Get by.

As we turn into the parking lot of The Top I think again of the book I want to write. The stories I got to tell. The people I can help. Maybe one day. Right now I gots no business trying to help nobody else with shit about fighting demons 'cause I still gots my own to beat the fuck off my back.

Chapter Four

Moët

"Hey, it's me again . . . Moët, just when I thought my life could only get better."

I don't know I'm crying until my tears fall on the photo, running across the scarred and battered face of yet another innocent child. It's days like this that I wish I stuck to my dream of being a teacher once I graduated from Seton Hall University last May. I don't know what made me think I was cut out to be a case worker (uh, Family Service Specialist Trainee) for the Division of Youth and Family Services (DYFS). I want to help children. Make a change. Do good things. Plus, I like working and having my independence to take care of me and my baby girl, Tiffany. But sometimes this—all of it— is more than I can handle.

After a day of testifying in juvenile court about a suspected molestation case and then having to take three children into custody from an abusive mother, I'm headed to investigate another suspected case of child abuse. Unlike Cristal, I love Newark—or at least what I saw of it growing up in a strict Christian home—and unfortunately, there are far too many cases of drug abuse leading to the abuse and neglect of children. Blacks had enough of an uphill struggle without getting hooked on drugs. Black children from cities like Newark already started the race to success behind the starting line and the last thing they needed was a dope fiend mother or father to hold them back. I have seen some serious mess since working at DYFS but that is nothing to the craziness children face every day. I feel drained. Tired. Wore out . . . emotionally, physically, and spiritually.

And I still don't have a full case load. As a "trainee" I have to complete a one-year training program and keep up with my field and office casework duties. Sometimes the thought of a full caseload gave me a serious migraine. But I'm grown and this is my job. I made the bed and now I have to sleep in it.

Of course, I have a lot going in my life than just my job. Dom and Alizé had therapy and I wonder a lot if I shouldn't find somebody's couch to get on. I'm a single mother with a big-time, celebrity baby-daddy who wants nothing from me and my newborn daughter but to stay the hell away from him. And yes, Lavitius Drooms aka Bones, the multi-platinum selling rap star, is the father. Hell I've only been with two men in my life. He actually thinks I just want eighteen years of child support. All I want is for him to be a father to our daughter.

I'm not the saint my parents want me to be, but I am a good person. I go to church. I pray. I pay my tithes. I'm not saved but I am healed. I am forgiven.

For fornicating with my minister at the age of sixteen.

For aborting the baby *he* didn't want.

For not honoring my mother and my father even though they made it so hard to do so.

For living a double life for years as I struggled to keep up with my friends and still front for my parents.

For the horrible example I set for my younger sisters.

For falsely accusing Bones of rape when he flipped on me for getting pregnant.

Of course he hates me. Yes, I was wrong. Dead wrong. But I have asked Bones and my Heavenly Father for forgiveness. It is up to them both to accept it.

I constantly thank my Heavenly Father that Cristal and Sahad were still together then. Bones is an artist on Sahad's record label, Platinum Records. Even though she had been mad at me for not telling her the truth, she convinced Sahad to help keep me out of jail for filing a false report.

My eyes fall on the 5"x7" portrait of my daughter sitting on my desk. Tiffany Drooms. To me she already looks more like Bones than me. She is a blessing for many, many reasons. Even without her father, she is *loved* by my friends—her four godmommies; my parents—even if they constantly prayed for her as if she is the spawn of the devil; and by me. I love Tiffany with every fiber in my being.

When I notice the time, I hurry through packing up my briefcase and grab my purse. Just two weeks back on the job and I already feel like I can use a mental vacation. Nevertheless, that will have to start another day. Duty calls.

One advantage to working in your hometown is knowing where you're going when you're sent on a home visit. I park my car on the street outside the small one-family house. It is the lone house on the entire end of the block, neighbored by a liquor store on the corner and an empty glass-strewn lot. Across the street is Westside Park. The biting winter air has kept the teenagers from playing basketball on the blacktop courts.

It's funny how empty a city can look when it's cold. But as soon as summer breaks out you know just how crowded the city really is. Even in the heat of summer, the lives of many children were still cold and bitter.

I turn and focus my eyes back on the house as I walk around my car. The front door looks like it once was a brilliant red but now graffiti and grime have dulled it considerably. If it wasn't for the color of the door everything about the little house could easily fade to black and white.

I reach inside my wool coat for my ID badge swinging on the end of a chain. I take one deep breath before I knock. Confidence has never been my strong suit. Up until last year I was still trying to find myself. Humph. That's what happens when you let too many people run your life. I'm finally learning to stand up for myself and clearly state what it is I want and don't want. Maybe having to stand up for these kids helped me to step up to the plate for myself.

When I knock on the door it swings open and a foul stench nearly knocks me off my feet. I turn my head to swallow down some fresh air before I cover my nose and turn my head back. "Hello. Hello, I'm Latoya James with DYFS," I say loudly, trying not to be shot or attacked.

There was an anonymous report made of twin toddlers being left alone a lot while their mother chased a horrible heroin addiction. That led to me coming here to conduct one of those beloved home visits.

Through the opening of the door I can see a trail of clothes and random trash on the floor. I can just barely make out the edge of the kitchen and the floor is filthy. Old juice or Kool-Aid stains, sticky and black from dirt. I figure the horrible scent is the smell of rotting trash. "Hello, is anyone home? This is Miss James from the Division of Youth and Family Services."

I turn away to walk back to my car. My steps halt at the faint sound of a child's cry. I step down off the small porch to double-check the address. Definitely the right place. And with a child crying, the door open and no adult answering my calls this looks like the right time. That cry is enough for me to enter the home.

With a small prayer, I step back onto the porch and I walk into the house. I have to cover my nose and mouth with the collar of my shirt to keep from gagging. The house is a wreck. Piles of clothes are everywhere. Open and used pampers are on the top of the scratched coffee table. There are more empty bottles of liquor than my mother has knickknacks and whatnots. The carpet used to be a rough shade of rust but large dark circles are flat and black in color like spills of some substance had never been cleaned up. Missing lamp shades. Raggedy furniture that should be on the curb. It's a mess. A big, funky, unlivable mess.

The more I move into the house the scent worsens and flies began to land against my face. I swat them away. Just a glance in the kitchen makes me want to throw up. The mother needs her behind whupped or like Dom would say, "That bitch needs to be pimp slapped."

Excuse my language. I'm not saved but God ain't through with me yet.

The sound of the crying is coming from the back of the small house.

"Hello. Is anybody home?" I push the bedroom door open and I nearly jump out of my skin when a cat comes running out the door full speed. I turn to watch its retreat and my blood runs cold at the trail of sticky bloody paw prints it leaves behind.

"What the . . ."

Okay, I'm not crazy. Nor am I a hero. But I have to check on the twins. Point blank.

I turn back to the door as it continues to swing open and my knees go weak. I have to reach for the dingy wall to keep from falling out. The scent nearly choking me is the smell of death.

This might be more than I can handle.

There on the floor atop piles of dirty clothes sat the twins . . . next to the swollen and obviously dead body of their mother. I walk over clothes and trash into the room. The twins look up at me with swollen eyes and their tears halt for a second at the surprising sight of me. I gasp at the sight of the syringe still stuck in her arm and the pool of blood dried in a jagged circle around her head. It looked like she overdosed and then fell and hit her head on the edge of the dresser.

Jesus.

Girl Talk

With drinks in hand, Cristal, Moët, and Dom settled into a plush leather booth inside the Savoy Grill on Park Place downtown. The low-key music was just loud enough to enjoy without keeping them from their girl talk.

Dom worked her arms out of the cropped jean jacket she wore. "Mo, you sure you ain't gonna explode or some shit?"

Moët flipped her the bird playfully as she took a deep sip of her margarita. "I go to church on the regular. I never said I'm saved yet . . . *bitch*."

Dom just laughed before she cut her eyes over to Cristal. Through a haze of smoke, she watched her. "What's up with you?" she asked, leaning forward to flick her ashes in the tray.

Cristal just shrugged. "I just have a lot on my mind."

Dom nodded as she bit the bottom lip of her glossy mouth. "Don't we all."

Moët lifted her curvy glass. "Here's to my daughter's smile, bubble baths, the feel of the sun, and the end of the work week," she said with a mischievous grin.

Cristal nodded in agreement as she let her head drift back slightly with a melancholy smile. "Hmm. Here is to the feel of my man's hands, lips, *and* dick, designer trunk sales, and rum raisin ice cream," she nearly purred dreamily as she raises her glass of champagne.

Dom rattled the ice in her glass of soda. "And here's to good friends who forgive you when you fuck up and who pull your ass up when you're down," she said with seriousness, as that hard glint in her eye softened a little.

"Now you know that's right," Moët agreed with enthusiasm brightening her face. "To friends."

The three women all looked at each other with a warmth that only sistahgirl friends can have.

"Even those here in spirit . . . if not body," Moët added as they all ignored Alizé's empty spot.

"I know I fucked up y'all. And that old Dom feels like I shouldn't give a fuck 'bout Alizé and me not speaking . . . but I do." Dom sat her glass down on the table. "She ever gone forgive me? Is it ever gone be the four of us again?"

Moët avoided Dom's questioning eyes.

Cristal shrugged when Dom turned those eyes to her. "I do not know, Dom. I really do not know."

Chapter Five

Cristal

Being stylish in forty-degree weather is not easy but I would not be me if I did not try. Last winter it was nothing for me to pull on a sharp eight-hundred-dollar Bergdorf Goodman overcoat to make a statement until I could enter the building, remove my coat, and reveal whatever fabulous ensemble I had on beneath it. The girls and I have been obsessed with clothes and fashion since high school. Of course with a little extra change it is easier to pull something together but I am making what I got work for what I want. I had to learn that taking my car note money to buy three-hundred-dollar shoes and thousand-dollar pants was just plain crazy. So I am looking as fine as I please in a fitted turtleneck jersey dress from H&M. Luxe for less. My new motto . . . well I *am* trying.

So after a few months of living the life as the future wife of a Black mini-mogul am I back on the grind. Not that going back to work is that big a hassle for me. I have always worked. I guess I learned something from nothing leads to nothing.

Bzzz.

I close the *Vogue* I am pretending not to read as I reach out to press a button on the intercom. "Yes, Mr. Ingram," I say in my most professional voice, not wanting all these intelligent lawyers to think that this ghetto girl from Newark with more work experience than education could not fit in. My life in the hood side of Newark is very different from this state-of-the-art chrome building in downtown Newark.

"My wife is on her way up. Please make sure she comes directly into my office."

"Yes, sir."

The Mrs. Gregory Ingram. Hmmm. Interesting. This would be my first time meeting the socialite. Her name, charity work, and social events are well known. She made being the wife of a wealthy man an art form.

The Ingrams lived in New York but Mr. Ingram and his partners recently moved the firm to Newark. The rent is cheaper and this part of Newark might be twenty minutes away from the hood where I grew up but it is miles away in terms of everything else. These suits could walk out of the door of their elegant office and hop onto the train right next door at Penn Station to be back in New York in ten minutes flat and never once have to blink or catch sight of that *other* side of Newark.

I whipped out my compact and made sure my makeup and straight Rihanna-inspired bob is still intact. Of course everything is in place and I am looking just as fine as I want to be. There are not too many women that I like to impress, but Carolyn Ingram is definitely one of them.

I am slipping my compact back down into last year's Birkin when the private elevator opens. Mrs. Ingram walks in and there is no doubt that she knows she is the shit. I recognize her from the same society and gossip pages I long to be in. My skillful eyes take her all in. From the Fendi shades to the tip of her stacked Gucci shoes. Her dark and flawless mocha skin is obviously the handiwork of good genes and an even better esthetician or surgeon. My eyes widen a little at the diamond solitaire on her finger. It is big enough to choke a horse and make my clit swell with renewed life.

I rise to my feet and extend my hand. "Hello, Mrs. Ingram. You are looking lovely, of course. Let me escort you right back to Mr. Ingram's office."

She removes her shades and the other diamond on her hand makes me literally squint. Gray eyes that have to be contacts glide down to my hand and then up to my face as she clearly assesses me. I cannot help but wonder if I pass her test as I notch my chin a little higher and give her the same assessing stare without being flat-out rude.

Suddenly she smiles and her Lumineers are almost as brilliant as her jewelry. She finally accepts my hand limply. "And you are?" she asks with a polite but distant smile.

I move from behind the waist high steel receptionist desk. "I am Danielle Johnson," I respond as I lead her back through the door leading to the executive offices of the partners.

"Aren't you a pretty little thing?" she says from behind me.

I make a face that thankfully she cannot see. "Thank you." I hope she does not think I want her husband. If I did slip any of the partners a little bit, it would not be Mr. Ingram's dusty old ass. I shiver at the thought of his silvery balls. Please.

With a polite knock on the mahogany door, I open it and wave Mrs. Ingram in. She passes me on a cloud of classic Fendi perfume. I give her one last smile before closing the door and gladly gliding back to my desk.

I hope her little chit-chat with her husband does not include my ass getting booted out of here because she is scared of joining the ex-wives club. She may think my fine Lisa-Raye-looking ass is giving Mr. Ingram's limp dick a hand- or mouth-job. Her husband or anyone else's is the last thing on my mind. I have Mohammed and not even Sahad crawling back to me on his hands and knees with a key to his dynasty will make me leave him. Outside of my friends, I have never known what it is to be loved until Mohammed came into my life.

I never thought my ass would be a wimpy, love me, I need you kind of chick. More like what can you do for me and how quickly. Not that I did not deserve the finer things. Mohammed just could not afford it. But what he lacks in cash flow he makes up for in dick throw. Okay? Alright.

"You remind me of myself."

Immediately slipping my mask of professionalism in place, I

swivel in my chair to find Mrs. Ingram standing at the reception desk looking down at me—literally and figuratively.

"Thank you," I say with hesitance as she continues to study me as she slowly walks along the large circular desk. I guess it is a compliment.

She truly is a striking woman with cat-like features and a very regal bearing, but the way she is watching me makes me feel like a field rat stalked by a hawk. Is the great Mrs. Ingram gay or just crazy as hell? Suddenly she smiles and I wish like hell that she would leave because I feel uncomfortable. What the hell?

"I once had that same desire to be more. Bigger. Better. Sexier. Richer. Prettier. Classier."

I sit back in my chair and cross my arms over my chest. I say nothing because the words, "Bitch, please" are ready to drip from my glossy lips.

She continues to circle the desk until I have to swivel in my chair to keep my eyes on her. "Of course, you have no way of knowing that I met my Gregory when I worked as a clerk in this small little shithole of a law office when he first started practicing."

Even in my hardcore gold digging days I never slept with a man over fifty. Please. Her Gregory is the safest man in the place. "Mrs. Ingram, I can ensure you that I am not here for anything but work."

She takes her time sliding on her fur and leather gloves. "Listen dear, you could sit under Gregory's desk all day and suck his dick until his balls are flat and dry and he would never leave me for you. That is not my point at all."

My eyes widen because who knew a lady like Mrs. Ingram would use such language with such ease. Plus the image she put in my head made me a little ill. Eew.

"What exactly *is* your point, Mrs. Ingram?"

"I can smell the stench of the ghetto on you almost as much as I can see the desperation that makes you pretend otherwise . . . just like me thirty years ago."

Her words make me feel angry . . . and exposed.

"You just need a little guidance and I'm in the mood for a pet project."

A pet project?

"Excuse me, Mrs. Ingram?"

She leans forward and taps my brow with a perfectly manicured finger. "Don't frown dear, it brings on wrinkles early," she advised with a haughty tone.

I am a grown-ass woman. I have taken care of myself since I was eighteen years old and aged out of the foster care system. So why did I immediately follow her direction and quickly remove my frown?

"I've just added your name to the list of invitees to a charity gala my husband and I are having at the Waldorf-Astoria's Grand Ballroom next Friday. It's black tie of course. Don't worry about the thousand-dollar ticket price." She tucked her silk clutch under her arm. "I'm sure a girl like you has something appropriate to wear or knows how to get your clever little hands on something."

She turned and walked towards the elevator as if she is on a high fashion runway.

I jump to my feet. "How do you know I even want to go?" I ask, with a boldness I do not regret.

The door to the private elevator glides open and she steps on and then turns dramatically in the center. "Please. You'd gnaw off your right arm to be there. Toodles."

The door glides close and shuts her off from my view.

I want to be that bitch and she knows it.

Chapter Six

Alizé

"*How wrong would I be to fuck my therapist?*"

That thought makes my face shape into an odd expression. Okay, so now I know this dick sabbatical is running me straight crazy. Fuck Dr. Locke's fifty-something-year-old ass? That was Moët's M.O., not mine.

Not that he's not nice looking . . . for his age. Tall, broad shoulders, bald head, and silver goatee. Glasses that sat on . . . strong cheekbones above a nice, kissable mouth—

I shake my head to clear it of the image of me licking Dr. Locke's lips as I ride him. I need some dick. Point blank.

Maybe it's time to call it quits on the celibacy and call my ex-sideline ho Tyrone. Now *he* had a dick out of this world.

"Monica?"

I shift my eyes up from Dr. Locke's crotch to his face. "Yes."

He crosses his legs where he sits across from me in a leather club chair. He looks at me long and hard behind his slightly tinted glasses. He jotted something down onto the notepad he held. "What are you thinking?"

"That celibacy sucks," I answer without a bit of hesitation. After months of bi-weekly sessions, I don't have time for bullshitting.

He nods his head as he continues scribbling my business. "Was it seeing Cameron recently that brought you to that conclusion?" he asks in that calm almost monotone voice.

"I want more from Cameron than sex . . . but the more I see him around the office the more I want to tear his clothes off and . . . well, you know."

Dr. Locke looks up at me over the rim of his glasses. "Yes, I think I have the idea."

I just shrug as I look around at his Maplewood offices. Everything about him from his voice to the décor of this place to his loafers is so . . . ordinary. "Does anything excite you, Dr. Locke?" I ask.

He gives me another long look before he turns the page in his notepad. I grimace to think that I have so many issues—after months of therapy—that one damn page ain't enough.

"We can talk about me or delve into yet another broken relationship you're facing."

I frown and my brows furrow together as I nod. "It's weird to think about facing Rah in court today. It will be the first time I've seen him since . . . since that night."

"And how does that make you feel?"

"Angry. Anxious. Furious. Vengeful. Pissed the fuck off."

"Your language, Monica," he reminds me gently.

I check the eye roll I'm about to give his ass. "Sorry. Pissed off."

"And?"

I lock my eyes with his. "Who says there is an 'and,' Dr. Locke?"

"And?" he asked again as if he didn't hear me the first time.

"Afraid. Okay. I feel afraid at the thought of seeing him again," I admit softly as I look down at my hands as I wring them together. I fight the urge to rub the long scar on my thigh. "But I can't wait until this is all over because there is no way he can get away with what he did to me."

"So you want him to pay?"

I jerk my head up to pierce him with my eyes. "Damn right I want him to pay," I answer in a cold voice. "Does that make me a bad person?"

"No, it shows that you're human."

I blink away tears that fill my eyes. "And does it show that I'm human because I want a bat and five minutes alone with that motherfuck—"

That makes him scribble away like crazy.

* * *

I never got to see Rah. When I got to court the prosecutor tells me that Rah accepted a plea bargain. Two years for aggravated assault. What the fuck? No trial. Weak ass sentence. Just a bunch of bullshit. I had to fight not to laugh in the prosecutor's face when he gave me the line about this ultimately being a victory. It wasn't his leg that was snapped in two like a dried chicken bone. Two lousy years while I will never be able to dance the way I used to.

Trying to literally shake it off, I left the courthouse and walked out into the winter winds that are cold and making my cheeks feel like I was pimp-slapped. I dig my hands down deeper into the pockets of my Ralph Lauren wool coat as I make my way down the steps.

"Alizé."

I turn to find Dom walking down the steps behind me. I see the hesitation in her face. She doesn't know how to take me. That's a good thing. This bitch used to be my friend and instead of having my back she stuck a knife in it. It still hurt. My dumb ass thought none of us would ever do anything to hurt each other. Friendship is important to me, but at some point you have to kick a bad friend to the curb just like you would a bad boyfriend.

She reaches in her Gucci tote for a soft pack of cigarettes. I recognize the bag from when Dom bought it two years ago. Obviously getting off the pole is messing with her money because the Dom standing before me ain't the hood fabulous bitch she used to be. I never did understand her six-figure wardrobe with a fifty-dollar-a-month rent in the projects.

"I was here to testify against Rah," she says, looking everywhere but at me.

I don't know what to say to her. I don't know if I will ever have anything to say *to* her.

At my silence, Dom finally locks her eyes with mine and I'm surprised to see she's angry. And that pisses me off. Suddenly I gots plenty to say.

"You know, the more you care about somebody the more power you give them to hurt you. I never let my guard down with any dudes 'cause I didn't want to be hurt. But with my friends? I take that shit serious. You, Mo, and Cristal were more than sisters to me." That door inside of me with Dom's name all over it flew wide open as I step nose to nose to her. "How could you fuck Rah? How the hell you gone fuck my man and then dime me out like a no-good snitch bitch?"

See all my education and Cristal-type talking goes out the window. When I'm mad it's straight hood all the time, every time.

Dom turns her head to release a stream of smoke.

I walk away from her but only get a few steps before I turn back and walk right back into her face. "It ain't about him. Matter of fact . . . fuck him. This about me and you. I wouldn't ever sleep with none of your men and you know it."

"And you know I was hittin' that dope hard then and I was hurt about Lex dying in the car crash," Dom says, locking her eyes with mine.

"So why hurt me? I been a good friend to you, Dom?" People passing by are watching us but I don't care.

Dom looks away again. "I was jealous of you," she admits softly before taking a long drag on her cigarette.

Her words shock me. Dom was my friend before she became my enemy. I know this hardcore bitch, so I understand how difficult it had to be for her to admit that to me. Dom *always* kept it raw, hard, and almost careless. That shit she just dropped is B-I-G. "Jealous? Of me?"

She roughly tosses her cigarette to the ground before she crushes it under the pointed tip of her snakeskin boots. "I *was*," she stresses.

"Why?" I ask in confusion.

Dom laughs a little. "Why the fuck you think?" she snaps.

It's my turn to look away. Of all my friends Dom's life is the most opposite of mine but she always had me thinking she was happy as hell in her life.

Yeah to the mother who was more weed buddy than anything.

Hallelujah to the cheap rent and living in the projects.

Thank you Jesus for creating weed to be smoked forever and always.

Walk it out about stripping for a living.

Who give a fuck about being a single mother with a missing baby-daddy.

"Listen. Can we not dig too deep into this shit," Dom snaps, obviously uncomfortable. "I fucked up and I'm sorry. This ain't easy for me, Ze."

"Walking in on you fucking Rah in the same bed where I fucked him wasn't easy for me either," I threw back at her.

"Damn, no she didn't," a woman said as she passed us by.

We both ignored her.

"We been friends a long time, Alizé."

"Damn right. Way too long for you to do what you did to me." I release a long, heavy breath and count to a hundred, remembering Dr. Locke's bullshit tactic. "I can't trust you as a friend, Dom. I could never be cool with you the way we used to be."

"That's fine." Dom reaches in her bag for her shades and slips them on even though the sun is hardly shining that bright.

She didn't put them on quick enough for me to miss the tears in her eyes. Dom crying? Huh?

I think about her hooked on drugs and almost dying from an overdose.

I think of the pain she felt when Lex died.

I think of the shit she went through with Diane as her mother and only a bad memory as her father.

I shouldn't feel sorry for this bitch . . . but I do.

She helped catch Rah after he went on the run for assaulting me.

She came here to testify and help put him away.

She is standing here before me admitting something that I *know* is hard for her.

"Listen, I don't know. I won't say that I'll call you or nothing like that. But maybe the four of us can go out to eat or something. I don't know. We'll see."

Dom nods as she lights another cigarette.

"Since there's no trial I have to go to my internship." I pull the collar of my wool coat up around my ears. "Bye, Dom."

I turn and walk away before she can hug me or something. I wasn't ready for that. One step at a time.

Chapter Seven

Moët

Sunday services at The Holiness Church of Christ are the highlight of my week. The church is small with barely a hundred members, but the spirit in the church is strong. The choir always sings with much praise and Reverend Hampton always delivers the word to teach and inspire. I look forward to going to church. I have a good time. It's in this church that I finally felt like the Lord forgave me for all my sins. Trust me when I say *that* is truly a miracle.

And it is here that I met Deacon Taquan Sanders. Now I truly thank God for that.

As Reverend Hampton preaches on the virtues of truth and integrity, I nuzzle my face into the sweet crook of Tiffany's neck as I gently rub circles into her back to belch her. I look over towards the small pew where the deacons sit to find Taquan smiling over at me. My heart nearly bursts in my chest as I smile back.

Dating Taquan feels like that first sweet love that I missed while in high school. It was hard to focus on boys my age when Reverend DeMark was delivering the kind of sexual pleasure teenage boys knew nothing about yet. The man was a scoundrel, a devil, a predator who picked girls just a few years from him being a pedophile, a freak against God and I hated him . . . but I can't deny that he taught me some things that make me hell in the bedroom. Things a sixteen-year-old had no business learning right there in The Greater Temple of Jesus Christ's church offices . . . and pews . . . and pulpit.

Things that I would love to do to Taquan.

As Tiffany finally lets out a belch, I kiss her cheek and gently settle her down into her carrier sitting beside me on the pew. I know I should be focused on the sermon but lately my mind is fixated on other things . . . like Taquan's thing.

Of the two relationships that I've had in my twenty-something years both progressed to sex very quickly. The Reverend and I only shared freak sessions in the church. Bones took me out but soon sex was our focus. It's different dating someone who ends the night with a kiss.

I had a man and I wasn't getting any more than Alizé's celibate behind.

I glance over at Taquan again. He is nodding his head and looking up at Reverend Hampton in pure devotion. I can put that same look on his face while I ride that dick . . . if he would finally move off of first base and bring it on home. All through the rest of church I try not to envision me stripping down to nothing and walking over there to climb right onto his lap. I know it's nothing but the devil putting these thoughts in my head but Lord I'm ready to see what else Taquan has to offer with his romantic, sweet, gentlemanly self.

"Hey you."

I look up in surprise to find Taquan leaning down to lift Tiffany out of her carrier. All around me people are mingling or leaving the church. "Church is over?" I ask in surprise.

He laughs and flashes me straight even white teeth. "Sure is," he says as he gently sways back and forth to rock Tiffany.

I would know that if I wasn't daydreaming about Taquan and me getting it on in the baptism pool behind the pulpit. Lord, help me.

"You ready to go?" he asks.

"Yes." I rise to pull on my coat before I grab my purse, baby bag, and the carrier.

We walk out the church together, speaking to the people we pass on the way. "I know we were going to Mrs. Jay's for dinner but I actually have a surprise," I tell him as he bends to settle Tiffany in her car seat in the backseat of his black Range Rover. As he did every Sunday, Taquan had driven all the way out to Livingston to pick Tiffany and me up for church.

"Really?"

He stands and turns around to look down at me. We are just inches apart. He is looking good and smelling good. And being close to him has me feeling good.

With everything I've been through with men, my mind was not on finding a man, but Taquan was truly special and for the first time I saw a man I was attracted to and I made the first move. No preacher lurking after virgin teenagers. No hook-ups from my girls. Just a woman letting a man know she is interested. To my pleasure, he felt the same way.

Now it's time to take this to the next level and if that meant making another power move than so be it. "Actually, my friends are all out for the day so I made dinner for us back at the apartment."

Taquan slid his hands into the pockets of his slacks as he tilted his head a little to look down at. "So you cooked for me?" he asks in that deep voice.

"Scared?" I ask, amazed that I even know how to flirt.

"Nope. Not at all."

He holds the passenger door open and I lightly touch his chest as I climb in. Taquan owns his own Subway franchise. His parents both died in a car crash and his uncle wisely advised him to use the insurance money to make more money. That was three years ago and now at just twenty-five he is planning to open another restaurant in Orange. Even once he found himself able to move, he still lived in the modest home in Newark where he was raised.

Of course, Cristal loves him to pieces. Alizé thinks it's weird we hadn't had sex yet. Dom thinks he's boring. But this new me, the one who stands up for herself, knows that all that matters is what I think.

As we ride to Livingston he reaches over and holds my hand.

"So Dom and Alizé have made up?" he asks as he steers with one hand.

"Kinda sorta." He is so easy to talk to so I have filled him in on my friends and all of our drama and right now the idea of Dom and Alizé even agreeing to be in the same room is a big deal.

"Well, I know it means a lot to you that they get it together so continue to pray on it," he advises.

"We're all supposed to meet up next week to go to dinner." I turn in my seat to check on Tiffany who is sleeping peacefully.

He says nothing but he squeezes my hand a little tighter to reassure me.

"How are things with your parents?"

"My mom offered to babysit."

"Really? That's nice of her."

I gave him a look like "Negro, you crazy."

"What?"

"I love my parents and we have gotten past a bunch but I'm not ready to put my child through the crap they put me through." I tried to hide the bitterness from my tone but I still haven't gotten over how I told my parents about the Reverend seducing me at sixteen and they called me the liar. "My sister, Latrece, just called me complaining about them having her on religious lockdown. It's too much for a child. Hell, we haven't sinned so what can we be saved for? Kids should have a chance to just be kids, you know?"

He nods but I know that his ties to God are much stronger than mine. "I grew up in the church and I was taught to love and respect the Lord and His words, but I don't feel like my childhood lacked for anything."

I blink away tears that threaten to fall. "But sometimes you can cage a child in so much; then when they finally have the chance to go free it makes them wild and crazy. I don't want that for my sisters or for Tiffany."

He pulls into the underground parking deck of The Top. I move to leave the car but his hand on my arm stops me. I'm surprised and pleased when he pulls me close to him and presses those Duane Martin–like lips to my forehead.

For me that is not nearly enough.

With a moan for courage, I raise my hand to his face as I tilt my chin to press my lips to his. He hesitates and I feel him pull back for just a second before he closes his eyes and kisses me back. Whoa. The feel of his tongue against mine is pure fire. I trace my hands down his hard cheek to his chest and abs. I use one shaking hand to yank his shirt from inside his pants. "Taquan," I moan against his mouth as I push my hand under his shirt to trace my fingertips over his nipples.

I feel him shiver. It makes me bolder.

I take his hand and press it to my breast. When his fingers search and find my hard nipple I arch my back and let out breath filled with pent-up frustration. He presses his lips to my neck and I dive my hand into his lap to stroke his hard dick straining against his slacks. Thank you, Jesus. He lives up to the "all black men have big dicks" stereotype. I have to see it. Feel it. Maybe even suck it.

With one hand I undo his belt and unbutton his pants. Seconds later that big dick is springing free right into my hand. I grip it tightly and stroke it like I'm trying to milk it. His ass clenches and he raises his hips up off the leather seats a bit. When I feel his hands sliding down between my legs I spread them wide until one knee is pressed against the window. One finger and then another stroke against my swollen clit before sliding deep into my pussy.

I don't care if a dozen cars ride by. I'm ready for this and nothing is going to stop me including the time nor the place. Pushing his hands away, I hitch my skirt higher around my waist and climb right into his lap. His dick is standing straight up between my thighs. I grip it and rise up until I feel the heat of his thick tip just between my thick wet pussy lips.

"No, we can't," he says weakly.

"Oh yes, the hell we can." I try to lower my ass but his hands shoot out to grab my cheeks and stop me.

I lock my eyes with his as my heart and clit pound crazily. "What?"

"We can't," he stresses with more determination.

"Why not?" I ask him sharply in frustration just as Tiffany begins to stir in her car seat.

Taquan licks his lips and looks away from me.

What's the problem? He's hard as bricks so he can't be gay or needing Viagra.

He looks back at me and his face is a tad bit embarrassed. "I'm a virgin. I'm abstaining until I'm married."

Say what?

Tiffany broke out into a full cry as the bomb Taquan dropped on me plummeted my spirits. "Don't worry, baby, Mama feels like crying too."

Chapter Eight

Dom

"No, don't go." I push his hands the fuck off me and climb right on up outta the bed. Like always his ass want to cuddle and shit but that ain't what the fuck I just wasted my lunch hour for. I was lookin' for a nut and he just gave it to me along with one helluva back blow out. "We gotta get back to work."

Corey Miller sits up in the bed with his hard dick standing up straight between his legs. I ignore him. I strut my naked ass right into the bathroom for a quick shower. Ain't no way I'm goin' back to work smellin' like sex. My ass shouldn't even be here in one of these short stay motherfuckers grabbin' a quickie from this Negro any damn way. I grab their thin rag and cheap soap as I step under the hot spray of the water.

Corey's the athletic director at the daycare center. He's the same height as me but he's cute and the sweetest fucking shade of caramel. Ever since I started workin' there he been tryin' to holla. He cute and funny and all that good shit but I'm just fightin' everyday to stay clean and raise my daughter. Right now I don't need the drama that a man brings into a woman's life. I'm scared that any little thing will have my ass huntin' up a blunt or some dope.

But I'm still a woman. I get horny and shit just like any other damn woman. And here's this nice, young, muscular motherfucker always smilin' with them big damn dimples lettin' me know that he feelin' me . . . so I decided to let myself feel him inside me.

Corey wants more than sneakin' these little random fucks on our lunch hour but right now good pussy is all I gots to offer him. He ain't my man so I ain't got to worry 'bout him cheatin', lyin', callin' me too much, not callin' me enough, and all that other bullshit relationships come wit'.

I'm rinsin' this funky soap from my body when the bathroom door opens. I turn my head and look through the glass door as Corey walks in with a sock hangin' off the tip of his hard dick. When his jokey ass makes the sock jump up and down, I laugh. He always crackin' jokes and shit. He always smilin' and in a good mood. Always. The little short motherfucker swear he Martin or some shit.

The shower door opens and that sock leads him right on in.

"Come here, Sensual Chocolate." He flings the sock over the shower door and his long and curvy dick is covered by a sheer pink condom. "You know you want this caramel all up in ya."

I laugh like a little girl or some shit as his hands grab my hips and pull me close to him. "You know you wanna get all up in this chocolate," I tease him, wrapping my arms around his neck as he turns and presses me back against the cool tiled wall of the shower.

Corey uses his strong arm to lift one of my legs. I gasp as his dick slides up in me. Feels like a pole or some shit. Pressing my back against the wall, I raise my ass up a little and work my hips as he begins to pop away in my pussy like a motherfucker on a true mission to please. I cry out a little as he uses his hips to press his dick against one side of my walls.

I ain't gone lie: Corey and me fuck so good together. Our shit is ridiculous.

As he starts to grind away like he don't want to miss one spot of this here pussy I'm thinking like Bernie Mac in *Player's Club*: "I'm in trou-ble. Trou-ble."

"Mommy, what happened to your hair?"

I look at Kimani as I zip up her puffy pink coat by the front door of the daycare center. I try to play crazy or some shit like I don't know that every curl and spike from my short do is done. Steam from the shower and the sex fucked up a perfectly good hairdo. "Uh . . . my hat messed it up," I lie to my child without a bit of shame. What I'm gone say? Mama had a freak session with Mr. Miller and this hair is what you call sweat the fuck out.

Corey walks up behind us dressed in his leather coat and wool skully. He has the nerve to laugh at my lie as he winks. "Hey, Kimani." He tugs one of her ponytails as he walks past us. "Bye, Dom."

"Bye, Mr. Miller."

"See you tomorrow, Corey."

It does feel funny that Corey and me are fuck buddies but we hardly even speak to each other at work. Just the way I fuckin' want it.

"Mommy, can Hiasha spend the night?"

Kimani and her friend Hiasha are inseparable. Wherever you see one, you see the other. They looked like two little chocolate china dolls playin' together. "Maybe another time. Remember you and me and the girls are goin' out to eat tonight."

My daughter's face lights the fuck up. "Auntie Ze too, right?"

I pull her pink wool cap down over her ponytails. "Yeah."

"Good."

Yeah. Good. Admittin' to Alizé 'bout bein' jealous of her was some deep shit for me. My drug counselor talkin' 'bout he proud of me and all that good shit. Okay, it wasn't easy but I'm proud of myself too. Diane and my father with all their bullshit fucked me up but I'm proud of gettin' my shit back together. And that includes gettin' shit back right between Alizé and me. See, a bitch like me woulda whupped my own ass for the shit I did to her, but she had to understand that I was a different person then.

I'm better now. And I plan to stay the fuck better. If that meant staying just sheet freaks with Corey; keepin' the fuck away from Diane's psycho ass; and making up with Alizé than that's what the fuck I will do. Period.

Girl Talk

The silence around their table at Ruby Tuesday was deafening. Alizé, Dom, Cristal, and Moët focused most of their attention on Kimani contently making funny faces to amuse Tiffany.

Moët kicked her foot under the table aiming for Cristal to get her attention.

"Ow. Shit." Dom swore as she reached down to rub her shin.

"Oops. Sorry," Moët mumbled as she dropped her head into her hands.

They all were glad when the waiter brought over the large plate of appetizers and saucers.

"I am starving." Cristal reached for a saucer and loaded her plate with spring rolls.

Moët was all over the chicken tenders and honey mustard sauce.

Both Dom and Alizé reached for the mozzarella sticks. Their hands touched briefly and they both snatched their hand back.

Moët and Cristal shared a quick look.

"You go ahead," Dom offered as she grabbed the rest of the chicken tenders to put onto a plate for Kimani.

"No, I know you like them too. You go ahead," Alizé said.

"No, I'm—"

Moët dropped her fork onto her plate. "Okay, now you bitches trippin'."

Every set of eyes at the table turned on her. Moët shrugged. "What? You two the only ones who can talk ghetto as hell? Not."

"That reminds of the time Moët cursed Mr. Piccolo out in science class because he kept picking on her for being quiet," Cristal said.

Alizé's eyes widened. "Ooh, I remember that. What was it she told him again?" she asked, excited by the memory.

The ladies all looked at each other with mischief in their eyes before they said in unison: "If you want me to talk I got some motherfucking words for your ass. Leave me the hell alone!"

They all broke out in loud laughter uncaring about the eyes they drew from people at nearby tables.

"Ooh, y'all said bad words," Kimani said as if she knew a secret.

"We have said plenty of bad ones over the years," Cristal said as she reached over and cleaned honey mustard from Kimani's round cheek with her thumb.

"We have shared plenty over the years," Moët stressed with a long look at Dom and Alizé.

"Good times," Alizé said softly.

"And bad times," Dom added.

Cristal nodded as she reached for her glass. "Here's to better time for all four of us . . . together."

Moët, Dom, and then Alizé lift their glasses to toast to that together.

Chapter Nine

Cristal

I am trying my best not to keep checking my gold watch. Mohammed looks up from his plate of jerk chicken and wild rice. He smiles at me and my heart swells up with love for him. I smile back and I know it does not reach my eyes. Guilt already lives there.

The Caribbean is his favorite restaurant. He says the bright colors, food, and lively atmosphere reminds him of his home in Negril, Jamaica. Coming here tonight was my idea. A bit of a treat before the letdown.

"You are looking beautiful as hell, Danielle," he tells me, reaching across the table to rub my hand with his thumb.

"Tell me something I do not know," I tease as I kick my Manolo off under the table and ease my foot onto his lap. The colorful floor length tablecloth of our corner booth hides my actions as I stroke his dick to hardness with my foot.

I cock a brow as he sits up a bit straighter in his seat. "I am ready to go," I tell him in my softest and most seductive voice.

"But we just got our food," he complains without much conviction.

I look him dead in the eye as I ease my body down under the table.

"Danielle," he whispers harshly.

I am a woman on a mission. Our Friday date night is being

switched to the edited version. On my hands and knees I crawl across a random chicken bone to get between his legs. I undo his zipper and work his dick from his pants. His thighs clench as I stroke it just the way he likes it . . . nice and firm with a loose wiggle at the tip.

His crotch smells like a sexy mix of his sweat and his cologne. I moan a little as I pull his dick to me like a cigar and take a big puff. My lips curve into a smile around it as he hollers out a little at the feel of me blowing him.

"Is everything okay?" I hear our waiter Henry ask.

"Yes, I stubbed my toe," Mohammed answers with that sexy Jamaican lilt even as he eases one hand under the table to grab the back of my head.

My motive for this spontaneous blowjob is to ease the date along a little quicker but the more his dick hardens against my tongue the more I am getting turned the hell on. No need for both of us not to enjoy ourselves, right?

I reach down between my legs and jerk my lavender La Perla's to the side to press my fingers against my clit. *Aaaah.* My own spit runs down my chin as I suck him deeply. I tickle the thick tip with my tongue before sucking it deeply. His legs shake and his hands grab my hair into his tight fist. I circle my hips as my fingers move faster and faster against my clit. His dick jumps as he fills my mouth with his cum. Like I am starved for it I swallow and suck until I know he does not have anything left. My fingers are wet from my juices. The smell of my pussy has filled the hot space underneath the table. I greedily clean every bit of his nut from his dick and balls as I shake and shiver with my own nut. My clit is sensitive as I cum but I do not dare stop rubbing it until I am spent and done.

His dick slips from my mouth as I fall back onto my ass and let my head lean back against the seat of the booth. Whoo. I would be wrong to fall asleep under here. I remember my plans and I suddenly have the energy of ten men. I ease back onto my seat and smile at the dazed look in my man's sexy eyes. With a napkin I clean the corners of my mouth before I rise up slightly to ease my skirt back down.

There is not a thing ladylike about blowing your man under the table in a crowded restaurant but who would know. I am not going to tell anyone . . . except Alizé . . . and Dom . . . and of course Mo. I *have* to tell my girls.

"Ready now?" I ask, pulling a compact from my purse to straighten my hair and check my makeup.

Mohammed just nods and his dreads swing against the sides of his handsome face as he reaches under the table to zip and button his pants. "Yeah, I'm ready," he says, raising his hand to motion for the check.

There is *nothing* a man can do about a woman on a mission.

As we leave the restaurant a man across the room raises his glass to me in a toast. I ignore him as I feel my face get hot. Nosy-behind people.

Mohammed hugs me close to him as we walk to our cars in the adjacent parking lot. "My place or yours?" he asks as he kisses my cheek and lightly bites my ear.

I take a deep breath and prepare to lie. "Actually I have an early morning meeting. I was thinking I would just stay home tonight . . . alone," I finish with what I hope is a beguiling smile as I wrap my arms around his waist and lean back to look up at him.

He frowns as he searches my eyes. Just when I think a million questions are about to fly out of his mouth he bends his head down to kiss me briefly. He lets me go and takes my key to unlock the door to my Toyota Solara. "Drive home safely."

Okay. I am confused as I give him one last kiss to those lips I love and climb into my car. I toot my horn as I pull out of the fenced in parking lot. I look in my rearview mirror to find that he is still standing in the same spot of the parking lot looking at me leave.

As soon as I step inside the luxuriously grand Waldorf-Astoria, I know I made the right decision to come. Located on Park Avenue, the Waldorf is one of the premiére social venues for the New York elite. This is a long way from foster care and group homes in Newark. I want to be here. I lied to my man and my friends about my whereabouts tonight—they would not understand and probably think I am up to my old ways which I am not. I charged eight hundred dollars to my credit card at a consignment shop for this one-shoulder, black mesh dress with beige chiffon underlay by Dolce & Gabbana—something that will take me at least a year to pay off. And I came to this stag—this is not Mohammed's type of thing but I will not cheat on him. I am seriously growing because last year I woulda whipped out my Bible and dialed me a date.

Am I crazy to be here . . . alone and in last season's dress?

I step off the elevator and walk towards the elaborate doors of the four-story Grand Ballroom. I carefully hold up the edge of the delicate form-fitting dress. I feel like I am in a fairy tale. It takes every bit of decorum that I have taught myself, not to look fazed by the glamour and elegance surrounding me. I did not miss the looks from admiring men and envious women. I look good and I know it. Sue me.

I make my smile more confident as I step inside and join the line of guests greeted by the Ingrams. For a hot second I have an image of the guards pulling me out there because Mrs. Ingram forgot that she invited me. She would not. She could not. She *better* not.

She is looking fabulous in a strapless dress of the deepest shade of red that I have ever seen. Everything about her is perfectly in place. She is the queen of the ball and she knows it.

"Hello, Mr. Ingram. Mrs. Ingram." I give them that winning Cristal smile as I reach out to them with both my hands.

"Hello, Danielle." Mr. Ingram pats my hand warmly before Mrs. Ingram reaches over to slide my hands into her grasp. Even her hands are cool.

"Welcome, Danielle," she says to me warmly before nudging me forward into the ballroom. I did not miss the way her eyes took in everything from my auburn weave flat ironed to perfection (of course) to my dress and jewelry. Thank God all of my men were not Indian-givers like Sahad. She did not make a crude comment so I assume I passed her assessment.

My eyes widen as I look at the partygoers. I cannot lie that I am intrigued. I see the crème de la crème of African-American high society. The already impressive ballroom is overflowing with flowers and artfully decorated tables around the large dance floor. Everything about this night says that no expense was spared. When the Ingrams throw a party, they throw a damn party. The crowd is a lot older and more sedate than I prefer. I am used to rubbing elbows with athletes and hip-hop celebrities—that hip twenty to thirty-something crowd. This is definitely a little more geriatric but it is also filled with people who are connected. Politicians. High-powered executives. Socialites. The Black elite.

There are more designer gowns and jewels in this place than I can ever hope to be near again. It is a long way from the foster kid growing up in Newark. I am going to enjoy myself to the fullest.

Chapter Ten

Alizé

"**B**raun, Weber. Monica Winters speaking."

"Hey, Ze, this is Cristal."

"Hold on." I stand up and quickly move around my desk to use my foot to close the door to my office. As soon as I settle back down into my chair, I press the phone back to my ear. "Whaddup, girl?" I ask.

"Did Mo call you?"

"No. Why? What's up?"

"Bones filed a petition to have paternity tests done on Tiffany."

"What?" I lean forward with my elbows on the desk.

"She just got the papers at work."

I pick up my pen and twirl it between my fingers. "Maybe it's a good thing. We all know he's the daddy. Now she can get some support from his Tupac wanna-be ass."

"*Are* we sure?" Cristal asks.

I frown. "Are we sure of what, Cris?"

"Are we sure Bones is the father?"

"Cris, don't *even* trip."

"I love Moët to death but she lied about Bones raping her. She did not tell us she was pregnant. Hell, we never knew she was screwing her preacher when we paid for her abortion." Cristal paused and I just know she is looking down at her nails. "Mo can keep secrets when she wants to. That is all I am saying."

"That was before. She's different now. Way more upfront."

Cristal remained quiet for a minute before she spoke. "Well, this blood test will tell it."

"The fact that he's getting the blood test might mean he wants to be involved. He hates Mo—"

"Understandably," Cristal interjected.

I do an eye roll. "Anyway, how are they gone handle getting along after everything that went down? Girl, that's some crazy shit."

"Tell me about it."

I bite my bottom lip and turn troubled eyes to the open laptop on my desk. "Well, I got some drama of my own."

"Cameron?"

"Please, he's so busy with his head up his fiancée's ass that he acts like I'm not alive. Hell, she be here more than I do."

Cristal's laughter fills the line. "So what's the drama?"

"My dad and his girlfriend Andrea are getting married."

"Ooh."

"And I have to tell my mama."

"Eew."

"This shit with my mama not getting over my daddy help put my ass in therapy." I drop my head in my hand.

"Yes, and I thank God for Dr. Locke getting you over that thug passion mess."

I cock a brow. "Focus, Cristal."

The other phone line rings.

"Hold on, Cris." I put her on hold and hit line two. "Braun, Weber. Monica Winters speaking."

"Hi down there, Monica. Mr. Steele's getting the team together for the ACTech acquisition. You want to sit in?"

"You know I do," I tell Delaney, already reaching behind me for the tan jacket of my suit.

She hangs up and I quickly pick up the other line. "Hey, Cris, I gotta go. Oh, and stay from under restaurant tables with your nasty self," I tease her as I rise from my seat.

"Who told you?"

"Mo. And don't trip 'cause you were gonna tell me yourself anyway."

"Sure was."

"Hey, did you swallow it? Gargle it?" I make a gargling noise in my throat before I drop the phone onto its cradle with a laugh.

As soon as I walk out my office my eyes lock on Cameron walking down the hall towards the conference room. I swallow over a lump in my throat as I take him in. All of him. I was an ass to think that this tall, handsome brotha with all the confidence and strength a man would ever need was not the man for me. He presented his heart to me on a platter and I threw it away. I could just pimp slap my damn self.

"Hi, Cameron," I call out as he walks right by me with his head down reading a file he carried.

He pauses and turns. He looks up and for a second his face lights up at seeing me but then the look fades away and he nods shortly. "Monica," he says just as shortly before he turns and continues on his way.

My plan to win him back before the big wedding day isn't scoring any runs. I hardly see him during the day and when we are within feet of each other there's always this distant and polite thing, as if we weren't friends last year. As if he didn't tell me he loved me.

"Cameron," I call out to him.

He turns again.

"Could I speak to you for a quick sec?"

He frowns.

I give him a smile. "Please."

He looks hesitant but he walks back down the hall towards me. Once I get him in my office, I am going to lock the door and jump his ass like white on rice. I done had enough of this ignoring me shit.

"Thanks . . . for . . ." The rest of my words trail off as his eyes shift from my face to some spot behind me. I turn to see what has taken his attention off me and all my fabulousness (even in my suit and heels I rip it, okay). My mouth drops open at the sight of Serena Lemons—Cameron's fiancée. Everything about her is the epitome of the corporate wife. She's tall, slender—but curvaceous, and beautiful, with jet black hair parted down the middle and flowing down her back. Somehow I know it's all real. This rich bitch can give Cristal a run for her money as the real deal socialite. She is wearing a mink, rocking the Fendi shades, Louis bag in place, looking like a black Barbie.

I hate her.

Cameron walks right past me and immediately pulls his future bride to him for a kiss.

He is happy to see her.

He is looking down at her as if he is deeply in love with her.

I am suddenly the last thing on his damn mind.

I hate that bitch even more.

I park my mom's old Camry (she upgraded to the 2008 model) in the driveway. I'm so happy to be home. This shit with Cameron is really messing with me. Standing there watching him kiss his fiancée hurt me like crazy. I know I told him that I didn't care . . . but I do. I know that I shouldn't give a shit . . . but I do. I know I shouldn't cry . . . but I want to. Damn.

I wish like hell that I could just drive to Livingston and talk this shit out with my girls but I had some other business to take care of. As soon as I walk through the side entrance into the kitchen, I see my mother stirring in a pot. She's already undressed from work and in one of her beloved caftans. She turns and smiles at me like I am the best thing since sliced damn bread. I love Elaine Winters to death. How in the hell am I going to tell her that my dad (the man she still loves) is marrying another woman?

"How was your day?" she asks.

"I went to my internship today," I remind her as I fling my overcoat onto the back of the chair at the wooden table.

"How *is* Mr. Steele?"

I move over to stand by her at the stove and my stomach grumbles at the sight of her lima beans and neck bones. "Still good. Still getting married."

She looks up at me and there is a hint of sadness in her eyes. "Seems like there's a lot of weddings and such going on."

"You know?" I ask her softly.

She nods and throws her arm around my waist to comfort me. That's ironic as hell. "I'm fine and I am happy for your father so don't you worry about me."

Playfully she swats my bottom and I hope like hell that she is telling me the truth.

Chapter Eleven

Dom

I got fuckin' troubles.

My job finally gives me a fuckin' raise and then has the nerve to up Kimani's daycare fees talkin' 'bout the fees is based on my income. Ain't that 'bout a no-good bitch? I ain't gone front. My share of the rent, my car note and insurance, plus daycare is kickin' my ass. Kimani needs clothes and shit. I need clothes. Shit, I'm already sellin' half my food stamps to help with my bills. I ain't never had to struggle like this and I grew up in the fuckin' projects.

For the last couple of weeks my ass been thinkin' 'bout a new job but hell more income mean more daycare fees. I'm 'bout sick of the rock *and* the fuckin' hard place. Can a bitch get a break? Or do a bitch need to give herself the damn break?

I parallel park in between a bright yellow Tahoe and a Sebring. I didn't have no business here but here I am. I look out the passenger window at the buildin' tryin' to get the nerve to get out my car.

My cell phone rings and I pick it up from the passenger seat. Corey's smilin' face fills the screen. I don't want to feel all soft and shit about him calling me. Our shit ain't supposed to be this way.

"Hey."

"Whassup, Sensual Chocolate?"

I smile at his nickname for me. This short, big-dick motherfucker always makes me smile and right now I can use it. "Nothin'. Whaddup with you?" I ask as I crank up the car and turn on the heat. Jersey in the winter is cold as hell.

"You in your car?" he asks. "You bringing my pussy over here to me?"

My eyes dart to the left as two hooded men walk past my car. My ass is tense as hell 'til they out of my eye range. Fuck that. I ain't tryin' to get carjacked or some shit. "*Your* pussy?" I ask, with my eyes still on the rearview mirror.

"Damn right," he answers with authority.

"Nigga, you trippin'. You ain't my man."

"But I wanna be your man."

Uh-oh. Oh no. Here we go again.

"Let me call you right back," I say suddenly, wantin' to change the subject as I grab my purse and get out my car. I shiver. It's even colder at night and right now the winter season is bitin' like a bitch.

"Before you hang up—'cause I know your ass ain't gone call me back—I want you to let me take you out tomorrow night."

"That's Valentine's," I protest.

"And?"

Holidays. Dates. Phone calls. Relationship. What part of fuck buddies don't his ass get?

"I'm walkin' in the store. I'll call you back," I lie as I push the remote to lock the car. *Ba-boop*.

"If you don't call me back I'ma put your ass on dick knock off," he says in a joking voice.

I don't even take his ass seriously. "Bye, Corey."

I close the phone and drop it into my bag as I step up onto the curb. The wind whips around me. The street is dark except for the flashing neon sign. Club XXXCite. I look at my reflection in the dark glass. I feel alone. So fucked up. Like I'm backtrackin' or some shit. But I feel like I ain't got no choice either.

Then why is it so hard for my ass to go in?

I light a cigarette and smoke that whole motherfucker plus another one. My hands and ears are cold. My leather jacket ain't doing shit to block the cold. My feet are freezin' standin' in the pissy snow. As men walk inside the club, the loud music and flashing lights come out the door. It's fuckin' money to be made up in that bitch but so much more to be lost.

I drop the lit cigarette and crush it into the grayish snow with the tip of my boot before I walk inside the club. It's dark as hell and it takes a minute for my eyes to get used to it. The smell of liquor, weed, and body is familiar as hell to me.

"Whaddup, Juicy!"

I smile at the tall and muscular bodyguard dressed in all black. "Whaddup, Dogg."

He wraps one beefy arm around me and pulls me close as hell for a hug. When he slaps my ass I feel like grabbin' his nuts in my hand and pulling down 'til he screams like a bitch. "Where's Vic?" I ask instead as I follow Dogg to the circular bar in the center of the club.

"He opened a new spot on Sixteenth Avenue so I'm kinda runnin' this one while he gets that one all straightened out and shit."

Dogg's breath smells like somebody's ass and I wonder which one of these dancers he done ate the fuck out. He use to treat the girls like they were his personal pussy playland and he probably still do. "Well I want to make some money," I tell him as I squint my eyes and peep the shit goin' on in this motherfucker.

Dancers in nothing but thongs and g-strings with titties hanging as they lap dance for the money. Two dykes are butt naked on the stage 'bout to let everyone in on the shit they supposed to do behind closed doors. In the corner dollar bills are flying up in the air from a crowd of hot boys watching some bitch booty clappin'.

Same-o-same-o I left behind.

"For tips only?" Dogg asks as he raises a shot to his mouth.

"Like some new bitch?" I ask, kinda insulted. "You know what Juicy can do."

"Well, I ain't seen Juicy in a minute so I don't remember," he throws back at me.

"Put me on after the clit lickers," I tell him before walkin' away from him.

I don't break my stride even when I see some random bitch under the table sneakin' this dude a blow job. I did smile when I thought of Cristal pullin' that same shit with her man in a restaurant. I ain't know she had it in her. Bitch swallowed and all.

Downstairs in the dressin' room, that same smell of funky feet, corn chips, and ass is still there. Most of the dancers are upstairs but I turn the corner by the beat-up lockers and see asses in the air as two dancers are bent over and snorting something from the counter. The sight of them gettin' high makes me anxious. It would be so easy to walk over there do a line and forget my money problems for a little while.

One of the girls stands up and almost stumbles on her five-inch heels. She turns. It's Candy. I frown a little. When I used to work here she was my weed partner. Me and this bitch could smoke four blunts straight without blinkin'.

The way she looks right now scares the shit out of me.

Powder is on the tip of her nose. Her eyes are so glassy and kinda yellow. She done lost weight. Her makeup is smeared and shit. This bitch look like . . . a junkie. Straight the fuck up.

Candy looks right at me but I know she so high she don't even recognize me. "Wanna hit?" she asks me. Her words is all slurred together as she stumbles back onto the edge of the counter. She reaches out with her hand and it lands in the residue. She laughs and raises her hand to lick the dope from her fingers.

I watch her and I feel hungry for it. My body is callin' for it. I want to lick her fingers, the counter, hell, the floor if some is down there on it. I want to get high *so* fuckin' bad.

I ain't gone never stop wantin' it?

I turn and run the hell out of there, almost trippin' as I try to get my ass up them fuckin' stairs. *Go. Go. Go.* I tell myself as I run through the club knockin' some big tittie bitch over as I fly out the damn door. As soon as I feel the cold air surround my body I stop and just fuckin' *breathe.* Cold air ain't never tasted so good. Bein' out of that strip club ain't never felt so good. It's like I was drownin' and finally breakin' through the water for some fuckin' air.

I can't go back. I can't. I *won't.*

I walk quick as hell to my car and climb in. My hands are shakin' as I crank my car. I pull off just as them tears I'm fightin' rolls from my eyes.

Everything for me is a fuckin' battle.

Chapter Twelve

Cristal

"Lowe, Ingram, and Banks."

"Hello, Danielle. This is Carolyn."

I look up from the message pad I was jotting on. "Hello, Mrs. Ing—"

"Call me Carolyn, dear."

"Uh, hello, Carolyn. If you will hold one second I will get you transferred in to Mr. Ingram."

"Actually I was calling to speak to you."

I pause. I am not quite sure how to take this lady. The charity event at the Waldorf-Astoria was two weeks ago. She hardly spoke to me there and I have not seen or heard from her since. I left the party confused as hell as to why she even invited me and I am confused as hell now that she wants to speak to me.

"How can I help you?"

"There's a celebrity charity luncheon tomorrow and I thought this would be a great event for you to attend with me."

One of my shaped brows lifts slightly. "Why?" I ask in the nicest tone and manner possible.

"Why not?" she counters mysteriously.

I know the luncheon of which she speaks. I even read somewhere that Star Jones, Holly Robinson Peete, Kimora Lee Simmons, and many more are supposed to attend. Do I want to have a fabulous meal and rub elbows with these celebrities? Hell yeah.

"I have to work tomorrow."

Carolyn laughs like I said the funniest thing in the world. "Oh dear, don't worry about that."

"Can I get back to you?" I ask, pretending to sound young, dumb, and unsure. I want to go. Do not get me wrong. But I am a little tired of this woman jerking my chain and catching me off guard.

She paused for a noticeable moment before saying, "Get back to me but remember the early bird gets the worm, Danielle. In life you never give another bitch the chance to take your spot."

Feeling properly reprimanded for not jumping all over her invitation, I still stick to my guns. "I had a prior engagement and I would not want to be rude and accept without making sure I can change my plans."

She paused again. "Well, call me as soon as you can. Here's my cell number."

Even as I am writing it down I am wondering if I upset her.

"Well, I have to go. I have a spa appointment. Danielle, make sure you make the right decision."

The line goes dead.

I cannot explain what made me drive through Newark instead of hopping on the interstate to get to Mohammed's house. Newark is called the comeback city and I cannot disagree that some areas look better. The rough and rowdy crowd is gone on blocks where they used to rule the streets. Hard-working people now live in the townhouses that replaced ten story multi-apartment dwellings that bred apathy and crime (too many people in one spot is never a good thing).

Still, there is a lot more to be done for sure.

I turn my car on the corner of Nineteenth Avenue and Nineteenth Street. There is nothing but the remnants of the house left after the fire but in my mind's eye I can see it and my days in it so clearly . . .

"Danielle! What are you doing in there?"

I hear Mrs. Davies but I ain't listenin' to her. I'm too busy flippin' through the pages of magazines and imaginin' that their great lives, fancy cars, and pretty clothes on the pages are mine. The magazines are years old but I don't care.

I stay in the bedroom a lot. Most of the other foster kids are in the livin' room watchin' TV but I just want to be alone in here whenever I can. Sleepin' four to a bedroom is crazy. Ain't no space in this place that you can call your own. No secrets. No hidin' places. Just two bunk beds squeezed in these four walls. And between the four foster kids stayin' here there still ain't enough stuff to fill the closet and the drawers. Closet and drawers I don't use. Ain't no need shoving my few pants, couple of T-shirts, and my precious magazines in no drawers.

I been here for a year and I still ain't tryna call this place home. I done been down the road of gettin' comfortable and just havin' the rug snatched from under me when they come to take me to another house and another family that ain't my house or my family. Or another group home that don't feel nothin' like home.

The bedroom door swings open and Mrs. Davies walks in lookin' mad as always.

She already got bad ass kids of her own. I don't know why she asks for all these foster kids when she mad about it. Wait a minute. Yes I do. I know about the money they get for each of us. Humph.

"Where you get them magazines from? You steal them, girl?" she says to me in the nastiest voice. Dang on shame I been livin' here for a year and every time she see me readin' these same old magazines she ask that same dumb question.

I always gave her the same dumb answer.

"No ma'am, these my same old magazines."

She bends down and snatches one from me, looks at the cover, sucks her teeth and drops it back down on the floor where I'm sittin' before she turns and leaves the room. Same-o-same-o.

I shrug and go back to readin'. I compared sequin gowns to my washed out T-shirt and high-heeled sandals to my no-name sneakers with the big Velcro straps across the top. These black stars talkin' 'bout big mansions and lots of cars and I had my squeaky bottom bunk bed.

I got dreams. I promised myself that I can't do nothin' 'bout this now but I ain't gone be poor forever. There's a better life out there for me and I'm gonna find it.

* * *

It was hard growing up and knowing nobody wanted to adopt me and my foster parents mainly had me and the others there for the money. I guess I was lucky to stay in that same foster care until I turned eighteen instead of getting bounced around some more. Still, I never did let myself feel like it was my home. And I never gave up on my dreams . . . until now.

I love Mohammed. I really do but I still feel like there are greater things out there for me to see and to have. Sometimes it feels like loving him made me forget my dreams. My ambition.

There's a better life out there for me and I'm gonna find it.

Why can't I have it all?

I take my foot off the brake and steer my car up Nineteenth Avenue and make a left on Eastern Parkway towards the other side of town to the Weequahic section. I hardly notice the people, the lights, or even the cars I pass as I make my way to Mohammed. He has a surprise for our Valentine's Day and I am ready to be with my man.

Still, my mind is on that luncheon tomorrow. What would it hurt to go?

As I sit to the light on the corner of Clinton Avenue and Eastern Parkway, I reach in my purse for my cell phone. I scroll through my address for Carolyn (yes, I programmed her number in my phone).

It rings just once.

"Hello, Danielle."

"How did you know it was me?"

She laughs lightly. "I only give my cellular number to friends and your number is the only one I don't recognize. So . . . have you made up your mind?"

"Yes. I would love to go."

"No conflicting appointments?" she asks a little mockingly.

The light turns green and I make the left turn onto Clinton Avenue. "No."

"Good. Take the whole day off and get yourself all beautiful for the luncheon. In fact, I will call Saks and let them know you will be by in the morning to purchase a new outfit . . . on me, of course."

My mouth falls open. "Wow. Thank you. Thank you so much,

Mrs. Ing—. Carolyn," I tell her as I steer the car with one hand and hold my cell phone with the other.

"Of course, no worries, dear. I will send my car to pick you up in the morning to run your errands and bring you to the luncheon."

"I do not know what to say, Carolyn," I say as I turn my car onto the driveway behind Mohammed's battered SUV.

"No worries," she says in a dismissive tone. "I have to go. Valentine's Day and all. There's a dick to be sucked and fucked and gifts to be plucked. I'm sure you understand."

I laugh. "Yes, I do." After I climb from the car I grab the gift bag holding the silk pajamas and sex toys I brought for Mohammed and me tonight.

"See you tomorrow, dear."

"Bye-bye." I can hardly believe my luck. I just found my own fairy godmother. Just call me Cinderella-ella-ella-eh-eh-eh.

I close my phone just as I jog up the stairs and use my key to walk into the house.

Surprise and pleasure stop me at the door. Candles and rose petals are everywhere and there by the fireplace atop a fake fur blanket is Mohammed, naked, hard, and ready with a red ribbon tied around his dick. I smile as I kick off my shoes and close the door. By the time I reach him, I have stripped off my clothes and I am laying down beside him just as naked as I please to unwrap my gift.

Chapter Thirteen

Moët

It's funny how good times are always followed by the bad times for me. My own little way of knowing that I'm not special or blessed. Classic examples of the Lord giveth and He taketh away.

My first lover is extraordinarily good in bed but he's the sinful pastor of my family's church.

I am blessed with my first pregnancy but the father is that same sinful pastor who wants nothing more than for me to have an abortion.

I fall in love with Bones, a high-profile, wealthy celebrity but he accuses me of entrapping him with my second pregnancy.

I began to date the man of my dream. I find out he's a virgin sworn to abstinence.

The paternity results proved without a shadow of doubt that Bones is the father. I just got served papers that he's suing me for full custody of our daughter.

"I ain't letting that . . . that . . . *motherfucker* take my daughter," I say in a hard voice.

Dom walks out of the kitchen in a wifebeater and leggings on her slender frame. Her eyes widen and her mouth drops open as I look at her. I'm not saved but I have really tried hard not to curse anymore. Now here is this Negro making me lose what little religion I do have.

"Today I had to take three kids away from their mother because she gave them liquor to make them go to sleep and he wants to take my daughter away from me like *I'm* unfit. There's a mother on the news who let her toddlers smoke weed and had the nerve to videotape it and this asshole wants to take my daughter from me."

Dom sits the carton of ice cream she's holding onto the table before she bends down to scoop Tiffany out of her carrier. "Kimani, go in the room and watch TV," she says.

"He is so busy chasing a bunch of Supahead wannabes that he hasn't seen Tiffany since she was born. Hell, he's denied her from the jump street." I am shaking with anger as I stalk back and forth across the living room. I hate the tears that fill my eyes. I hate them more when they fall down my cheeks. "He's just mad that the test proves he's my daughter's father."

Out the corner of my eyes I see Dom lay my baby in the rocking cradle by the unlit fireplace. My baby. *My* baby. I walk across the room and move Dom out of the way to gather her into my arms. I press my face into her neck and I can't imagine not being able to hold her and smell her and kiss her whenever I want.

"Heavenly Father, show me the way, Lord," I whisper near her cheek. "Show me what to do—"

"What you should do is call his ass and talk it out 'cause y'all really do need to get this shit together."

I love Dom. I do. But I wish like hell that Cristal or Alizé was here instead. I know she mean well but Dom—therapy or no therapy—is still a little rough around the edges with her advice.

I settle down onto the couch with my daughter held close to me with my tears wetting her as I pray like I have never prayed before.

I pray for the Lord to show me the way.

I pray that the strength I will need to fight for my daughter comes to me.

I pray that the anger I feel dies down so that I can think clearly.

I pray for Him to forgive me for my sins.

I pray that He shows Bones another way.

I pray and I pray and I pray some more.

"Jesus. Jesus, please don't let him take my daughter. Please."

I feel a hand on my shoulder shake me gently and I look up surprised to see Taquan coming around the couch to sit beside me. He uses his thumb to wipe the tracks of my tears and I close my eyes to lean my face into his hand. When he settles back to pull me and Tiffany into his embrace I let myself lean against him.

"How long I been praying?"

"Dom called me and I came right over," he whispers into my hair as he rocks us both gently.

I forgot that we had plans for a Valentine's dinner.

Without me even asking, he lowers his head. "Heavenly Father, we call on You for we are in need," he begins to pray with reverence.

God, I am so glad that he's here.

Girl Talk

Moët, Cristal, Alizé, and Dom all sat around on the large white sofa in their living room. They all were dressed casually and enjoying eating straight from various containers of ice cream. Each had things on their minds and it felt good just to be in the company of friends.

"Winnin' the lottery would come in handy right 'bout now," Dom says, wearing shorts and a tank and crossing her legs Indian style. Her brows came together as she thought of her bills.

Cristal thought of the glamorous life she craved.

Alizé thought about paying off her school loans.

Moët thought about being able to afford attorney fees to win custody of her child.

"Tell me about it," they all said in unison before digging down deep into their ice creams.

Chapter Fourteen

Alizé

Cameron's eyes are on me as I give my best runway walk to his desk. I keep my eyes on him. I can hardly believe he has summoned me to his office and I'm glad that I chose the ankle-length fitted skirt and silk blouse by Claiborne. My heart is beating mad crazy as we keep looking at each other. I'm thinking he looks sexy as hell with his tailored shirt slightly open at the neck with his rust tie loosened and the sleeves rolled up to expose strong forearms. I wonder what's on his mind.

"Cameron, this is ridiculous," I say as I smile down at him and flip my jet-black hair over my shoulder. I am in full flirt mode.

At my informal tone he leans back in his chair and sits his square chin in his hand. "And exactly what is ridiculous?"

"You pretending that we weren't friends last year . . . that you never said you loved me," I say softly as I trail my hand around the edge of his desk as I come around to stand above him. "Like I said . . . ridiculous."

Cameron shakes his head at me and smiles sardonically. "Now *this* is inappropriate."

"Inappropriate?" I ask with a little laugh. I cock my head to the damn side and pull my skirt up around my waist to expose my matching lace thongs. Oh, I'm a bitch on a mission. Trust. Before his behind can blink I kick a leg over his lap, sit on the edge of his desk before him, and spread my knees wide.

Cameron's eyes dart down to my sweet business in his face before his eyes dart to his closed office door. "Monica—"

"I locked it on my way in," I tell him in that husky and sexy fuck me voice as I shift my hands down to pull my thong to the side to trace a finger against my throbbing clit with a purr.

"So you don't love me. You don't want to date me . . . but you want to fuck me?" he asks with attitude just before I use my finger to trace my pussy juices onto his mouth.

He starts to lick it but bites his bottom lip to keep his tongue locked in. "But I do—"

Bzzzz.

He rolls to the left and quickly pushes a button on the intercom system. "Yes, Delaney."

"Your fiancée is here to see you."

Cameron jumps to his feet and reaches out quickly to snap my legs shut. "I actually called you in here to tell you that my fiancée is having a little issue with your working here."

"And?" I ask with attitude as he places strong hands on my fore-arms and lifts me from the desk with way too much ease.

"And I need you to stop throwing me those vibes before more than my fiancée picks up on it," he says sternly, as he quickly straightens his tie and unrolls his sleeves.

I smooth my skirt back down over my hips. I could strip naked and wait on wifey but if Cameron is angry at me for the little stunt that it defeats my purpose of winning him back before the wedding date. A date that is getting closer and closer. "So . . . you don't love me anymore," I say softly, trying to overcome my natural reaction to put up my guard and protect my heart.

"And you never loved me . . . remember?"

I turn and offer him a smile that is the opposite of my sadness.

"I moved on, Monica, and I need for you to respect that."

I walk back across the room and stand before him. I look him in those eyes and take a deep breath. "I love you," I admit to him softly.

His eyes widen in surprise just as the doorknob rattles.

I place my hands on his shoulders and raise up on my toes to whisper against his lips, "I can love you better than she can, Cameron."

His head lowers to mine and I feel excitement course over my body.

The doorknob rattles again.

Cameron jerks back from me and rushes over to open the door.

I got the message. Serena comes first.

Tears fill my eyes and I walk past them and out the door, leaving him to answer any questions she may have. I got enough problems of my own. I lost the man that I love forever and it hurt like hell.

That night when I get home I am immediately on my guard because these days it's a regular damn barrel of surprises with my moms. *I'll be fine*, she said. *Don't worry about me*, she said. That was a big old lie. My mama done straight lost her damn mind.

At first I was happy that she started to hang out with a couple of her friends from work. *Yes, Ma, get out the house. Socialize*, my dumb ass told her. I didn't know she was gonna step out the house with skin tight jeans, stilettos, and enough makeup to shut down MAC and Cover Girl. Hell, she was *my* mama not a damn hoochie mama.

And then one night last week she didn't come home at all. My mama stayed out all night and then gone come home early in the morning looking like she been in a wrestling match.

Elaine Winters is straight trippin' all up and through here. My daddy's getting married and she's going through a damn midlife crisis. Hell, I still don't know where she stayed that night. Had the nerve to tell me to "get up outta her business." Say what? Say fucking who?

I'm starting to think she needs to get her ass on the couch and talk some shit over with Dr. Locke.

I walk into the kitchen and there is nothing popping on the stove. My mama *used to* cook everyday. Once I pull off my coat and step out of my heels, I make me a quick ham and cheese sandwich, grab my briefcase, and head out the kitchen.

I take a big bite out of my sandwich and stroll into the living room. "Ma . . ."

All I see is flashes of ass and titties and a dick sliding out of my mama. What the motherfuck? I drop everything in my damn hand and turn before I see anymore than I already seen.

"Excuse me, Rockman," I hear my mom say.

Rockman. What the fuck?

Seconds later there is a strong hand on my arm leading me somewhere. I am scared to open my damn eyes. Oh, Lord, I saw my mama fucking. I wish I had went to Livingston and spent the night with the girls. Most of the time me and Dom still didn't talk directly to each other but we were in a better place than this time last month. So even with a little awkwardness between me and Dom, anything is better than walking in on an amateur scene from a flick.

"Please stay in here while I escort my company upstairs."

"Maybe if you and your company were upstairs in the first place I wouldn't feel like tearing my eyes out with spoons!"

"This is *my* house."

Okay that makes me open my eyes and get this. She has on a damn oversized Roc-a-Fella T-shirt. I give her a long disgusted look and step right out the kitchen into the living room to really get a good look at this Negro. I gasp in horror. This young buck with the braids, faded jeans, and Timbs is my damn age. Humph, well he might be in his early twenties but he real late on getting fucked up.

"Aw hell no. Get the fuck out," I tell him, walking over to start pushing that fool towards the front door.

He frowns looking more and more like Nelly to me. "What? Hold on. What the hell . . ."

"Monica!"

I feel my mama's hands on my arm but I shake her off and keep shoving this nigga.

"Monica!"

I turn and look at her, my mama, like I don't even know her.

Okay, this is why I'm so mad. This . . . *shit* is just another damn example of her still loving and wanting to be with my father. Deep down she is so upset that her hopes and dreams of a reconciliation are being squashed that she has done a total 180 degrees. This same stupid shit of hers had me scared to fall in love. Scared to admit to Cameron that I loved him.

In the past, before Rah broke my leg, I would find a dance studio and make myself forget everything but getting lost in the music. I don't even have the time or the passion to dance no more. But right now I would bust open my scar to just get in the zone and forget this shit. I need my stress reliever more than ever.

"I'm going to Daddy's," I tell her before I storm out of the living room. I pause for a hot second at the bottom of the stairs before I climb them. When I finally reach my room I don't hesitate to start packing some of my clothes.

I'm pissed at my mama for this shit. Right, wrong, or indifferent, it's just how I feel and right now I just want to get the fuck away. My mama is a fuckin' cougar on the prowl for younger men. I am so sick of her shit.

"Why did you need an emergency appointment this morning, Monica?"

I shift my eyes from the view of the spring leaves on the trees to look at Dr. Locke. Of course, I know the answer to his questions but I don't feel like talking. Just being in this office, in this chair, across from him gave me comfort.

In this moment, none of the bullshit bothers me.

Not my mama drama.

Not the hell of sleeping on the couch in my dad's living room.

Not how stupid I feel sometimes for being Dom's friend again.

Not even how it really fucks with me that I laid my pussy out for Cameron and he rejected me.

Emotions made my chest tight and I took a deep breath hoping to get myself straight. Yes, this forty-five minute session where I ain't had shit to say was worth a hundred and fifty dollars to me.

I shift my eyes back to the window.

Something on his desk buzzes.

"Excuse me, I have to take that."

I look over at him as he sits his notepad on the small table by his chair and unfolds his tall frame to walk over to his desk and pick up the phone. Unlike his normal attire of a suit, Dr. Locke wore a fitted polo and slacks in all black. The color looks good on him with his bronzed complexion and silver goatee. His shoulders look broad and his arms are still a little toned beneath his short sleeves.

I bring my hand up to lightly bite the tip of my thumb as I watch him closely. He speaks quietly on the phone and my eyes drop to his mouth. Straight even teeth. Nice lips. Groomed beard. I squirm in my seat as I feel my nature slowly rising.

Again that question pops into my head.

How wrong would I be to fuck my therapist?

How wrong indeed?

He turns his back to me and I reach up to shake my hair free.

By the time he ends his call and turns to me I am sitting in that chair naked as the day I was born with each of my legs draped over the arms of the chair. His eyes drop down to take in my pussy and I see that hot look come over his face. Got him. I have nothing to say . . . but there is no need to let my good money go to waste. I might as well get *something* out of this last thirty minutes.

Part Two

"Keep on Movin'"

Chapter Fifteen

Dom

One Month Later

I'm tryin' to avoid Corey's ass flirtin' with me from across the room as I finish readin' to the circle of children at my feet. The shit might sound crazy but I'm enjoyin' the story about Rumpelstiltskin my damn self. That's the thing. Workin' here made me realize that I like to read. I get lost in the stories and shit. It makes me forget my own drama with bills, my mama, and anythin' fuckin' else.

After puttin' Kimani to bed at night, books about the hood been keepin' me occupied. (I'm still a late owl. Shit I don't get sleepy 'til 'bout one in the mornin'.) Right now I'm blazin' through this book one of the girls at work let me borrow called *Desperate Hoodwives*. That shit about these four crazy bitches got me carryin' that mother-fucker with me everywhere so I can read some whenever I get a chance. And the more my ass be readin' books and writin' in my journal, the more I feel like I can write a book too. Shit, growin' up in the projects, my ass plenty of stories to tell.

"Miss Lands? What happens next?"

I look down at one of my students and then all the rest of them. Each one is lookin' up from their spots on the floor, waitin' on me to stop daydreamin' and finish the story. That makes my ass smile. "I'm sorry," I tell them playfully.

Some of them giggle. It's funny as hell that I didn't use to like to spend time with my own child and now I love being around her and the rest of the carpet crawlers.

I search the page to find the spot where the hell I left off. I look up and catch sight of Kimani's class walkin' like little soldiers in one single line behind their teacher. Mrs. Harris don't play and she keeps her class in check all day everyday. Kimani waves at me with her curly Afro puff on top of her head and I give her a wink. When she leans forward to talk to a child in front of her, my eyes shift. Her friend Hiasha got the same damn black girl puff on the top of her head.

They look like twins.

I frown with my eyes goin' from one to the damn other.

Now this the shit. As much as I see Kimani and Hiasha together, this the first time it hit me that them two heifers look a lot alike. Like sisters.

Even after Kimani and the rest of the pre-schoolers go down the stairs to their area, I think about Hiasha. While I'm readin' this story to the kids. While I'm serving them a snack of pineapple juice and oatmeal cookies. Even when me and Corey sneak off for one of our lunch hour fuck fests, I think about Hiasha. When the bank calls my job talkin' 'bout repo'ing my Lexus 'cause I'm two payments behind I got right off the phone with they ass and thought about Hiasha.

Did my babydaddy, Deon, have another bitch pregnant the same time that I was? How sorry would it be that if that motherfucker know he got two daughters the same age and ain't said shit about it?

Is Hiasha my daughter's sister? Her last name is . . . Kingsley. It ain't the same as my babydaddy but that don't mean shit 'cause Kimani ain't got that nigga's name either.

At the end of the day, I make my way downstairs to the colorful play area of the pre-kindergartners. Kimani's class is in the back rear corner. I am lookin' at they asses sittin' side by side on the carpeted bench lookin' in a book together. Them two been thick as damn thieves since Kimani's first day here.

I'm schemin' on gettin' into the daycare's record and gettin' some info but Yoba, the clerk—with her lazy fat ass—don't leave her desk for shit. If I ask, will she tell me the name of Hiasha's daddy? Probably the fuck not. She 'bout a stupid big headed bitch.

My daughter looks up and she smiles at me with all this love and trust and shit. She relies on me. Depends on me. Needs me. Loves me.

If Hiasha is her sister a bitch like me need to get on the grind and find out for sure. I ain't tryin' to be one of those fuck the next bitch type of chicks no more.

Might be time for me to look up my babydaddy. Plus, if his ass working he gone give me some child support. Hiasha sure don't look like she lackin' for a motherfuckin' thing. Yup, my ass gone kill two birds with one damn stone.

Chapter Sixteen

Cristal

Now *this* is the life.

A Central Park West penthouse. A guest roster filled with an eclectic mix of New York's A-list celebrities and socialites. Veuve Clicquot champagne flowing like water. Appetizers by Wolfgang Puck. Wynton Marsalis and his band playing the best of the best from the stage in the corner of the ballroom. The Ingrams' dinner party is the crème de la crème.

And I am right in the midst of the world of being rich, beautiful, and philanthropic. The socializing is great but a sister like me is also networking. Carolyn says the best way to become rich and famous is to hang around the rich and famous.

In fact these past couple of months I have been to more soirees than the entire year I was with Sahad. Benefits, charity events, and store openings. It was the perfect start to a summer in New York. Some of New York's high profile celebrities and socialites knew me by name because of my association with Carolyn and because of my prior relationship with Mr. New York himself Sahad Linx. I have even received a few mentions in the gossip rags, who knew being Sahad's ex had benefits.

I take a sip of my champagne as I stand in a circle made up of Carolyn, the Reynolds (Star and Al), and Kimora Lee Simmons, looking just as fine as I want to be in a strapless gray sequin dress by

Diane Von Furstenburg with Giuseppe on the heels (like Ms. Mary of course). I am so loving my life right now.

My cell phone rings inside my clutch. The sounds of Kanye West's newest song drifts up. Carolyn raises a disapproving eye and I make a mental note not to forget to put it on vibrate again. At the sight of Mohammed's number my stomach nearly drops to the floor.

"Excuse me ladies, I will be right back," I whisper to them before drifting off to the guest bathroom in the gold trimmed hall.

As soon as I close and lock the door behind me, I pull out my BlackBerry. I have five voice mail messages. I sit my purse on the marble counter and take a deep sip of my champagne before I check them.

"This is Cristal the fabulous one enjoying an uberfabulous life. If you're calling you're not with me living it up too. Aw. Too bad. Too sad."

Beep.

"Danielle, you forgot we supposed to go to the reggae concert? Why you not answering your phone?"

Beep.

"Danielle, what going on with you girl?" Mohammed asks with his accent even heavier in anger. *"You no wanna be with me no more? 'Cause that's what gone happen." Click.*

Beep.

"Cristal, girl you are missing it. Dom just pimp slapped some damn girl for spilling liquor on her dress. Möet is in the middle of them trying to break it up. Girl, call me. Call me!"

Beep.

"Cristal. Bitch, how 'bout Ze's mama here with Rockman trickin' ass. Humph. Ze 'bout to flip in this bitch. Oooh, Ze, your mama know how to supersoak that ho better than your fuckin' ass."

Beep.

The line just hangs up during the last message. I know it was Mohammed and even as I stand in the midst of the world I longed to be a part of, I miss him. I wish that he could stand beside me and enjoy this world just like I do. But I know he wants no part of it. He is a simple man who just wants to work hard and be a good man. He could care less about wealth and fame.

Lose Mohammed? I cannot do that.

Lose the new spot I am claiming in a world I felt I belonged in? I did not want to do that.

For the last two months I have used every lie imaginable to get away. The girls and Mohammed would not understand. They would think I am back on the prowl for a wealthy husband and I am not. Several men—several wealthy men—-several wealthy *celebrity* men mind you—have stepped to me and I have nothing but Mohammed on mind. Me, the *ultimate* gold-digger, is quite happy with my handyman with the little house in Newark. I am not here on the prowl. There is no other man for me but Mohammed—this I know for sure.

I look down at my silver BlackBerry and my thumb is right over the speed dial button. I cannot call him. Not right now. I have to make my apologies in person. As much as I would love to hear his sexy Jamaican tongue wrap around my name, I push my BlackBerry back into my purse.

I turn to check my flawless makeup in the mirror. Everything about me being here seems right. A piece of me is still that little orphan girl nobody wants with the high water jeans and dirty no-name sneakers wishing her wealthy parents would swoop in and rescue her from a life of poverty and no heritage. A piece of me wants to make everything right. Restore order. Set it all straight.

With one last check of my appearance, I swallow down the last of my champagne and leave the bathroom to get back to the party.

Chapter Seventeen

Moët

Tonight I am on a mission.

Cristal has hooked me up with an attorney, a Helen Jacobsen, from the firm where she works. I have an appointment with her to-morrow. She's supposed to be one of the best attorneys in the tri-state area . . . so at least for tonight Tiffany is safely asleep in her crib in my bedroom. For the first time since I got those papers, I feel like I have the will to fight for—and win—custody of my daughter.

I had to testify for the first time in family court about the back-ground and emotional stability of a child ordered to testify against her mother in a neglect case. My supervisor praised me for my per-formance and we believe the judge's decision not to let the child testify was mainly due to that. So work—for now—is a non-issue.

My sister, Latrece, called complaining about my parents' not let-ting her join the debate team because it would mean her having to travel out of town sometimes. I called them and gently suggested loosening the strings a bit or they would lose her. They compro-mised and said she could join and attend all local events but any-thing out of town would have to be supervised by my mom. It's not much but it's something. Family drama handled? Check.

My friends are getting along. In fact, Alizé, Moët, and Dom are out enjoying a movie, dinner, and of course . . . drinks. Another check on my "things to worry about" list.

Tonight? Tonight is all about handling my personal life. Taking it to the next level.

Ding-dong.

I check my appearance in the mirror and for one second I doubt myself. Am I wrong?

I leave my bedroom and walk across the plush carpeting in the rhinestone stilettos I borrowed from Dom. They were from her "Juicy" days and just what I needed for tonight. With one last lick to my lips, I open the door and try to look my sexiest.

Taquan's eyes travel from my soft curled hair to my elaborately made up face. I bite my bottom lip a little bit before his eyes drop down to take in the sheer pink teddy I'm wearing.

He swallows over a lump in his throat and suddenly shoves his hands into the pockets of his vintage jeans. "Jesus," he says huskily before he averts his eyes.

I reach out and take his hand to pull him in. He resists. "Taquan, come here," I order him softly. He relents.

His mouth is moving and his eyes are focused on the ceiling as I pull him behind me to push down onto the couch. It's not until I try to straddle his hips that I realize he is praying. Good grief.

I lean forward to wrap my arms around his neck and he brings his hands up to block me. His hands accidentally touch my breasts and I feel his dick jump inside his pants. "Taquan, please," I beg shamelessly. I haven't had sex since the night I told Bones I was pregnant. That was over a year ago. Oh, choir boy gone give me some. Shoot.

I reach for his dick and he grabs my wrist. I try to wrestle free but of course, he is stronger than me. Shoot, I'm sitting here in a crotchless teddy begging for sex and he isn't giving in. Look like his will is stronger than mine too.

"Jesus, we pray for the strength to resist temptation and rebuke sin," he prays.

"I know that the flesh is weak, Moët. Trust me I am human and I have . . . *needs* too but this isn't right," he implores me as he looks into my eyes with the utmost seriousness.

I try to press my breasts closer to his face. His eyes drop down to take in my hard nipples through the sheer material and I don't miss the little lick of his lips. "Taquan, I want to be with you in every way."

He gave himself one last long look at my body before he shifts his eyes to mine again. "And we will . . . one day—"

"Today," I stress.

"One day," he stresses.

"Today," I stress again.

"The Bible says 'For this is the will of God, even your sanctification, that ye should abstain from fornication.'"

The man I want to make love with is throwing Bible verses at me while I am straddling him in a crotchless see-through teddy. Talk about a mood killer.

"I'm sorry, Latoya, but if you can't understand—and respect—how serious I am about this then I don't think we can be in a relationship."

His words make me climb right off his lap. I cross my arms over my exposed breasts as I step back from him. "You know, Taquan, a lot of my life has been filled with lies and deception on my part. This last year I have really tried to find myself and be true to myself. Be it right or be it wrong."

He stands and removes his suit jacket. "So what are you saying?" he asks softly as he moves behind me to place the jacket around my near nudity.

I have to swallow back a shiver at the feel of his hands on my body. Even the most innocent move from him makes me want him even more. "It's hard for me to be around you so much and to want you so much and not have you," I admit, turning so that I can look up into his face.

"This is very important to me, Latoya," he stresses with conviction clearly in his face.

What can I say? Sex is important to me? That would sound trashy—especially to a church boy like Taquan. God, this would be so much easier if Taquan looked more like damn Flavor Flav's oogly ass than Idris Elba.

"Maybe I should go and give you time to decide," he says.

I feel alarm. "Decide what?"

"If a relationship with me without sex is what you want," he answers without hesitation, his voice hard and certain.

Dang on it. The man or the sex? That's a crazy choice for a woman to make. I will never make love with Taquan unless we get married. Hell, what if he never proposes? What if I don't accept?

Maybe I do need to think this over.

He must have seen that on my face because he leans down and kisses me on both my cheeks and my forehead before he turns to leave. I turn away because I can't watch him go. Is this the end for Taquan and I? I'm not promiscuous, but can I grab the celibacy torch from Alizé and run with it? I've had some really good sex and it's going to be hard to forget that.

I slump down onto the couch and wince as the cool leather sticks to my vagina lips. It's a shame that's all the action I'm getting tonight.

Cash rules everything around me. Humph. How true that is.

Cristal stands up from behind her desk as soon as I walk out into the reception area of Lowe, Ingram, and Banks. "Oh, God, Mo, what's wrong? What did she say?" she asks with concern as she comes from behind her area to take my hands in hers.

Does my face show how scared I am?

I look up at her and I feel the tears in my eyes. "Last night I'm trying to make Taquan make love to me like that's important. How stupid is that when I don't have two red cents to rub together to pay for this . . . this child custody suit. He can afford the best and I can't afford . . . to fight for my baby. She needs ten thousand dollars just to get started."

My chest heaves as I fight to breathe in air. I feel like I am drowning. "I told her about the rape thing. I told her how rich Bones is and . . . and . . . that he hates me. She thinks he's going to file papers for temporary custody. Oh, my God. I'm gonna lose my baby."

My legs give out from under me and Cristal struggles on her stilettos to hold me up.

Chapter Eighteen

Alizé

I need my girls because I know I shouldn't be here. They would have talked me out of doing this if they knew. But Cristal's at work—so she says. Moët had to meet with her attorney this morning. And Dom? Like I said before me and Dom was cool but I'm not to that point where she would be the one I would call on. Not yet. Me and my moms haven't really spoken since I moved out. My dad had no clue about this whole Cameron thing and I'm not bothering to fill him in now.

So here I am.

My palms are sweating. My heart is racing. I have that same fear I had the very first day I walked into high school without any friends. All these years later and I still don't have much more confidence than I did at fourteen. Although this is a lot bigger than first day of school jitters.

Still, I *have* to do this.

"Okay, Alizé, here goes nothing," I tell myself as I get out of my car and walk towards the steps of St. Bartholomew's Church in New York City—the same Park Avenue church where Cristal was supposed to marry Sahad a couple of months ago. The same church where the man I love is marrying another woman. Today.

I just feel like I should tell him I love him one more time. I should say the words he wanted to hear last year. I tried at work but ever since I made that bold move on him, Cameron has kept me the hell away from him and his office. I went by his house in South Orange but he doesn't live there anymore. He did move to New York even though the wedding had been postponed. I would send an email but all company messages are monitored and any hint of something between Cameron and me will leave my ass scooty-booted out of Braun, Weber.

Okay, truth? I could have found a better time to proclaim my love again, but a piece of me has been scared shitless that he will reject me. This is all of my fears and insecurities about love coming to a damn head. I have to keep telling myself that in the end, if I win him back, that it was all worth the risk. Nothing ventured. Nothing gained.

And I do love him. I adore him. I want him. I miss him.

I *can* love him better than she can.

"Hi, Monica."

I turn and there is Delaney walking up to me smiling like she doesn't have a care in the world. "Hey, Delaney."

"God, you look really pretty."

I'm not conceited in the least but I put extra effort into making sure I look damn good. My natural jet-black hair is bone straight. My caramel skin is gleaming from a good lotion down from Carol's Daughter body butter. The April weather is still chilly in New York (especially as the sun is setting), so I really had no business wearing this silk chiffon Vera Wang dress but it's so ultra-feminine and the olive color is blazing against my bronzed caramel complexion. I borrowed one of Cristal's stoles to fight the cold some. I feel beautiful. Beautiful enough to steal my man back.

"Thanks, Delaney. You too," I tell her even though I really haven't given her a second look. I have other things on my mind except girl chat over clothes.

"Come on. We can sit together." Delaney offers.

I give her the best smile I can. "You go ahead and save me a seat. I have to make a phone call," I lie, reaching into the gold beaded bag I'm carrying.

She squeezes my hand and gives me a soft smile before she walks away. It makes me wonder if she knows anything about Cameron and me. At this point I don't care. I have to go for mine or get left behind. Point blank.

I've never let myself fall in love before and I can't just continue to sit on my ass doing nothing while another woman marries Cameron. I have to make a move or this wedding is going to go down right in my face.

I walk into the vestibule. Ushers are leading people into the chapel. I look around not sure where to go to find him. I'm about to open any and every door I see when two tuxedo-clad men walk inside the church. I keep my eyes locked on them like a hawk as they both turn to the right and make their way towards a door. As it opens and then closes behind them, I see a hall.

With a quick look around me, I walk right over to that door and run smack dab into Cameron and the two men standing there talking it up. Three sets of eyes fall on me. "Hello, Cameron," I say, as if it's the most natural thing in the world. On the inside my stomach feels like I'm going to shit up my damn self.

He steps forward with confusion on his handsome face. He looks so good in his tuxedo. So handsome. So refined. So Cameron.

"We need to talk, Cameron," I say as he reaches me.

He looks down at me for a long time before he grabs my hand and pulls me into another room off the hall. As soon as the door closes behind us, he begins to pace in front of me. I start to speak and he stops pacing to hold up his hand to stop me before he resumes his pacing all over again. Several times as he walks back and forth in front of me, he looks at me a long time before he shakes his head and looks straight ahead again.

"Cameron, I love you," I tell him in a rush before he can stop me. I step up and grab his arm to stop the damn pacing so that I can step in front of him. I look up into his eyes and my heart feels like it grows in size. "I love you so much, Cameron, and I know you love me too. Don't you?" I ask with fierceness as I step up on my toes to try and kiss the hell out of him.

He just steps back from me. "Why are you doing this, Ze? Is this a joke to you?" he asks in a voice I barely hear.

I reach out and grasp his chin to tilt his head up so that he is looking at me. "You know more than anyone that this is not easy for me but here I am laying my heart on the line for you. *Fighting . . .* for you."

His face looks tortured and I know he is fighting with his feelings. That gives me hope. "Why now?"

"Because you shouldn't marry Serena," I tell him without hesitation. "She's not the one for you and you know it."

"And how should I know that?" he asks with attitude. "Serena and I have been in a relationship with each other. I've been there for her and she has been there for me. We spent time together. We've built things together. We own a home together. I haven't laid eyes on you until two months ago."

"Then the love you claimed to have for me wasn't that deep because not very long after you tell me you love me your ass—"

"You're in church," he interrupts me sharply.

There is a knock.

"Go away," I shout.

"Come in," Cameron shouts at the same time.

I drop my head into my hands in frustration.

"Excuse, Cameron, the wedding planner is ready for you."

I look up at one of the tuxedo-clad brothers sticking his head inside the supply room. I turn my attention to Cameron. My face says *"What are you going to do?"*

He diverts his eyes from mine and my heart plummets. Oh no, this nigga ain't still going to marry another woman?

"Tell her I'll be right there," he says.

Oh yes, the hell he is.

This is the pain I always wanted to avoid. This is the rejection I never wanted to feel. This is not the way things are supposed to be. Cameron is the first man I have ever loved and he isn't supposed to marry someone else.

"This isn't the time nor the place for this, Monica." He reaches for my hands but I snatch away from him.

"Tell me you don't love me," I demand, tears filling my eyes as I stare at him. I hate that I feel desperate.

"I'm not leaving her at the altar," was his reply.

"Tell me you don't love me, Cameron," I demand again as one traitor-ass tear races down my cheek.

He raises his hand to my face and uses his thumb to swipe away the tear. "Why couldn't you say all this that day, Monica?" he asks softly.

I close my eyes at the feel of his hand. The warmth. The strength. The chemistry. "It's not too late."

He nods as he bends down to me. "Yes, it is," he whispers against my forehead before he presses his lips there.

I shiver and close my eyes as my heart breaks. I don't open my eyes again until I hear the door close behind him. I feel stupid for even bringing my ass here. The old Alizé don't take shit like this off nobody. I used to go for mine and fuck everybody else. That way I never had to feel this shit. And I never want to feel this way again.

I run out of the church just as a Hummer limo pulls up to the reserved parking spot in front of the church. I know it's the bridal party arriving. But for some reason I stand there and watch the dozen or so girls climb out of the limo in their beautiful Lazaro gowns of silver. They all huddle in front of the church. I'm still standing there when Serena is assisted out of the limo. I have to admit that she looks beautiful in a strapless beaded gown.

I will admit to no one—not even my friends—but at that moment I'm so jealous of this bitch. For real. Not because she's prettier than me or lighter than me or richer than me. She has Cameron and I want Cameron. Point blank.

She turns her head and catches sight of me. Her face shows surprise and then some other emotion I can't quite figure the fuck out. She stares at me and I stare back until one of her bridesmaids asks her, "Who's that?"

"Nobody," she answers before she continues on into the church.

The fucked up thing is that I feel like a fucking nobody.

What we share ain't about love or passion or chemistry. It's sex pure and simple. Good sex but that's all. In the last month these hot ass moments with him have become my lifesaver. If these four walls could talk.

I grab the sofa cushions and bite the pillow as he pushes his dick inside of me like I've been a bad girl. With each pop of his hips my ass jiggles as I toot it up to the sky for his taking. Sometimes when we fucking I think about Cameron. Or shopping for shoes. Or school. Or my internship. But other times I'm thinking "no this old motherfucker ain't fucking me this way." Viagra or Cialis or the dick pump has got to be involved because his dick is *always* hard as jail time.

Right now Cameron and Serena are at their reception popping corks and probably laughing at my dumb ass. I pound my fist against the couch as a wave of heartache hits me. That pain made me fly straight from the church to him. I want to feel something more than pain. I want to forget.

"Suck my dick," he orders as he slips it out of me.

I turn over and sit on the floor with my head tilted back onto the sofa as he straddles me and then squats down to press his dick into my mouth. His balls swing near my chin as he begins to fuck my mouth as I circle the thick tip of it with my tongue.

"Look at me," he orders.

I open my eyes and look right up into Dr. Locke's face. The sweat from his body drips down onto my face. I bring my hands up to press against his thighs as he tries to push his hardness down my throat. Dr. Locke is a straight freak. When it comes to sex, he giveth and he taketh. Ass licks. Rim shots. Light spankings. One time he just wanted me to let him lay in my lap and suck my titties like he was breastfeeding. You name it and he has asked for it. We have done it all. Fuck it. It makes me forget Cameron and my mama and Dom . . . and everything else going wrong in my life.

I flick out my tongue as he grips his dick and uses it to lightly tap all around my mouth. Each time his dick lands near my tongue I lick it and taste it.

He turns suddenly and walks away from me with his dick still in his hands. I smile because he's naked as me with nothing on but his dress socks. As soon as he lays back on the top of his desk with his dick standing up like a bat, I climb off the floor and walk over to him in my heels. I know what he wants.

Just as I am straddling him backwards, ready to slide down onto every bit of his nine inches, the doorknob to his office rattles. I look over my shoulder down at his face.

"Who?" he calls out.

"It's me, Hunter," a woman calls back through the door.

He jumps up so fast that I stumble off the desk to the floor. "That's my wife," he whispers to me as he jumps to his feet with his dick sticking off like an arm.

Oh shit.

"Coming, baby," he calls back.

I began to grab up my clothes as he pushes my ass into the small bathroom off his office. I quickly pull on my clothes as my heart is beating fast as hell. Out the crack in the doorway I watch him rushing to pull on his clothes. I laugh as he catches hell getting that Viagra hard-on inside his pants.

He gives the office one last look over before he walks over and shoves my head back roughly from the door before he closes it.

"Hunter, what took you so long to unlock the door?" I hear her ask.

I'm *dying* to see what she looks like but I'm not trying to get caught fucking her husband, so I keep my ass behind that closed door.

"I was on a call, Mildred."

Mildred? What the hell?

With nothing else to do I drop down onto the commode and study my nails while I eavesdrop on him lying about why he came into the office on his normal day off. "He came in to get this pussy, that's why, Mildred," I mumble aloud.

Nearly thirty fucking minutes later, after listening to their boring ass talk about dinner and their grown ass kids, the bathroom door swings open. My heart races up into my throat. Am I going to have to fight this old bitch?

But it's Dr. Locke standing in the doorway already unzipping his pants. "Let me use the bathroom and then we can ride home together."

He steps inside and closes the door behind him. I give him an anxious look as he drops his pants down around his ankles and puts his still hard dick in his hand. I don't say one word when he drops to his knees in front of me and works my panties off. I spread my legs wide and hold onto that commode as he slides that dick inside me and fucks me like he's a twenty-year-old man.

Girl Talk

Cristal, Alizé, and Dom all looked at each other before they turned their eyes on Moët. It was a rare moment in their friendship lately that they could come together and join forces to protect, to comfort, to take care of one of them. Neither forgot the path Moët took after her abortion last year. Depression. Self-hatred. Pain. Withdrawal.

When she looked up at them as she held her daughter close to her chest, they saw the fear in her eyes. They all understood it and wished they could rid her of it. Money is power and in this war between her and Bones, Moët lacked any arsenal.

They all wanted to say something but any words from their lips would sound fake—what help was that?

"I can't let him have my baby, y'all," she says in this whisper soft voice that is haunting as hell—very Sophia from *The Color Purple* "You told Harpo to beat me" kind of haunting. "I mean it."

Cristal, Alizé, and Dom looked at each other again and this time it was their eyes that were filled with fear.

"Where the hell are we going to get ten thousand dollars?" Alizé asks as she propped her bottom on the arm of the sofa.

"We?" Moët asked, looking up with red-rimmed eyes at each of them.

Cristal moved from her spot on the sofa to sit beside Moët on the ottoman in the center of the living room. "One for all and all for one, Mo. You *know* that."

Alizé rose up to sit on the other side of Moët on the ottoman. She eased the baby from her arms to snuggle against her neck. "Nobody's breaking up the six of us."

"Nobody," Dom stressed as she came over to stand beside the ottoman with them.

Chapter Nineteen

Dom

April 22

When we was kids we thought growing up was the end all of all. Damn we was stupid as hell. Bein' grown ain't brought us shit but more drama than we coulda ever thought of in high school. I ain't caught up with my babydaddy yet but I ain't sleeping on this shit either. I get a chance to sneak a peek at Hiasha's records and her father's name is William or something like that. Even though I done got over Kimani and her friend Hiasha being sisters I am strugglin' like a bitch to take care of my daughter alone and it's been enough of that shit. Broke as I am, my ass is ready for some damn child support. Fuck that—

"You hungry?"

I look up from my newest journal with my favorite pen in my mouth as Corey walks into his bedroom with his big dick swingin' between his thighs. "No, I'm 'bout to go," I tell him. I ain't even sure I made the right move to come to his apartment tonight. Thing is he called me. We talked. We laughed. I missed him. He offered for me to come to his place and for the first time I made that move. Two hours filled with watchin' TV, fuckin' like crazy, with a small nap right after and a bitch like me is ready to roll out. This shit feel too comfortable. Too right. Too much.

"Why you leaving?" he asks, giving me that damn dimple smile of his as he drops down onto the queen-sized bed beside me. He reaches over to massage my nipple and my whole breast feels hot from his touch. I can't explain the way this jokey motherfucker makes me feel.

I don't even answer his ass as I smile and shift my eyes back down to my journal.

This little short motherfucker with a dick like a six-foot man is really getting to me. He really dropping that pressure for us to be a couple. I ain't had a man to call my fuckin' own since Lex. I never really thought I would find a motherfucker that could make me feel like him. Why the fuck is it so hard to separate the pussy from the heart?

My pen drops to the bed as he leans over to stroke his tongue against my hard nipple just the way I like. By the time the pen falls from my hand and rolls off the bed to the floor I am laying flat on my back and spreadin' my legs wide as them motherfuckers will go. I moan and arch my back but my eyes pop open as he shifts his sexy ass away from me. I turn my head on the pillow to look over at him with a little frown. "What's wrong?" I ask as I grind my hips against the bed.

"I got more going on for me than just my dick, Dom," he tells me as he climbs off the bed and walks over to the chipped dresser in the corner.

Oh shit. Here the fuck we go.

"I know that, Corey."

His back is to me as he gets somethin' from the top drawer. What, this fool 'bout to shoot me? Shit, where I come from that shit don't sound all that crazy to me. "What you gettin' a gun or some shit?"

Corey looks over his shoulder at me and frowns. "What?" he asks as he turns. "You must mean a shotgun."

My eyes drop down to the blunt in his hands. I lick my lips a little as I watch him raise that fat motherfucker and put it between his lips to light. "You smoke weed?" I ask, surprised and a little mesmerized by the thick smoke rising from the lit tip.

Corey strolls his ass back over to the bed. "I don't smoke while I'm working. Weed ain't that serious for me to be high around kids . . . *but* what I do between seven at night and seven in the morning is my time."

The scent—that one of a kind scent of weed—is callin' my ass. When he drops down on the bed beside me and tilts his head back to blow a thick cloud of smoke I almost feel like a little fist of fuckin' smoke is knockin' me against the head sayin': "Sniff me, bitch."

"Want a shotgun?" he asks as he holds the blunt between his teeth and shifts his body to kneel beside me on the bed.

Sniff me, bitch.

Me and my mama used to give each other shotguns. That shit pushed more of that good ass weed into your system.

You know you want to sniff me, bitch.

I used to love me some fuckin' weed. I could smoke a half ounce by my goddamn self. That and a bottle of Henny and a bitch was straight.

Just say yes.

And after a while I smoked so much of that shit that weed didn't do shit for me no more. I moved my ass right on to pedope. I almost overdosed off that shit.

One tear races down my face as I twist my damn eyes away from that temptin' ass blunt to look over at him. "I can't," I whisper as that struggle to stay fuckin' sober grips my throat and my chest.

Corey sits up. "What's wrong, baby girl?" he asks with concern on his cute-ass face.

My drug counselor told me moments like this would come in my life. That second where you have to decide to tell somebody in your life about your addiction. Trustin' 'em not to hold it or use it against. Believin' that they will still look at your junkie ass the same way. Wantin' everythin' to stay the same.

Why I do this shit to myself? Why the fuck my life got to be all about using drugs and gettin' the fuck up off them?

"I used to . . . uhm . . . get fucked up off . . . I used to get high . . . off dope. I can't be 'round you smokin'. See, bein' with me ain't as easy as you think." I drop my eyes from his 'cause I don't want to see all that shock, and disbelief, and only God knows what else.

I can't stop them damn tears if I want to. But this the shit. The realness. I hear the blunt hiss as he drops it in a glass of soda. That little nigga gathers me in his arms and pulls my head against his chest and holds me like he ain't got shit to do in the world but try to make it better for me.

And that makes me cry even harder.

"I like you a lot, Dom," he tells me as he rubs my back and presses his face down on top of my head. "Fuck that. I won't smoke it around you. Shit, I'll even stop smokin' it if you want. Fuck that shit. Dom. Fuck it. I got you, a'ight? I promise I got you."

Right then in that moment his words and the feel of his arms is way better than the hardest of dicks.

Chapter Twenty

Moët

Faith.

I've been at this crossroad before. Believe or not believe? Do I take this into my own hands or do I let Him show me the way? Do I choose right or wrong to fight like hell to keep my child? Do I turn my back on the faith that I do have . . . again?

I feel like I don't have a choice.

The lawyer from Cristal's job was right. My whole gut clenches as I think of the papers in my tote bag advising me that Bones has filed for temporary legal and physical custody of our daughter while we await the custody trial. So I need a lawyer even sooner than ever.

I make too much for legal aid and I'm not really trusting my case with a cheaper lawyer . . . yet. What can some joke of a lawyer with an office over a fried chicken shack do against the type of heavyweights Bones can afford?

Bones changed his cell phone number and he moved out the building where he used to live. Even when I worked up the nerve to go to him and beg him to leave me and my baby be, I couldn't find him. Besides, if I did get close to him I knew his bodyguards would do their job and keep me away.

After taking two grand worth of cash advances off my credit cards, my little bit of savings, overdrafting my checking account for the allowed five hundred dollars, selling my designer items (courtesy of

Bones and Reverend Sin) to a consignment shop, begging and borrowing the rest I'm still four thousand dollars short of the retainer.

If I could borrow some from my parents I would. I still haven't told them about the case because the fact that I lied about being raped is a subject none of us discuss.

Cristal and Dom told me to ask Taquan for the money but I would be dead wrong to do that when I've barely spoken to him since my failed attempt at popping his "cherry." I like the deacon but I have other things on my mind than getting him or his dick.

Like accepting this offer from yet another devil.

I cut my eyes to the bundle of cash laying on the table and then up to the calculating eyes of Jean Pierre. He sees how desperate I am to snatch that five grand and run. He sees it and he is daring me with his eyes not to take it.

It would be so easy to walk out of his house with that cash in my hand and leave his sons here with him—even though I clearly can tell that he is whipping they ass twelve ways to Sunday. And that's all I have to do. Leave and not make a report. Leave his boys here with him and the five grand is mine. The Haitian lawyer with the beautiful house in South Orange is willing to do whatever to keep his sons with him.

Just like I am willing to do whatever to keep my daughter with me.

I don't have a choice.

Chapter Twenty-One

Cristal

"The most accomplished woman is known for what she does and not just whom she does."

I took a sip of my mojito as I look at Carolyn over the rim of the glass. It is time for some of her wisdom and she certainly looks the part of my mentor to high society. Her thin frame covered in an elegant red jersey dress by Christian Dior. Classy gold jewelry by David Yurman. Valentino shades ready to slide into place. Birkin bag on the empty chair at our table ready to be slid onto her arm. Her well pampered feet softly cushioned by Giuseppe Zanotti heels. Trendy blunt bob personally designed by Frederic Fekkai. And to top it all off a Fendi sable worth more than I made in a year was checked and ready to slide onto her back effortlessly.

She had generously gone through her closet and given me outfits that I could only dream of affording. So today as I sat in the perfect size six Chado Ralph Rucci ivory dress, black lace Carolina Herrera trench and this bad pair of Christian Louboutin slingbacks, I look the role of the black socialite on the rise. By every outward appearance anyone who really did not know me (like just about everyone in this restaurant) would think I have every right to be here amongst them.

The girls are waiting for me back at the apartment to go over Mo's court hearing in a few days and Mohammed is home fixing me a special Caribbean dinner for later tonight, but at that moment nothing matters but the knowledge Carolyn is about to drop.

"What is the legacy you will leave behind for your children?" she asks as she raises her bejeweled hand to wave away the waitress who just stepped up to our table.

And with that simple motion the waitress is gone. As always I am truly impressed.

"Don't get me wrong. I've done office work too but now you won't catch me on *anyone's* job." She leans back in her chair and crosses her legs exposing her one-hundred-dollar silk stockings. "I grew up in Harlem with a drunk for a father and a junkie prostitute for a mother. Whenever the bitch did remember to send me to school I wore sneakers with holes in the bottom and jeans with my knees exposed. I was a hungry, napped-headed, ashy mess. And look at me now."

The look she gave me is pure cockiness. "I made sure that I aligned myself with only the best. I walked like them and talked like them and learned from them. When I married my beloved husband I was ready to *become* one of them."

I nod my head to let her know that I am listening and I am understanding.

"Now since you've made it clear that your . . . handyman is your future—and he barely has a decent pot to piss in or a window to throw it out of—then you need to supply your own pot and window."

Carolyn's words are the end all of all to me . . . except where it comes to Mohammed. True, my friendship with Carolyn had put the first dent in that armor surrounding our relationship but I love him with all that I have and ever hope to have. She has tried to hook me up with wealthy men—some handsome and some not, some young and some who were well into the sugar-daddy range. According to Carolyn these older fish were the best to catch because it put a woman closer to the time his will is read. It seems that being a wealthy widower is the real fun.

"I love Mohammed, Carolyn," I remind her as I lean forward to reach for my drink.

She rolls her eyes. "Trust me, I know the pleasures of a young firm body to stroke my clit. I have plenty of young ass from here to Brazil . . . *but* I don't let anything or anyone fuck with my money." Carolyn sits forward on the edge of the leather club chair and reaches over to lightly rub and then pat my hand. "Remember that, Danielle."

Remember it? It's been my motto, my mantra, my everything . . . until Mohammed. "I think you're right about defining my own legacy . . ."

My words trail off as a commotion breaks out near the front of the restaurant. I turn in my seat to take a look.

A thirty-something woman is pushing past the maître d' to storm over towards the rear of the restaurant. My eyes get wider and wider when it looks like she is headed straight to our table. I turn back to Carolyn. The cold and hateful look on her face shocks the hell out of me. If looks could kill that woman headed our way would be dead. I twist back around in my chair.

"Why are you doing this to me, Carolyn?" she yells from halfway across the restaurant. "What? So you don't know me now, you old bitch?"

Two bus boys roughly shove her back towards the glass front doors.

One last look at Carolyn and her façade is back in full effect. She is calmly sipping her glass of water as if there is not a woman screeching her name as she is hauled out of the five-star restaurant.

My eyes must hold questions because Carolyn waves her hand dismissively as she says, "I hired that asshole, Kelle, as my personal assistant and I fired the bitch for stealing. The little slut even put her raw ass into my silk panties. Nasty bitch."

I cock a brow. "There is one thing I will never wear second-hand and that is someone's worn underwear. No offense."

Carolyn laughs. "None taken."

"Too bad she couldn't appreciate working for you," I say, leaning back as the stoic waitress brought out our plates of sliced fresh fruit, croissants, and shrimp salad.

Carolyn cut her eyes at me. "I thought about offering you the position when I first met you," she admits before using her utensils to dice the jumbo-sized shrimp in the salad.

I lock my eyes with hers. I am anxiously awaiting the rest.

"*But* I have bigger things in mind for you than being anyone's flunky . . . including mine."

She raises her crystal goblet to me and I gladly toast to a life of bigger and better things.

"Well, look what the fuck the cat drug in."

I close the front door and give Dom's sarcastic ass a mean eye roll. The ladies and the kids are all in the living room, obviously waiting on me. With work, living it up with Carolyn in NYC, and squeezing whatever time I have left for Mohammed, I have hardly seen my beautiful apartment . . . or my godchildren and friends. I did not have a clue what is going on with everyone outside of Mo's custody battle.

How are Dom and Alizé getting along?

Is Dom willing to admit that she likes Corey for more than his jokes and his dick?

Is Alizé still mad at her moms and sleeping on her father's couch? Is she willing to go back to teaching dance classes yet? How is she dealing with Cameron's marriage?

Has Mo convinced Taquan to finally give up the dick?

"Damn, Cristal, you looking like a *Vogue* fashion layout," Alizé says as she sucks on a red BlowPop, in a mean jean jumpsuit and thigh-high leather boots.

Moët's eyes are sad as always as they take me in from head to toe. She says nothing. She just looks back down at Tiffany sleeping peacefully in her arms.

Dom moves Kimani in between her legs to begin loosening her hair from her ponytail. Mother and daughter are both sporting velour sweatsuits. "Look like a bitch back on the grind workin' that addressbook."

I pause before I sit down next to Moët on the couch. "I am not cheating on Mohammed."

Dom sucks her teeth in obvious disbelief.

"I thought this meeting was to talk about Mo . . . not me," I stress as I lean back into the comfort of the chair and cross my legs.

Alizé frowns as she gives me a hard look. "Damn, bitch, since when does hanging out with your friends become a meeting?" she snaps.

"You all know what I mean," I say, giving them that signature Carolyn Ingram dismissive wave.

"No. What we know is what your sneaky wannabe bougie ass been up to." Dom leans forward to pick up a newspaper from the floor to hand to me.

The *New York Post*'s Page Six Section shows a picture of me standing next to Carolyn, Star Jones-Reynolds, and Holly Robinson-Peete at a charity event for autistic children. The caption reads: *"Socialite extraordinaire Carolyn Ingram shows the star power she can pull to raise money for yet another of her worthy causes. Pictured left to right: Star Jones-Reynolds, Holly Robinson-Peete, and Danielle Johnson (ex-fiancée of Platinum Record's owner Sahad Linx).*

I am looking so good in this cropped camel Bottega Veneta anaconda jacket with a matching tank and linen skirt. I fit right in with these stylish and wealthy Black women. I smile as I read the caption again. I do not mind at all being linked to Sahad.

When I look up from the paper (which I plan to keep) there are three pairs of eyes on me.

For the first time *ever* I feel like we are not as close as we all should be, or rather *I* am not as close to them as I should be. But they have to understand that a friend like Carolyn Ingram will get me to places their friendship cannot. If not for Carolyn giving me hand-me-downs that are still worth thousands of dollars used, I would not be able to sell things to loan Mo a thousand dollars towards her lawyer's fees.

We are all growing up. We are not the same four teenagers chilling in the caf at University High. I am a grown-ass woman who is learning to look (and plan) for my future.

"You cheating on me, Danielle? Huh?"

I drop my fork onto my plate wishing like hell that Mohammed would let me enjoy the jerk chicken and wild rice he made for our dinner. I want some good food, some good sex, and a good night of sleep. Instead he is filling up my evening with petty arguments.

Mohammed sits across from me at the small round table with his eyes locked on me as he wrings his hands. I look away from him at anything and everything but his eyes. The bright orange of his kitchen's walls. The pots and utensils on the counter from his cooking, messy as always. The black tile on the floor. Anything. Everything.

"What you done find some rich sugar daddy to buy you all those nice things you worship?" he asks.

Even though he is pissing me off I love the way his accent makes the word *thing* sound more like *ting*. I love it and I love him. I turn my eyes back to him. "I am not cheating on you, Mohammed."

"Ain't like it ain't something you ain't done before," he tosses at me under his breath.

I toss my plate away from me and it crashes to the floor as I jump to my feet. "Yeah, I chose you over Sahad. Sue me for picking you over *my* Benz, *my* clothes, *my* furs, *my* jewelry, *my* trips out of town, *my* walks down the red carpet, *my* life as a celebrity. I chose a bigger dick and love. Excuse the fuck out of me, Mohammed."

He smirks. "If all those things were yours, where are they now?" he asks mockingly.

I feel like crying but I *dare* a tear to fall. All of this is too much.

Carolyn's advice.

Now since you've made it clear that your . . . handyman is your future— and he barely has a decent pot to piss in or a window to throw it out of— then you need to supply your own pot and window.

Alizé's criticism.

Damn, bitch, since when does hanging out with your friends become a meeting?

And now Mohammed's mocking.

If all those things were yours, where are they now?

All I want is a better life. To accomplish my dreams. To have it all.

"I'm going to bed," I tell him as I rise from the table.

"Danielle," he calls out.

I stop at the kitchen entrance but I do not turn around.

"You're losing me, ya hear? One of these times you gone 'come 'round and I ain't gone be here."

I walk out the kitchen without saying a word.

Chapter Twenty-Two

Alizé

Ineed someone to talk to. I have a lot I want to say and no one to say it to.

Cristal busy hanging out with them high society bitches and celebrities.

Moët scared as hell about losing Tiffany so my drama seems silly compared to that.

Dom and Corey been hanging pretty tough, plus I'm getting back comfortable around her but I don't fully trust the bitch. Who can blame me?

My mama is still hanging with Rockman and I am still on my daddy's squeaky and lumpy-ass sofa bed.

Now that Dr. Locke and I are fucking like crazy, we haven't had a real therapy session in weeks.

"Welcome back, Mr. Steele, and you look so beautiful, Mrs. Steele."

I look up from the report Delaney gave me to look over on the KML Electronics acquisition. My heart literally stops in my damn chest at the sound of Delaney's voice. So Cameron and his new wife are back from their three-week-long honeymoon across Europe. My eyes drop back down to my hands trembling atop the papers. On my left finger is a diamond domed shaped ring . . . not the wedding ring that Cameron slid onto his wife's finger. I poured my heart out to him and he still chose Serena.

That hurt.

I feel a presence at my office door and I blink away the tear. "Delaney, I'm almost done with—"

My words are swallowed by surprise as Serena Lemons-Steele closes my office door behind her. I stiffen my back as she takes the one step needed to stand before my desk. "How can I help you, Miss Lemons?" I ask as I lean back in my chair.

She raises her left hand to smooth her long and fine hair. "It's *Mrs*. Steele," she answers with emphasis as she holds out her hand and wiggles her left ring finger at me. That isn't hardly necessary. I saw the four-carat ring as soon as she stepped inside my office.

"I forgot all about the wedding," I say, using one of my manicured hands to push my curly hair behind my ear.

Serena's eyes hardened like the diamonds in her ring. "Funny that you forgot . . . when you were there . . . trying to convince Cameron not to marry me."

He told her?

I cover my surprise good as hell as I cock my head and look up at her.

She presses her hands down onto the desk and leans down towards me. I don't move one inch. "Cameron is mine and I will have your hood ass out of here quicker than you can count your nappy little buckshots."

I sit up in my chair as my anger flashes hot as hell in my chest. In the softest voice, I tell her, "Because you just pissed me off I *will* fuck Cameron the first chance I get. Here in my office on this desk or in this chair. In his office. Or the conference room. Maybe the elevator. Or out of town on a business trip. In your bed or your car. Wherever . . . .whenever . . . and *definitely* whatever."

Serena looks like she wants to slap me silly but since she ain't silly she didn't fuck with it. Smart girl.

"Cameron would not touch you with a ten-foot pole," she says in this tight little voice.

I laugh huskily, filling her face with whatever I had for lunch. "One night when Cameron comes home and he kisses you and you smell the sweetest pussy ever on his upper lip don't doubt that it's mine. When you suck his dick and lick up all those good juices don't doubt that it's mine. And when he fucks you and doesn't say your name, know that it's because he's scared he'll call out my name instead."

"I guess I just have to show your little ghetto girl ass just who is the top dog around here," she tells me before she turns and slams out of my office.

I didn't intend to put myself out physically or emotionally for Cameron again, but since that bitch tried to play my little ghetto girl ass close, then I will fuck him the first chance I get and make sure that bitch remembers well what I told her.

"Stupid bitch," I mutter as I reach down in my tote for my cell.

Who am I going to call? Usually I would hit Cristal up without a doubt, but she's back to her social climbing bullshit licking the crack of Carolyn Ingram's ass. That bitch tripping again.

I look down at my phone. I have twenty voice mail messages. "What the hell?"

They all are from Dr. Locke. Sometimes when he can't reach me his ass gets a little weirded out. He can be a little intense at times, but right now an intense fuck is just what I need. Dropping the phone, I rise from my desk and lock the door as I strip out of my tailored pinstriped suit, sheer blouse, and every bit of lingerie. I shove my clothes into my briefcase before I pull on the Burberry trench I wore this morning.

I'm out.

I grab my briefcase and leave the office. After shooting Delaney a quick lie about a meeting with my advisor on campus I make my way onto the elevator. I am loving the feel of my pussy lips rubbing together as I walk. The way the silk of the lining is rubbing against my body is freaky. I dial Dr. Locke's private line.

"Where are you?" he asks as soon as he answers the phone.

I smile as I reach down inside my trench and tease one of my nipples. "On my way to you. I have on nothing but my stilettos and a trench. Are you ready for me?" I ask as I press my backside against the wall.

"Bring my pussy to me."

I purr.

He hangs up the line.

I give my nipple one last twirl just as the elevator door slides open. Several suit clad men are waiting to get on and my ass is ready to get the fuck off. As I walk out the building with a bounce in my step, I am more than ready to go fuck a freak.

Girl Talk

Moët walked up the steps of the courthouse and tried to keep her head held high . . . but she failed. She stopped and squeezed her eyes shut as she did the only thing left to do. "Heavenly Father, I call on You because I need You now. I need You more than ever. I stand here ready to walk in court with my baby and I may very well walk out without her."

Moët stomped her foot as emotions gripped her and tears raced down her cheek. "I ask You sweet Jesus not to leave me right now. I ask You to bless me with the right to raise my child. I beg You not to take her from me. I plead with You to find a way for this to go in my favor. I love You for every blessing that You have ever bestowed upon. I am grateful for Your forgiveness for all of my sins. I thank You for all the support I have here with me today.

"My parents."

Mr. and Mrs. James stepped up close to her on the steps of the courthouse. Little Tiffany was sound asleep in Mrs. James' arms.

"My friends. Thank You for them *all* being here."

Alizé, Dom, and Cristal stepped forward to surround her with tears in their eyes.

"And thank You Heavenly Father for making a way for me to pay the lawyer to help me fight."

Helen Jacobsen stood off to the side with her briefcase in hand.

"Jesus, please . . . please, don't take her from me." Moët's shoulders began to shake with her tears as she doubled over. Cristal wrapped her arm around Mo's shoulder. Dom and Alizé each grabbed one of her hands. With their support she straightened up until she stood tall.

"I pray to You Heavenly Father with all that I am and all that I ever hope to be. Amen."

"Amen," they all said in unison.

Chapter Twenty-Three

Dom

Instead of havin' one sucky job now my ass got two. A full-time piece of bullshit and now a part-time one. Anything to keep my ass off the pole. So it's kids durin' the day and motherfuckin' adults actin' like kids three times a week at night. Who knew people be all up in Wal-Mart like that? Go get this. Find me that. Where is this? Where is that?

I wish I could tell all of them to kiss my motherfuckin' ass and leave me alone while I just try to get through them four hours.

It's hard bein' around the girls and my clothes games done slip the fuck off. It's hard pinchin' pennies to survive. It's hard bein' off the damn pole.

I been back to Club XXXCite twice since that first night but both times I couldn't find the strength to carry my ass in there again. And I do need the money bad. I'm the only one who couldn't give Moët one red cent towards her lawyer's fees. That shit makes me feel like I ain't shit. But being off dope, raising my daughter alone (no updates on the daddy hunt) and livin' right makes me feel like I'm the shit. Silly, right?

"That's my mommy right there."

I turn away from the chalkboards I'm cleanin' at the sound of my daughter's voice suddenly behind my ass. She and her little friend Hiasha are standin' next to a tall and thin dark-skinned man in a

New Jersey Transit uniform. That friendly—and fake as hell—smile that I give all the parents begins to fade as he stares at me. "Can I help you?" I ask with a little bit of attitude. He is creepin' me the fuck out.

He holds up his hands like he wants to touch me or some shit, but lucky for his ass he drops his hands back down to his sides. "I'm William. William Kennedy," he says like that means something.

"Daddy, I'm hungry," Hiasha says as she reaches up to grab his hands.

My eyes go from her to his face and then down to my daughter, and back to his face just as he leans over to me and whispers over their heads. "I'm your father."

"Bullshit," I snap even as my fuckin' chest feels like it's going to damn explode or some shit.

He looks confused as his eyes keep lookin' all over my face like he tryin' to take a damn picture of me or some shit. "Diane and I used to go out," he says.

The fact that he know my mama's name throws my ass but this man standin' before me all handsome and clean and workin' and shit is not the dope fiend my moth—*Diane* always told me about. What the fuck is goin' on?

"Listen, I don't know what the hell you trippin' off of but you ain't my . . ."

The rest of my words don't come as I see two sets of eyes—almost identical almond shape eyes—lookin' up at me swallowin' up everything I'm sayin'.

"Come on, Kimani, let's go home. Go get your stuff," I tell her as I drop the sponge onto the table.

"Come with me, Hiasha," Kimani says, reachin' for her friend's hand as they walk over to take the stairs down to their area.

"Please, Keesha. You don't know how happy I am to see you," he says.

I am fuckin' confused as hell and I just want to get the fuck away 'cause I don't understand why this stranger who ain't got my daddy's name is claimin' to be my daddy. This shit ain't funny. If we wasn't in a fuckin' daycare I would cuss his ass the fuck out for tryin' to play with my fuckin' emotions.

But why would he lie? I ain't got shit to offer nobody. No reason for nobody to lie 'bout knowin' my broke-as-a-joke ass. I ain't barely got a pot, the window, or the money to buy the water to make the fuckin' piss. I look up at him and I see me all up in his face. I always thought I look like Diane but this motherfucker standin' here proves that wrong as hell.

"When Hiasha brought this picture of her and your little daughter home I saw that she's the spitting image of my mama . . . just like me . . . just like Hiasha . . . just like you," he says with tears in his eyes as he takes two photos out of his uniform jacket.

I take the pictures—one of Kimani and Hiasha and the other of him and an older woman that looks like me forty years from now. I feel my body drop down into one of them little ass chairs the kids sit in. I saw the resemblance between the girls and I thought it was my no-good babydaddy slingin' his sperm all over town. Ain't that some shit? The little girl I thought was my daughter's sister is *my* fuckin' sister.

"You know I wondered all these years if you was dead or strung out on some dope, tryin' to come up with some reason why I ain't know your ass and why you don't know me," I admit as all my fuckin' emotions and shit make my throat tight as hell.

"Keesha, I ain't never been on damn drugs and your mama told me that she was pregnant and that the baby—you—wasn't mine. It hurt me to know she was cheating on me but I took her word for it about who the daddy was. Even though I did wonder if you were my little girl after all," he says.

I look up at him as the tears fall. "Then your ass shoulda did more than wonder. Your ass shoulda acted. Your ass shoulda stepped the fuck up. Not even a bitch like Diane shoulda kept you away from your child." My voice gets louder and louder as I rise to my feet. I don't give a fuck who sees me. I don't give a fuck who hears me. I just don't give a flyin' fuck. I swipe away my tears as I point to him. "You don't know what the fuck I been through while you off livin' life and makin' more babies. At least thinkin' you was on drugs was an excuse for why you didn't give a fuck if you ever saw me again."

He reaches for me and I jerk away from him.

"Why are you here?" I yell at him at the top of my lungs. "It's about twenty years too fuckin' late."

I push past him and grab my purse and coat.

"Keesha," he calls behind me.

I just have to get away. Through my tears I barely make out Corey comin' towards me. I know that his arms would feel so good right now but I just have to get out of there. I push past him.

"Dom," Corey calls behind me.

I hear footsteps but I keep goin' until I grab Kimani with one arm and push out the door to leave. I don't stop until I am in my car and racin' our asses away from there.

I just got to get the fuck away.

Chapter Twenty-Four

Moët

At first, it really didn't sink in on me that I have to share temporary custody of my child with a man that hates me. Not when I heard the judge's decision in court. Not when I read about it in the papers and all over the internet (everyone knows that I bore his child and that I am the woman who falsely accused him of rape last year).

It didn't really hit me until I had to pack her bag for the weekend. On top of that I could still lose her for good when we have to go back to court next month.

I am grateful that the Lord saw a way for me to even get up the majority of the money for the lawyer without me having to sell my soul that night. Jean Pierre's son was safely placed in a foster care home while I continued my investigation into the abuse claims by the boy's school. When I picked up that money the look of satisfaction and mocking on his face changed once I tossed the cash back at him.

I just couldn't sell out one child's safety, not even to keep my own child close to me. Cris let me borrow a thousand and Alizé came up with eight hundred. I finally caved and talked to my parents. We prayed together until my knees went numb but in the end they let me borrow a good bit.

And so the court case began.

Bone's lawyer brought up all of it. My secret life from my parents, my affair with the minister, the abortion, the false rape accusation. All of it.

I never once said Bones could not see Tiffany. Never once. He didn't have to go this far. I knew from the look on his face as his lawyer berated my character that he just wanted to hurt me. He wanted to humiliate me.

Now how in the hell are we going to raise a child together?

With all the damage he did in court plus his mother's testimony that she now lives with her son in a comfortable home in Saddle River and will help with the baby, Bones and I are temporarily sharing custody of our daughter. I guess after seeing a millionaire like Britney Spears lose primary custody of her children to a man she supports financially, I should feel lucky.

There is a knock at my bedroom door and I look up as Alizé, Dom, and Kimani walk in with their faces just as sad as mine. I clutch Tiffany to me and press my face into her neck. She coos all softly and my heart bursts with love for her.

I know Alizé is hurting about Cameron and this new drama with Dom and her suddenly reappearing daddy is big time, but I am grateful they both are here for me. I wish Cristal hadn't went away for the weekend. A piece of me still can't believe she went knowing what I would be going through today. Whenever the four of us are together it feels like we are invincible. Besides fighting back from depression after the abortion, this is the hardest thing I ever had to do and right now I need my friends.

Kimani presses a kiss to Tiffany's hand as Dom grabs the baby bag and Alizé rubs my back while I rise from the bed. It feels like a funeral march as we walk out the bedroom and through the living room together. Even as we ride the elevator downstairs I just silently pray that the Lord watches over my daughter and grants Bones the maturity to be the best father he can be to his child while he has her this weekend.

The elevator doors open.

"'Bout damn time."

I look up to find Bones and his entire ten-man entourage scattered about the lobby of our apartment building. I feel the girls shift closer to me as Bones stands and turns to look at me with all the hatred he has for me filled in his eyes.

He still looks like the same man I fell in love with all those months ago. Tall, fine, and hood rich with enough diamonds glistening from his jewelry to give him a glow of light around his tall frame. His lawyer rises as well and whispers something to Bones and he nods as he looks at me.

"It's time, Miss James," the short white attorney says as he slips his hands into the pockets of his chinos.

I walk up until I am standing in front of Bones. He takes Tiffany from my arms as Dom steps up to hand me the baby bag I packed. Several of his entourage whistle at her but Dom just shoots them a mad stare.

"She likes to be rocked to sleep and she loves a bottle of cool baby water—"

"I don't need your lying ass to tell me shit about my daughter," he snaps. Several of his crew snicker.

"There's no need to act an ass, Lavitius," I stress to him as I carefully watch the way he holds our daughter.

"And there was no need for your no-good ass to lie about me raping you either."

"And I was wrong for that but you were wrong when you said I lied about her being yours and you were wrong when you said I wanted to gank you for your money. I haven't asked you for one red cent since she was born."

He sucked his teeth. "Man, I ain't got no convo for your ass."

See, to me I am trying to do what's right for Tiffany. I hand him the diaper bag filled with her things.

He looked at it like it was a dead cat or a pile of shit or something. "You can keep all that cheap shit 'cause I bought my baby girl Brittany everything she need and more," he boasts as his crew starts to walk out of the lobby.

I wrap my arms around myself. "Her name is Tiffany," I say sadly.

He turns and looks back at me. "What?" he asks with attitude.

I shake my head because it's a damn shame. "Your daughter's name is *Tiffany* not Brittany."

His lawyer clears his throat and looks away while Dom and Alizé step up to stand beside me. Bones gives me a long look before he turns and walks out the building with our daughter.

I just hang my head and turn to get back on the elevator. I pray hard and fast because at that moment I feel what little faith I have leave me and I am trying not to go there again.

Chapter Twenty-Five

Cristal

The Ingrams' cabin in the Poconos is gorgeous. It is definitely a completely new level of rustic, with floor to ceiling windows everywhere, fireplaces in every one of the four bedrooms, top-of-the-line furnishings, expensive art work, and a full staff. From every window of the two-level house there is a spectacular view of the towering pine trees. Who knew the woods could be so beautiful?

I know Mo and the other girls wanted me there when Bones came to pick up Tiffany but how in the world could I turn down a weekend surrounded by all of this. Besides I called and Mo was a little weepy but holding up the best she could under the circumstances. So now it's time for a little R & R.

The guest bedroom is done in all white and it looks good as hell against the wooden surroundings. Although it's early May the stone fireplace is lit and the sound of the crackling fire is peaceful. It is all romantic as hell. Just the spot for lovers.

I sit up in bed in nothing but my bikinis and look down at Mohammed's naked body sprawled out next to me. His dreads are sprawled out against the down pillow and his chocolate body is sexier than ever against the white Egyptian cotton of the sheets. He is one of the sexiest men I ever laid eyes on. The sexiest and the most broke.

When I told him I was going out of town he first tried to talk me into not going and then he invited himself like he wanted to prove I was not going to be laid up with another man. He actually gave me an ultimatum. Either he went or I stayed.

So here we are the guests of Mr. and Mrs. Ingram.

I can see it in their eyes that they are only being polite because he is here with me. They see and judge everything about him: his clothes, his dreads, his accent, his job, his status. I can see that none of it is up to par to them and that embarrasses me.

And his judgment of them is just as harsh. Rich snobs. Uptight assholes. Plastic surgery whores (and he is dead on because both Mr. and Mrs. Ingram have gone under the knife).

I am working on that legacy Carolyn's been talking to me about. And what better legacy than my own business. Somewhere upscale. Somewhere trendy. Somewhere all the right people want to be.

Questions is: What?

Who better to ask than Carolyn? My friend, my mentor, my confidante. And hopefully my investor in whatever I plan to do.

I am not going to let Mohammed and his foul mood ruin this for me. He better shape up or ship the hell out.

Okay, last night we did make love on the fur rug in front of the fireplace and in the Jacuzzi tub in our private bath and out on the balcony but he invited himself along on this trip and he was not going to ruin *my* good time.

He turns in his sleep and reaches for me but I just roll my eyes as I climb out of bed and grab my thick cotton robe to slip on. I give Mohammed one last look over my shoulder before I leave the bedroom. The entire chalet is quiet and still a bit dark because the sun is just beginning to rise. Hopefully, everyone is asleep. I just want to slip down to the kitchen, grab something to drink, and head back to bed.

I jog down the stairs and walk into the kitchen that is almost as big as my apartment. I open the SubZero and pull out a bottle of water.

Boom-boom-boom.

I freeze at the rapid sound of something knocking or being knocked. I cock my head to the side.

Boom-boom-boom-boom-boom.

I turn my head towards the solid wooden door leading to the pantry. What in the hell? Is someone trapped in there and trying to get my attention for help? Who knows. These rich people are crazy as hell.

I sit the bottle of water on the huge tiled island in the center of the kitchen and walk over to the pantry on my tiptoes. The sound of muffled noises makes me stop right where I am.

Boom-boom-boom.

Okay that hood side of me is like "get the hell out of there and mind your neck," but I keep on walking to the pantry and jerk the door open. My eyes damn near pop out my head and my mouth falls open at what I see.

Carolyn and her cook, Gerard, are both looking up at me in shock as they jump apart from each other on the floor. I quickly take in her naked body, his big and long dick that is still wet from her juices, and the heavy scent of sex. Okay, this is way more than I need to know. "Excuse me," I mumble before I step back from the small pantry.

"No, don't go," Carolyn whispers out to me.

One of my newly threaded eyebrows jumps up. "Excuse me?"

"Come in and close the door," she says from her spot on the floor.

I step back into the pantry with my eyes *squeezed* shut and pull the door close behind me. "Listen, Carolyn, you're busy—"

"Shut the door. I need you to stay in here in case my husband drags his ass down here. You and Gerard can come out together if he does, while I stay in here."

My eyes pop back open and flashes of Gerard climbing back between Carolyn's legs which are spread wide until each of her Chanel bed slippers are touching shelves filled with canned goods and snacks. I shift my eyes because I really do not need to know what her pussy looks like. Okay? Alright.

"Carolyn, I don't know about this—"

The sounds of his flesh hitting hers stops me and I cringe as the sounds of pussy juices echoes amongst their grunts. What . . . the . . . hell?

"Yes, Gerard, get this pussy," she moans.

"I'ma take this dick from you," he answers.

"No, please, no."

He laughs all low in his throat.

"Put it back in, Gerard. *Pleeaassee.*"

I try to press my body and my face into the door.

For the next five minutes I am in some weird sort of porno hell as Gerard fucks Carolyn's old ass like she stole something. I mean that man went to work on her. I can hear even if I refuse to look. Somewhere along the line my nipples harden and my clit jumps to life.

"I'm cuuuuuummmmmmiiiiiiinnnnnnggg," she moans.

Hump. I bet you are.

The sound of things rattling on the shelf and falling makes me turn around. There are food items on his back and some on the floor beside them, but Gerard is still power driving that dick in her. I let myself enjoy the sight of his strong chocolate butt flexing and tensing as he slides that dark dick in and out of her as his balls swing like bells.

I turn back to the door as they finally wrap their little sexcapade up. Gerard is making noises like a man possessed and the sounds of his pumps gets faster. Thank God his ass is cumming. The sounds of their moans and kisses are replaced by heavy panting. The scent of their sex is strong.

"I'll see you tonight, lover," Carolyn tells him.

"If not sooner?" he asks.

She just laughs.

Carolyn steps up next to me and I am so grateful she is back in her silk robe. "You go first," she tells me with a small push to my back.

I am busy thinking that I hope she does not have some of Gerard's nut on her hand with her touching me. Okay? Alright.

Thankfully the kitchen is still empty and quiet. I throw them couple of pantry freaks a quick thumbs up and dash out of there. I make it up the stairs and back to our room in record time. Mohammed is still sleeping but I slip out of my robe and my bikini. I flip the covers back and bend down to ease his boxers down his narrow hips as my clit steady throbs like a heartbeat between my legs.

He stirs in his sleep just as I lift his dick with my hand and take the tip into my mouth. "Morning, Danielle," he says, his voice still heavy with sleep even though his dick gets so hard against my tongue.

Truth? I am feeling horny as hell. I am going to enjoy this sexy bedroom *and* my sexy man. Why should Carolyn be the only one to have fun?

Chapter Twenty-Six

Alizé

This is the last thing I need right now.

I feel like every eye is locked on me as I walk towards Cameron's office like my ass is going to war. I wish the paper balled up in my fist was his damn neck.

"Good morning, Monica," Delaney says as I breeze right on past her desk. "You can't go in. He's on a phone—"

I turn the knobs to the massive double doors leading to his office and they swing open like I have super powers. Humph. Just call me Angry Woman because I am pissed off.

Cameron looks up at me and his face becomes surprised. "Let me call you right back," he says to whatever insignificant person he's on the phone with.

"How could you, Cameron?" I ask him accusingly as I toss the crumpled paper at his face.

He swats it away and rises quickly to walk around the desk and towards the open doors to close them. I watch his every movement as I turn. He storms right up to me until we are standing face to face. "How could you tell *my wife* that you plan to fuck me and then send me home for her to suck your juices off my dick?" he asks in a crude voice.

I tilt my chin up as I meet his eyes. "Why did you tell the bitch—"

"Monica," he interrupts sternly.

I give him a "say what" look. "Why did you tell *that bitch* that I tried to stop the wedding?"

Cameron threw his hands up in the air. "First off, I didn't tell my wife that another woman came to me before our wedding to stop it but if I did why would you care. Hell, it's the fucking truth!"

If he said "my wife" one more damn time, I'm gone to really flip the fuck out. "You transferring me out of the department is fucking with my career. I had every intention of leaving you and your wife alone, she came into my office."

"You are messing up your own career, Monica, by sexually soliciting your supervisor, arguing with your supervisor's wife, and basically acting unprofessional." Cameron walks past me and back around his desk to reclaim his seat. "You're lucky you are just getting transferred and not fired from this internship."

I begin to bite down on my bottom lip as my chest heaves with emotion. I hate to admit it but he's right. This scheme to win him back is not a part of my master plan. And frankly, I'm tired of Cameron making it clear as hell that he loves his wife and not me. Monica "Alizé" Winters doesn't chase any damn man. Fuck the dumb shit.

He's staring at me with this look that is way too caring but I don't even let it get to me. Enough is enough. Serena Lemons-Steele can have her husband.

Without another word or look in his direction, I turn and walk away.

"Monica," he calls out.

I don't even stop or turn or nothing. Fuck him.

As soon as I park the car outside of Dr. Locke's brownstone, I lift my hips to take off my panties. The summer breeze feels good against my thighs as I climb out of the car in a silk print wrap dress. Nipples hard. Stomach flat. Just the right amount of leg peeking through the split. Luckily for me, the winds didn't send my skirts up and expose my ass to any Tom, Dick, or Harry walking or driving by.

I climb the stairs of the brick duplex. I'm just reaching the top step when the front door opens and Dr. Locke walks out onto the front stoop. I smile and lick my lips as I start to pull the flap of my dress up my thigh. "Hungry—"

"Hello, Miss Winters. Did we have an appointment that I forgot?" he asks in that professional voice that is nothing like the way he sounds when he is begging me to spank him before I fuck the hell out of him.

My eyes shift past him to a round as hell, short woman with grayish short hair walking out behind him. The sight of her makes me ease that dress right back down. Plus, the crazy look on his face and his lie gives a sistah like me the distinct feeling that I am face to face with Mrs. Locke. "Yes, my parents and I thought our meeting was today. They're on the way actually," I lie as I cross my arms over my hard as hell nipples pressing through the thin material of my dress. I threw in the parents just in case she's wondering what the hell a sexy bitch like me is doing showing up to her husband's office unexpectedly.

"Actually, my wife and I were just headed out and I don't have any appointments for the rest of the day."

She gives me this smile that reminds me of my grammie and I feel a tiny twinge of guilt because I am fucking the hell out of her husband like I'm on a damn mission.

"Nice to meet you, Mrs. Locke," I say, keeping one arm folded over my chest as I reach with the other to offer her my hand.

She takes it. It's soft like the type of hand you want to comfort you when you're crying or hurt or lonely. It's that special touch only a grandmother has. "Nice to meet you too," she says softly. "Hunt, I'll wait for you in the car."

And like that she walks down the steps leaving us alone momentarily. She trusts her husband.

"I have to go but you look amazing," he tells me low in his throat for my ears only, standing there with his hands in his pockets with that blasé psychiatrist look on his face.

I remove my other arm and his eyes instantly drop to my nipples. I see that look come into his eyes and right now I could care less about anything but having him. "Can we reschedule another appointment and then I can call my parents and tell them not to come?" I ask loudly.

He looks at his watch (fronting like a motherfucker). "My scheduling book is inside," he says, pretending to sound reluctant before he holds up his hand to his wife. "I'll just be a minute, baby."

With my back safely to her, I roll my eyes as he turns, unlocks the door, and leads me inside. As soon as he closes the solid wood door and locks it behind us I bunk my ass up right there on the bottom of the steps that lead to the second level where he holds group sessions. I wiggle my ass as I politely toss my skirt up exposing my ass.

He slaps it with one hand but motions for me to turn. "You know I cum faster when you ride."

He drops his pants and takes a seat on the step. I climb right on that dick and began working my hips like I'm trying to win a damn hoola hoop contest. Sweat pops on the top of his bald head and steam covers his glasses as I enjoy the feel of his hands on my ass, his lips on my hard nipples, and his hard dick pressing against my clit.

In no time at all we both are kissing each other to keep from hollering out too loud as we cum together. Even though we rushing I don't stand up until I work my pussy walls and squeeze all the hardness and cum from his dick. Humph. It's good to the very last drop. Fuck Folgers.

I don't say another word to him while I straighten my skirt over my hips and push my titties back inside my bra. I got what I wanted. Wet ass and all, I strut right out that hallway and give his wife a friendly smile and a wave before I hop in my ride and haul ass with a squeal of my tires.

Girl Talk

Alizé, Dom, and Moët were enjoying the warmth of the end of spring in New York as they walked up Fifth Avenue doing more sightseeing than shopping. As they walked up to Saks a cab pulled up to the curb and a young man hopped out followed by a five-year-old boy they assumed was his son. They watched as he bent down to pick the boy up into his arms.

He looked up at them with a smile as he crossed their path to walk inside the store. All three of the ladies smiled in return and each of their smiles was melancholy.

"I wish my father had taken me out for a daddy-daughter day," Moët said, as they continued up the busy New York avenue. "I hope that Bones takes advantage of having his daughter and builds a relationship with her like that, you know?"

"Well, my daddy and I had plenty of that 'quality time,'" Alizé added as she reached into her Ferragamo tote for her shades. "But I swear I could do with a little less daddy-daughter time these days 'cause I am sick of his lumpy-ass couch and being an ear witness to his freak show with his fiancée. Can we say thicker doors, Daddy?"

Dom and Moët stopped walking to look over at Alizé and say, "Eew."

Alizé slipped on her shades. "Eew is right."

Dom ran her long acrylic fingernails over her short spiky hair as she bit her bottom lip and let the troubles that she felt fill her eyes. "I would take either one of your daddy problems compared to my shit. I mean what's fuckin' worse: growin' up without a father at all because he cracked out or findin' out that he off livin' a wonderful new life with a new family?"

"Dom, you really should talk to him and hear his side of the story," Alizé offered as they stopped at the corner.

Dom reached inside her khaki military-style shirt for her soft pack of Newports. "I know I do but first I got somethin' else to take care of."

"Whatever you decide just make sure it's right for you," Moët added.

Dom nodded as she let out a stream of smoke. "Good, 'cause this might be the hardest shit I ever had to face, y'all."

Both Moët and Alizé lock their arms through hers as they all crossed the street. It was their way of letting their friend know that they had her back.

Chapter Twenty-Seven

Dom

"Uhm . . . uhm . . . uhm. Look what the cat done drug back home."

I'm standing there lookin' at my mother and feelin' like it's a damn shame that I don't miss her even though I ain't laid eyes on her since last year. And being here, back in this wild-ass project, surrounded by shit I'm runnin' from is so fuckin' hard for me. But I don't have no choice.

"Can I come in?" I ask, noticin' that the entire Baby Phat outfit she wearin' is mine. When I moved out I left more clothes than I took.

Diane is forty goin' on damn twenty. She never felt like a momma. She was more like a big sister. We talked about men and money. We used to smoke weed, drink, and party together—and those were the good times. I tried not to remember how bad she treated me when I was too small for her ass to hang out with. The names she used to call me. The way she used to make me feel like she didn't want my ass.

And now this shit that I come to handle today.

She steps back to let me walk in. I look around at the new furnishings in the apartment. Diane always kept a bad ass apartment and she obviously ain't lackin' for shit without me. So I know her "get money" mentality ain't changed a bitch because Diane ain't gone ever hit a fuckin' lick at a stick on someone's job.

"Where's my grandbaby?" she asks with attitude as I sit down on the new brown leather sofa.

Safe from your crazy ass, I think. But I say, "She's with the girls."

She rolls her eyes as she struts across the room. "I haven't seen her in a good minute. You would think your ass woulda brought—"

"Who is William Kennedy?" I ask her. Fuck it. I want to get right to the point.

Diane makes a face as she walks over to the kitchen counter to pick up a black ashtray. "Who?" she asks as she picks up the lit cigarette in the tray.

Somethin' 'bout the way she shifts her eyes away from mine makes me think she straight lyin'. "The man who came to my job and told me he's my father. The man whose daughter looks like me and Kimani. The man who showed me a picture of his mother—who I look just like. Don't play games, Diane, 'cause William Kennedy is somebody you fucked twenty-two years ago."

That fake-ass confused look on her face changes to fuckin' blasé as she lays down on the couch and watches me through a stream of smoke she releases through her pursed lips. "That motherfucker is crazy out his ass," is all that she says. "Your daddy ain't no fuckin' William Kennedy and I thought I got that through to his dumb ass way back when."

I just stare at this crazy bitch.

"Me and your daddy—"

"Which one?" I ask as I squeeze my keys so tight that it pinches the damn flesh of my palm. "The one you say is my daddy or the one that is," I snap.

She sits up as she stares at me all angry and shit. She points at me with that lit cigarette between her fingers. "Why you all in my space and my face fuckin' with me 'bout this *bullshit* now?" she asks as she rises to her feet to glare down at me.

"I got every right to know if my real daddy is some ex-drug dealer turned dope fiend or not," I shoot back at her as I rise to my feet too. I don't put it past her to try and fight me.

"Why you all up in my business, Dom?"

I look at her like she really is crazy. For real. "Your business? *Your* business? Why everything got to be 'bout your ass? This ain't planet Diane so get up off yourself."

She leans back with attitude and looks at me like she ready to step to me. Then her face changes again and she is lookin' calm. Too fuckin' calm. She raises her hand to take another drag of her Newport. "You know what, I *was* fuckin' both them niggas and either one coulda been your daddy, but I went with the one that paid them bills and treated a bitch the way she needed to be treated. I went for the baller shot caller and not the broke motherfucker who ain't had shit goin' for him but a big dick. I put my head before my pussy. If I did pick the wrong motherfucker as your daddy . . . so the fuck what."

I feel like I can snap her neck without blinkin'. "No, your ass played eenie-meenie-minie-moe with my fuckin' life!" I shout at her as tears fill my eyes because I hate her. I hate her so much.

Diane looks at me with so much anger in her eyes. "You act like you had it so rough but you don't know shit about the hard knock life, baby girl. I did what I had to do to take care of your ass and if it meant slob or rob I took care of you. So don't stand here cryin' like you had the worst life ever."

"Are you crazy out your ass or what?" I ask her. "You know there was a chance that man was my fuckin' daddy and you just said fuck it 'cause he ain't have enough money. And then the top dog drug pen you pick turns out to be a fuckin' junkie and broke as hell. You threw it in my face my whole damn life that my daddy wasn't shit and I was just like him and the whole time you knew he might not be my fuckin' daddy. *Bitch*, you crazy. You crazy as hell."

I just got the hell out of her face before I straight throw a two-piece and lump her ass up real good. I reach the front door when somethin' crashes against the wall. I turn and look at the glass shattered on the wall over the chair. I cut my eyes over to Diane and the tears runnin' down her face shock my ass.

She starts to walk towards me with her finger pointed at me and shakin'. "You try being gang raped at eight, *bitch*. You try having your own momma teach you shoot her up with dope, *bitch*. You try sleeping on top of subway grates to keep warm 'cause your junky mother got evicted again . . . *bitch*. Don't you fucking tell me about your hard ass life. I kept a roof over your head, food in your belly, and clothes on your ass, *bitch*."

Diane is standin' in front of me with her chest heavin' and shit. The smell of liquor and cigarettes is hot on her breath. I feel sorry for her but it's time for the realness. "The roof, the food, or the clothes . . . they wasn't enough 'cause most of all I wanted your love and you didn't give it to me. You took the only chance I had to feel loved and wanted when you took my daddy away from me before he ever had a fuckin' chance."

I swipe away my tears and get the hell out of there. As soon as the heavy metal door closes behind me, my legs give out and I let my body slide down to the floor while I cry like I ain't ever cried before.

Chapter Twenty-Eight

Moët

Bones is late bringing Tiffany back . . . again.

I am sitting in the lobby with my cell phone clutched in my hand, watching our neighbors come and go, watching the sunset and then the darkness fall and still he's a no-show. I have damn near bitten my nails down to the nub. Each time I worry he will use his money and run with her—somewhere I can't find her. I worry that something bad has happened. I just plain worry.

I flip the cell phone open and dial his number—that the court had to make him give me—again. One . . . two . . . three rings. Voice mail.

"Bones, this is Mo . . . again. You're late with Tiffany again and . . . I just want to make sure she's okay so a call to let me know you're running behind would be . . . that would be a big help." I release a heavy breath. "Bye."

I have to talk to my lawyer about it. Even though he is fighting to take my daughter away from me for good, I am trying my best to be amicable because that's what is best for Tiffany. I still haven't sued for child support because I have to admit that the bastard always returns her with plenty of new clothes, pampers, and formula to last several babies. Still, he is always late bringing her back and I am afraid that him and his mother will talk shit about me to Tiffany. My child—especially when she's older—doesn't need to be around all that drama.

I try to focus on the files from work on my lap, but every five minutes I'm looking up hoping to see Bone's black-on-black Escalade. It isn't that the stories weren't compelling enough to hold my attention. Each one is its own war story. Abandoned babies. Another child born with HIV and addicted to crack. Another burnt with boiling water by their mother. Kids left home alone. Kids raising themselves while their parents or grandparents chase drugs. Horror story after horror story after horror story. The sad part is my coworkers tell me that what I've seen is only the tip of the iceberg. It only gets worse.

It's funny but my work makes me want to fight even harder for Tiffany. I'm sure Bones loves his daughter and he never has brought her back to me harmed in any way (oh I check her from head to toe because I don't know him and his momma like that) but I have to fight for my daughter.

I am just filling out paperwork for the placement of a set of orphaned twins when my cell phone vibrates beside me. I drop everything to snatch it up but the pounding of my heart slows to see Taquan's number.

I start to send him to voice mail but decide to answer the call instead. "Hi, Taquan."

"I'm surprised that you answered."

I hear a car door close and my eyes dart to the glass door. It's not them. "I'm downstairs waiting for Tiffany. Bones is late again . . . of course."

"If there's anything I can do just let me know," he offers. "I know we're not going out anymore but I wanted to call and check up on you since you haven't been coming to church as much anymore."

I drop my head back and wipe my tired eyes with my fingers. He's right I have slacked up from church big time. I haven't stepped away from faith—although it's been tested—I've just gotten lazy with it. Bones usually brings Tiffany back on Saturday nights and I am so happy to have her back that church is the last thing on my mind on Sunday mornings. Trying to do just enough to keep my job, worrying about Tiffany over at Bones' *and* worrying about Bones winning full custody of her has become my obsession.

"Listen, with all the trials and tribulations you're going through this is the time to turn to the Lord and not away from Him."

He's right.

"Listen, just promise me I will see you and Tiffany in church to-morrow."

"I promise," I tell him with honesty just as Bones' Escalade pulls up in front of the building.

"I've done my deacon duty now I am just talking to you as a man and I miss you, Latoya. I wish things between us could have worked out. I want you back in my life," he tells me in this husky voice that gives me actual goose bumps and causes my nipples to harden into tight buds.

A part of the reason I left this man—this good religious man—alone is because he turns me the hell on. I will corrupt his ass. I will keep right on until I have him naked and hard in my bed.

"I miss you too," I tell him with honesty. "But—"

"No buts. Just knowing you miss me too is enough for now."

Bones walks in the building with Tiffany in her carrier while his bodyguards stand outside like he the president or something. Please.

"Maybe we can talk tomorrow after church."

I lift the files from my lap to sit in the leather club chair beside me. "Okay. See you tomorrow." I rise and take the carrier from him. Our hands briefly touch and there is none of the spark we used to have.

"Bones, you really could call and let me know you're running late," I tell him as I sit the carrier on the chair and immediately pull my baby out of it into my arms. She coos as I lay her against my chest and snuggle my face against hers. "Hey you."

He sits two large shopping bags on the floor next to my feet. "What-ever," he mutters around the toothpick hanging out his mouth be-fore he turns to leave.

"Bones," I call behind him.

He stops but he doesn't turn.

Still holding our daughter, I walk over to him. "We both have done things to each other that we should be sorry for. I know I am.

We have a daughter to raise and for me she is the most important thing out of all of this. I don't want to go to war with you. I never wanted to keep you out of her life. I never wanted to take you for your money. I never wanted you to get back with me because of her. I just want us to find a way to raise her together."

He turns and he looks down at me as he pushes his hands into the pockets of his dark denims. "I don't want my daughter raised by the type of manipulative low-down dirty bitch that would lie on a mother-fucker about rape. See to me that shows me what type of cluck cluck bitch that you are. So *I am* going to take Tiffany from your no-good ass."

I swallow back the tears and fears that rise in me as I look up at him. "What happened to the Bones I fell in love with?" I ask him softly. "You wasn't a cold hard angry ass man filled with hate."

"You never loved me. You loved my dick and my money!" he yells down into my face.

Some of his spit sprays against my cheeks and mouth. "I'm not going to lie down and let you take her. I'm willing to work out joint custody—"

He reaches in his pocket for a big wad of money. "Look, how much I got to pay a greedy bitch like you for my daughter? Ten thousand. Twenty. Fifty. Name your price."

Disgusted that he thinks he can bribe me to give up my child, I reach up to slap him with my free hand and he catches it in his grasp and holds my wrist so tightly that I cry out. I snatch away from him as Tiffany begins to cry like she can feel the anger, hatred, and tension between her parents. "If I were you I would consider joint—"

Bones throws his hands up in the air. "I ain't got to consider shit."

What did I ever see in this corny motherfucker? (See now I'm cussing.) "Bones, you either can ride with me or I will do any and everything in my power to run you the fuck over," I tell him fiercely.

"Oh, you threatening me again? What you gone do now, lie and say I hit you or some dumb shit? Man, let me get the fuck away from your crazy ass."

I offer him joint custody and he throws it in my face. I tried to go the high road but if it's down and dirty that he wants then that's what he's going to get. I have to do what I have to do.

Part Three

"Life is What You Make It"

Chapter Twenty-Nine

Cristal

Two Weeks Later

"If Mohammed's woman won't come to the mountain then I'm bringing the mountain to Mohammed's girl."

I look up from the book I am reading on creating a business plan to find Alizé looking down at me. She is looking office chic in a linen pantsuit. Her hair is looking fresh with her signature doobie wrap.

I stand up to reach across the receptionist desk to give a quick hug and an air kiss—just the way Carolyn taught me. "You did not have to go to your internship today?" I ask.

"I have to meet with my advisor from school so I left early today and decided to stop by and see you, Miss Stranger." Alizé gives me a disapproving look. "You know we understand that status and wealth have always been goals of yours but I never thought you would turn your back on your friends . . . or your man."

"My man?" I ask as I reclaim my seat and look up at her.

"I've been hanging out at the apartment until really late—to give my dad and his fiancée more privacy—and Mohammed's been coming by the apartment before he goes home for the day and he asked what was up with you."

I turn my head and look out the glass window of the law firm's outer offices. He has been insisting that I end my friendship with

Carolyn but everything I want in life is within my grasp and he just
wants me to let it all slip through my fingers like sand. I cannot do
that. Especially when she has agreed to help finance my idea for an
ultra-chic, ultra-exclusive day spa with a price point that is high
enough to draw in celebrities but not too high to dissuade real women
like me and the girls who want to splurge and feel like celebrities for
a day. Carolyn loves the idea and all she wants from me is the details. A business plan.

Maybe it is divine intervention that Alizé, my smart college grad,
MBA-student friend is right here before me.

"You are just the person I need to see," I tell her as I take my
notepad and the book I was reading to sit on the counter before her.
"Can you help me draw up a business plan?"

Alizé frowns a little as she looks down at my notepad and closes
the cover of the book to read the title.

I stand and put my hands on my hips in full fabulous mode as
I give her my best smile. "I think the day spa is a good idea. Don't
you?"

Alizé's frown deepens. "You mean like Bubbles and Bliss or
Serenity—where we already go?" she asks. "One part of a solid business plan is finding a need that is not being met. I think there are
enough day spas in New York."

My chest *was* pumped up with pride but Alizé's words—her dis-
approval—deflates me right on down. "Why do you have to hate?" I
ask as I snatch my things back from her critical view.

Her mouth drops open as she looks down at me. "Cris, are you
trippin'?" she asks me in a high-pitched squeal of nothing but pure
disbelief.

I look around and thank God we are alone. "I just asked for your
help not your damn opinion," I whisper up to her.

Brrrnnnggg.

I hold up my hand and pick up the ringing phone. "Lowe,
Ingram, and Banks. How may I direct your call?"

The elevator dings and I look up as a teenage delivery man walks
through the opening doors with a massive spring bouquet in his
hand. I hang up from the call just in time to hear Alizé tell the boy:

"Negro, please. You have to be old enough to ride this ride and if I felt like breast-feeding a child, I would have a baby. Boy, you better get your little self up out of my face with a quickness."

"This little boy will have you hollering and moaning, baby," he tells her with more teeth than lips.

"Probably from you poking me with that little ass dick," she shoots back just as calm as she please.

"Little? Shit, it's so big if I pull it out right now it'll cover the sun and make it dark."

Alizé arched a brow. "Good, do that so your mama can call your young ass on home for your bedtime."

I reach between them for the clipboard and quickly sign it before these two start swinging. "Thank you, Jamal," I tell him with a sweet smile.

He shoots Alizé another mean look before he turns to me with every last one of his pearly whites on display. "Nice to come face to face with a nice polite woman of style and grace," he says with emphasis before he accepts my five dollar tip and walks away with one last glare at Alizé.

She just waves her hand dismissively as I look at the card. I am not surprised to see they are for me. For the last two weeks flowers, expensive chocolates, and other trinkets that a woman loves have been sent to me. I open the card as Alizé eyes me with open curiosity.

"This is for you?" she asks. "This has to be a five-hundred-dollar arrangement."

> *Danielle,*
> *I want you in my life. Just ask.*
> *The world is yours without question.*
> *Marc*

I smile as the scent of his cologne reaches me.

I met Marc Ellison during that weekend in the Poconos and although I have told the handsome and ultra-wealthy investment banker that I have a man (who was sitting and glaring at us talking from across the room) he has made it his business to woo me with every possible gift a man can give a woman. I have not laid eyes on him since that trip but he has definitely made his interest known. I have no intention of giving in but I have to admit that it feels like good old times to be pampered again. He is definitely a brother on a mission.

"I know damn well you not letting Mohammed spend most of his check on your ass."

"Who?" I ask, looking up at her as I place the card to my nose and inhale Marc's scent.

"Mohammed. Your boyfriend. The man who loves and adores you. The man you are losing because of your dreams and delusions of fucking grandeur."

Damn. I forgot all about him.

Alizé puts her tote back on her shoulder and her shades back down over her eyes. "I have to get going so that I'm on time to meet my evaluation . . . but I'm not hating on you for wanting to start a business or to give yourself a better life. Just remember the same people you step on and hurt on your way up are the same ones you have to face on your way down."

She turns and struts to the elevator. Like she planned it, the door opens and she steps on and turns. "Get your shit together, Cris," she tells me just before the doors close her off from my view.

Chapter Thirty

Alizé

Okay, I know I could have moved in with my girls but I am only making eighteen dollars an hour at the internship and I no longer have a baller to feed my designer clothes and shoes addiction, so a chick like me ain't looking for no parts of no rent. Straight up. Plus, my father and I get along so well so I thought I could spend some time with him while I work out my drama with my mama. But I never knew just how much time his fiancée, Andrea, spent at his apartment and with my situation with my mother *still* an issue, I am rethinking my living arrangements.

"Yes, yes, yes!"

I roll my eyes at the sound of Andrea calling for Jesus and turn up the television from my spot on the sofa bed. Them two is at it again and I'm trying so damn hard not to throw up the smothered pork chops she brought over for dinner. Who knew my daddy was such a freak?

I lean across the bed to grab my cell phone from the end table. I start to call Dr. Locke out the house for a freakfest but I change my mind and dial the girls' apartment instead. Dr. Locke is getting to be a little too caught up in this here pussy. I'm looking for sex not a relationship. He even offered to take me with him to a week long conference in Brazil. *Puh-lease.*

The phone just rings so I hang up. Everybody must be out. I don't even bother with their cell phones. Just because I'm stuck in hell don't mean I have to call and ruin their plans bitching about it.

"Oh . . . oh . . . oh . . . oooooooh Charles. *Charles.*"

Unfortunately, I know just *what* might have my mama so fool over my daddy. I wonder if them two freaks in there don't know that the walls of this one bedroom apartment—that can use a lady's touch—is paper-thin.

Needing a diversion, I roll off the bed in my shorts and wife-beater to grab my briefcase from by the door. I hop back onto the bed and pull out the report my new supervisor gave the finance department members to review. I have to admit that Cameron hurt me by shifting me over to the finance department under Roger Franks—a short, balding, nerdy little white man with more glasses than face. In the end, the move was great for my education because I am learning so much—even if I missed seeing Cameron on the regular. Maybe not seeing Cameron and having blood pumping to my pussy and not my brain is helping to do what I really came to Braun, Weber to do . . . learn. In this new department I am so intrigued to see the principles we were taught in class actually put to use.

Even though I still love Cameron (and I do love him even if I say fuck him all the time), my focus is back where it needs to be.

Bzzz. Bzzz.

Still reading the report, I climb back out of bed and make my way across the short distance to the front door. I stand on my toes to look out the peephole and my heart stops to see my mother standing there . . . just as Andrea hits a high note that lets me know their little romp is over.

Biting my bottom lip, I open the door just as she rings the doorbell again. I slip out the door and pull it close behind me. "Hi, Mama."

She looks me up and down. "Why are you in the hall dressed in your nightclothes, Monica Winters?" she asks me as she looks past me to peek through the crack in the door. I jerk it shut and she jerks back a little bit.

"I was just about to go to bed."

"Well, I think we need to talk. Don't you?"

I eye the dark form-fitting jeans and snug V-neck Baby Phat white tee she has on with gold sandals and my first thought is she don't want to talk to me. She just wants to come over and flaunt all her newness to my daddy. "Are those my shoes?" I ask as I bend down to eye them.

"Listen, I came here to talk to you about moving your little grown behind home and I'm not talking in the hall—"

The door flies open and I nearly fall back inside the apartment. "Who's at the door, Ladybug?" my father asks.

I look over at Mama and she eyes my daddy from head to toe in his robe. I look over at Daddy and he eyes Mama from head to toe in her new and improved look.

"Charles?" Andrea calls from behind him.

My mama's face gets nasty as hell. My daddy looks uncomfortable as hell. And I wish I could press my body into the door and just disappear to hell . . . especially when Andrea walks right up to the door in her silk caftan.

Mama looks her up and down. I know she is not missing one bit of her—Andrea's high-yellow complexion, blondish long hair, and tall curvaceous frame that is hard to deny even in a caftan.

Daddy clears his throat and looks at me and I look at him. Andrea just smiles warmly.

"I'm Elaine Winters, Charles's first wife," my mother says, not even bothering to extend her hand.

Andrea's smile drops off her face like a ton of bricks. "I'm Andrea and it's nice to meet you, Elaine," she says.

The tension in the air is thick as hell. Real thick.

"I'll let you all get back to . . . *whatever* you were doing," Mama says with plenty of attitude. She turns to me. "Monica, I want you to come by the house tomorrow so that we can talk."

Just before she turns, I see tears glistening in her eyes and my heart hurts for her.

I take off down the stairs behind her. "Mama," I call out. She wipes her face before she turns to face me. I can see her sadness through that fake smile she gives me. I take her in my arms and I hold her like she's held me so many times over the years. "Wait in the car and I'm gonna pack my stuff real quick and follow you home. Okay?"

She nods her head as she looks at me. "Thank you," she tells me earnestly.

It's easy for me to tell her to get over it but I look at the way Cameron turned me down and married another woman and then transferred me out of his department . . . and I still love him. Who am I to question her heart?

I let my pain over Cameron push me onto the dick of an older married man. Who am I to question her getting out the house more and finding a young tenderoni to ease her mind?

Plus, I miss her . . . *and* my bedroom.

Girl Talk

"Do we tell her?" Alizé asks as she stands between Moët and Dom outside the entrance to Macy's in Livingston Mall.

"Will she even give a fuck?" Dom asks, her eyes and her feelings safely hidden behind large black shades.

Moët's grip on the carriage tightens in anger. "It doesn't matter. We *have* to tell her."

Alizé crosses her arms over her chest in her sweatsuit. "I already told her what y'all told me and I don't see no change in her ass. Men ain't shit."

"Yeah and some bitches ain't shit either," Dom snaps, right on point with her usual sullen and angry demeanor.

They all thought of her neglect of them. They felt it and if he felt it too then maybe it led to the scene before them. It didn't make it right but they understood what might have led to it a little better.

"Shit, I got so much of my own fucking problems," Dom muttered.

"Yeah, but she is *still* our friend." Moët eyed both of them long and hard.

"I can't tell lately," Alizé adds.

All three pairs of eyes were troubled as they watched Mohammed and Evette walking through the mall together. She lightly touches his hands and says something that makes him fling his head back and laugh. It's the happiest they've seen their handyman in months.

"Damn," they all said in unison.

Chapter Thirty-One

Dom

"I'm glad that you decided to come in and see me, Keesha."
I look at Dr. Copeland through my shades as I keep my sweaty palm squeezed tightly shut. "I needed more than that group shit."

I know he hates for me to curse but he don't say nothing so he must know I need his help. "Tell me what's going on, Keesha?" he asks.

I look at him, this man who helped me stop using drugs by making me look at life. I mean really take a look at him. I can't even wonder what the fuck it would be like to fuck him. I can't even believe Alizé and her therapist is screwing. Oh, she didn't tell me 'cause she still don't trust me all the way but I overheard her and Moët talkin' 'bout it.

Okay, it's wrong as hell but it ain't my problem. The only motherfuckin' thing I want from Doc is some help. I got real problems a dick ain't gone solve.

"I found out that my mother damn near flipped a coin on who my real father is and well, Doc, she picked wrong."

"What happened?"

"About a month ago this man comes to my job and tells me that I am his daughter and that my mother told him he wasn't my father. So all these years she's been throwin' it in my face that I'm just like my crackhead daddy . . . but this man ain't on drugs. He's married, has kids and works, and takes care of his family. He woulda taken care of me . . . too."

My throat gets tight as I fight back the tears that fill my eyes. "I can forgive her for an honest mistake but she damn nears tells me to get over it because my life ain't as bad as hers."

"So this man is your father?"

I grasp my hand into a tighter fist as I nod. "We took a paternity test and the results came back last week."

"Do you want a relationship with him?"

"I don't know, Doc," I admit as I open and close my fist. "I do know I'm tryin' to stay clean and raise my child. Just when I'm gettin' myself together the best I can here's this . . . this . . . mess."

"So you think this is enough to break down all the hard work you've done to stay clean?"

I lift my shades and lock my eyes with his as I raise my arm and open my damn fist. A small plastic Ziploc of dope falls onto the floor between us. "Yes," I admit soft as hell as my tears run down my damn cheeks like they were freed from jail. "I brought that after I got finished talkin' to Diane. I can't take it but I can't throw it away either and that scares the shit out of me, Doc."

He raises his eyes from the bag of dope to look at me. I know he sees me for what I really am. A junkie on the edge of falling back into my fuckin' addiction.

"Throw it away, Dom," Dr. Copeland orders me.

I look at it and I want it so bad. I just want to get right on the floor, bust that bag open and bury my face in it until Diane, my daddy drama, my money problems, my friendship bullshit all is nothin' but a fuckin' afterthought . . . at least for a little while.

"Throw it away and show yourself that you don't need it."

Dope is a prison that I'm on probation from (I will never be completely free). I don't want to go back to that hell again. I won't. I can't.

I reach down and take that bag into my hand. It's damp and shit from my sweaty palms. I rise from my seat and walk over to the window of his small office. Under his watchful eyes, I look down at that bag of dope in my hand and open it. With one last breath, I push the window open and fling the bag out into the air.

The powder leaves the bag and swirls in the air before drifting down to the abandoned lot below.

"I'm proud of you, Keesha," he says from behind me.

I close the window and stare at my reflection in the glass. "I'm proud of me too," I admit softly, before wrappin' my arms around myself.

Chapter Thirty-Two

Moët

I love my friends and the support they give me unconditionally but I'm proud of myself for doing this alone. Tiffany is my baby and my responsibility. I need to handle this by myself. I prayed for some divine intervention and things are finally starting to go my way.

I can't afford any more lawyer's fees and to be honest my lawyer is going to have to sue me to get the rest of the money I owe her if this case wraps up before she sends her next bill.

I am going over just what I want to say to Bones when Helen walks into the conference room looking more man than woman with her short black hair and black suit. I can care less how she looks as long as she helps keep me in Tiffany's life.

"Mr. Drooms and his attorney are on their way up," she tells me before sitting beside me and placing her files on the table in front of her.

I finger the large manila envelope in my lap. "Helen, is there any way that I can speak to him alone before you guys get involved? I just think Bones and I should give it one more try working it out ourselves."

She pauses in putting on her glasses as she looks over at me. "I would advise that everything be on the record and you both have representation for any meeting."

"I know you know better than me but I still would like just a few minutes alone with him," I insist.

The door opens and Cristal shoots me a smile as she leads Bones and his attorney into the room. It's funny but it's so late at night when she comes home and so early when she leaves for work, that I feel almost like she is a stranger to me.

Even as my attorney requests permission for me to speak to Bones alone, I'm wondering if Cristal will eventually move out of the apartment and chase her dream of opening a day spa—mind you Alizé had to tell me and Dom about that *and* the flowers she received from someone other than Mohammed. Was being rich and famous that important to Cris? I thought that mess with Mohammed and Sahad had taught her a lesson.

"What do you want, Moët?"

I look away from where I was staring off into the distance to find that me and Bones are alone. I shake my head for clarity as I open the manila envelope and pull out the three newsmagazines inside. I swallow over a lump in my throat as I push them down the length of the table to where he stands in a three-piece suit.

I have to admit that the bastard looks good.

He eyes me with open hostility before he picks the papers up.

"I want to suggest . . . that we sit down, just you and me, and work out a joint custody agreement. I never wanted to take Tiffany from you. Never. It's you that wants to completely wipe a mother from a child's life." I lick my lips as I sit back in my chair and watch him. "I don't want any child support as long as you continue what you're already doing on your own."

His face is so angry but that look on his face just empowers me. I have him by the nuts and if I wasn't a child of God working on being an even better child of God I wouldn't be so gracious to offer joint custody.

"You full of shit, bitch," he yells as he flings the papers across the room. "This is a bunch of lies."

I calmly rise from my seat and pick up each one. "I don't know if they are or not. I haven't seen you in almost a year and I'm not an insider to your camp or one of your reps that's reported in this article. All I do know is that I am mother fighting for her child and I have to give my lawyer any evidence that shows that you are unfit."

He puts his hands on his hips as the bright sun of spring shines through the window and makes his diamonds glisten as if they are wet. "If you believe that trash then why would you offer joint custody then, Moët?"

I bang my fist on the table as the fire fills my eyes. "Because . . . I . . . have . . . *never* . . . WANTED TIFFANY OUT OF YOUR LIFE YOU *ASSHOLE*!"

I bite my lip to stop any more of a tirade as I point and look heavenward. "Forgive me Lord. I'm trying. You know I'm trying."

The door opens and the attorneys both rush in. I calmly smooth my white pencil skirt over my hips as I reclaim my seat and look down at the covers of the magazines in front of me.

Bones pulls his attorney to the other side of the room while Helen whispers to me, "I didn't leave you two alone to fight, Latoya," she reprimands me.

I don't even respond to her because I am too busy thanking God as I look down at the tabloid headlines: "MULTIPLATINUM RAPPER MILLION DOLLAR CRACK HABIT" and "THE FREAKY (AND WEIRD) SEXUAL FETISHES OF RAPPER BONES" and "GUESS WHO IS THE LATEST GAY RAPPER? (THAT'S RIGHT RAP STAR . . . BONES)!!!"

All of it is enough for the judge to take a closer look at his lifestyle and I know for a fact that he blazes more trees than twelve Snoop Dogg's and the last thing his ass wants to do in the next thirty days is piss in a damn cup.

These tabloids just evened the scales for me and I look at it (no matter how unorthodox) as a blessing.

"Taquan, can I ask you something?"
"Go ahead."
"I know you're a virgin but have you ever cum before?"
"Yes."
"So you masturbate?"
"*Latoya*."

"I'm just curious."

"Yes, I've masturbated before."

"So masturbation is not considered fornication. Right?"

"Technically? No, it's not."

"Good. Open your front door." I snap my cell phone closed and loosen the tie on my trench coat.

As soon as the front door to his apartment opens, I step inside with my tote bag swinging from my hand. He looks at me nervous as hell about my intentions.

I reach up and lightly kiss his lips. "Don't worry. I'm not going to try and seduce you again."

He visibly relaxes. "What's in the bag?" he asks, looking way too tempting in his wifebeater and red basketball shorts. He must put all that pent-up sex drive into working out because the deacon's body is *ripped*.

I sit down on his leather sectional and reach for the remote to turn off the game on the big screen television. I kick off my shoes and reach down into my bag of tricks as Taquan comes over to sit in front of me on the oversized coffee table in front of the sofa.

"How did the meeting go today?" he asks as he looks down at me rummaging through the bag.

"They asked for a continuance," I tell him as my hand closes around just what I'm looking for.

"You seem okay with it?"

"I have a feeling I finally have Bones right where I want him."

Bzzzzzzzzzzzzzzzzzzzzzzzzzzzz.

"What is that?" he asks.

I smile as I look over at him. "I'm not Scarface but let me introduce you to *my* little friend."

His eyes get wide as I rub my vibrating ten-inch dildo from my knee to my inner thigh as I look at him from hooded eyes and lick my lips. "This is called the middle ground between what you want and what's right. This is my compromise," I tell him in a husky, soft, and sexy voice as I turn the dildo off and sit forward to caress the side of his face. "I don't want you to make love to me but I want you to touch me and kiss me and hold me. I want you to watch me play with this and if you feel the need to do you, then I want to watch you too. You feel me?"

He sits forward and grabs my face with his hands and kisses me like I am the best thing since sliced bread. "Latoya," he moans against my lips before he licks them lightly.

As he kisses my lips a dozen times I keep my eyes open and on him. "I'm not trying to make you be something you don't want to be or make you do *anything* you don't want to do. This is something we do anyway . . . so why not do it together and share something natural . . . *together*."

I stand up and open the trench. He makes a face that looks painful but I know is all about pleasure as he takes in all my naked glory. I bend over with my round caramel ass high in the air as I lick and kiss his mouth. "The choice is yours, baby," I whisper against his lips before I pick up my dildo and walk away to head to his bedroom.

I lay across his bed with my legs spread wide as I run my hands from my soft thighs to the aching nipples of my breasts. I lick my lips at the pleasure I give myself. Knowing I'm in *his* bed and *he's* in the next room excites me even more.

Bzzzzzzzzzzzzzzz.

I open my eyes to see Taquan standing at the foot of the bed, naked with his own hard dick in one hand and my vibrating dildo in the other.

I moan in anticipation. "This is about releasing that pressure until the time we can be together. Release me, Taquan. Release me."

As he climbs on the bed beside me, I know that I really want all of him and even though I won't have that of him tonight, for now . . . this will do.

Chapter Thirty-Three

Cristal

I never thought Mohammed would cheat. Maybe it is because I think highly of myself and I just assumed he did too or maybe it was because I truly never cheated on him and I just felt like he should trust me not to do the same thing to him that I did to Sahad . . . with him.

The girls told me what they saw. I confronted him and he didn't deny it. He said they were just friends. She was in town visiting and they were just chilling. And then he challenges me to believe him just like I always challenge him to believe me when I dip to hang out in NYC with Carolyn.

Funny thing is we had some of the best sex ever that night. I think we both were trying to prove something to each other.

Me: My pussy is so much better than hers.

Him: You should be here to take care of this good-ass dick.

But a part of me is hurting to think of Mohammed and his ex still dealing. A part of me is hurting real bad.

I wish my girls were here with me or I was with them. They would understand. They would know what to say. Carolyn will just wave her hand like she is shooing a fly and say good riddance.

I look around at the celebrities, the wannabes, and the gonnabes of New York's Butter restaurant. I miss Mohammed and his realness.

I lean in close to Carolyn as we sit on the banquette. "Carolyn, I think I'm going to head on home," I tell her as I pick up my clutch from the table.

"But our food hasn't even arrived yet," she tells me, looking quite pretty in all white with bold gold jewelry.

"I'm not feeling well," I lie.

"Well, you've had quite a bit to drink." She pats my hand. "Take my car. I'll just give Marc your regrets."

Fuck Marc. Fuck this star studded place. I just want to be in Mohammed's arms. "Thanks, Carolyn," I tell her, air kissing her cheeks before I rise to my feet.

"I'll call you."

Carolyn has become that surrogate mother I always dreamed of. Although she agreed with Alizé that another day spa is the last thing New York needs, she still will back my business . . . once I decide on one.

"Look-a-here, look-a-here."

I just stepped outside the restaurant when Sahad steps right in my path. Nothing about him had changed. Not his raw sex appeal or the rich quality of his clothes on his tall frame or that handsome, angular face. He raises his hand and the lights from the restaurant make his ring truly "bling" as he removes his shades. There is nothing but hate in his eyes as he looks at me.

"Who knew your little Rasta handyman could afford to treat you to such a fine establishment," he says snidely in a voice that is way too loud.

I am immediately filled with anger. "Just go inside and enjoy your evening, Sahad." I try to push past him to get to the valet stand but he steps to the left in my path.

"You know I feel sorry for Mr. Lover Lover because he can't afford a money-hungry bitch like you and soon someone with deeper pockets is gonna bum rush his coconut-loving ass right out of your life."

"The way he bum rushed your ghetto fabulous ass right out of mine," I shoot back as the lights of the paparazzi's cameras flash like crazy.

"Dayum," he says in an exaggerated fashion as he looks down at me with eyes colder than every bit of diamond Chris Aire jewelry that he is wearing. "Truth hurts, huh?"

Yes, it does. I think of Marc and all the gifts I have accepted from a man I do not know. Still, none of this is any of his business.

I step close to him and look up into his face without enough anger of my own in my eyes. "Leave me the fuck alone and get the fuck on with your life and stop letting the fact that a man with smaller pockets and a bigger dick took me from you."

He grabs my wrist and I do not break a sweat.

"A nice little civil suit is just what a golddigger like me wants . . . especially with all these witnesses."

He lets me go with a quickness. "Man, fuck you."

I push past him. "No, fuck *you*," I tell him over my shoulder before I walk away.

I do not relax until I am in the back of Carolyn's limo headed out the city to New Jersey and back on the Garden State Parkway.

As soon as I walk into the house I strip and make my way to the bedroom to climb into the bed beside Mohammed and wrap my arms and legs around his strong, muscular frame. And tonight as he stirs in his sleep there are no questions. No who, what, when, where, or how. He just presses a loving kiss to my forehead and wraps his arms around me to pull me even closer to his warmth before we fall asleep.

The steady buzzing of something vibrating awakens me the next morning. My cell phone. I lift my head from the bed as I lay on my belly. I am disappointed to find the bed empty. I had plans to wake before him and give him just the lip service needed to awaken him.

With a small stretch, I roll over in bed, tangling my legs in the covers, as I reach down into my purse on the nightstand. I frown at the sight of Alizé's mother's house phone. Oh God, did something happen to Ze?

I jerk the phone open. "Ms. Winters?"

"Girl, this me. This ain't my mama," Alizé snaps playfully.

"What are you doing there?" I ask as I sit up in bed exposing my breasts as the sheet falls to my waist.

"If you'd call a bitch or return a bitch's phone call your scandalous ass would know I moved back home."

"Girl it is too early for that much *at-ti-tude*," I tell her as I wipe sleep from my eyes.

"Well, is it too early for some celebrity gossip?"

"Can you call me back—"

"About you and Sahad," she slides in with way too much ease.

"What? What do you mean? What are you saying? What are you talking about?" I ask her, all the words coming out of me in a rush as my eyes dart around the room.

"You know I have to get me some *E!* in the morning while I'm getting ready for work. Well, news of your reconciliation with Sahad and the lovers' spat you guys had last night is all over the news. Hot 97. WBLS. *The Steve Harvey Morning Show.* Girl, DeeDee got y'all business all up on the *Doug Banks Show.* Bitch, ya'll *everywhere.*"

"Oh . . . my . . . God!" I gasp as I feel like I am going to hyperventilate.

"Why you ain't tell me you was back fucking that Negro?"

"Because it is not true. Oh, I cannot let Mohammed get a whiff of this shit. He will never believe . . ."

My words fade as my man walks into the bedroom carrying a bag of groceries. His face, his handsome face, is so cold as he looks at me. "I went out for some things to make us breakfast and instead I get that plus some *bullshit* about my damn woman and her ex . . . or current . . . or whatever the fuck Sahad is now."

Oh God, Mohammed LOVES listening to Steve Harvey in the morning.

I kick the covers from my legs and damn near trip my naked behind over myself as I get over to him as fast as I can. "That is *not* true. That is not what happened, Mohammed!"

I touch his chest and he brushes my hands away so hard that I stumble to the left. I watch as he flings the entire bag of groceries. Eggs splatter to the floor. A jar of orange juice crashes against the wall. A pack of bacon flies like a damn Frisbee.

I scream out at his unusual show of violence. I have not seen him this mad since the night he fought Sahad. "Mohammed, don't do this. You better believe me. I would never cheat on you. I promise. I swear," I plead with him as tears run down my face and my heart aches at how fucked-up fate can be.

He starts pacing, causing his dreads to swing across his back. "I can't do this shit, Danielle. Get out. Just get your shit and get the fuck out!"

I point at him. "No, Mohammed. No! No! No!"

He stops pacing to look at me and the pain in his eyes tears me up. "I don't want to feel like this no more. I don't want you no more."

My eyes widen as he walks around the room jerking up everything that is mine. He turns and flings it all at me. "Just get the fuck out, Danielle," he says in this voice that is way worse than screaming. It is the voice of a man who is truly fed up.

"I am not leaving this house," I tell him in a determined voice. "I am not leaving you and this relationship. I will not do it, Mohammed—"

He walks out of the room. "Don't be here when I get back, Danielle," he throws over his shoulder. Moments later I hear the front door open and then slam closed so hard that the house literally shakes.

Chapter Thirty-Four

Alizé

Now that my focus is back on work and not on Cameron, I have gotten my shit together and it's all about school and this internship for me. Over the last few weeks it's paid off. My supervisor just offered me the chance to return for the summer internship program. This will give me over a total of one year's experience here. With that type of relationship, I plan to work here once my MBA is in my hand in another year.

Oh, a bitch is back on the grind for my MBA (yup, it's *still* MORE BANKING OF ASSETS as far as I'm concerned).

My cell phone flashes and I pick it up from my desk. I roll my eyes at the sight of Dr. Locke's cell phone number. Maybe it's because my mom and I are working out our issues or because I'm resigned to the fact that Cameron and I will not be together or that my internship is in a great place, but I have been calling on my therapeutic dick less and less. In fact, the last time I gave him some of my goodies was last week and he has been blowing up my phone ever since.

That's why you can't put that pussy on some men like that. They ass can't take it when you shut off the supply. I laugh as I rise from the desk and start gathering my things.

I didn't even realize it's after seven already. I was so busy working on the paper describing my internship for my advisor. It's way past time to get my ass to the crib.

Before I leave my cubicle that is worse than the small office I had in Cameron's department, I know my ass is more determined than ever to leave this shit behind and get my fine ass in one of those top-level executive suites.

With a little smile I clutch my briefcase tighter and turn on my Via Spaga heels to stroll to the elevator. Most of the staff in the finance department are already gone for the day. Unlike the other departments there isn't much burning the candle at both ends kind of nights. I wouldn't be surprised at all if Cameron is still working hard for the money upstairs in his office.

My heart double pumps at the thought of him. Yes, I ain't no better than my mommy because I am still so in love with a man who don't love me.

The elevator doors open and I step forward. I pause as my eyes travel from polished Gucci loafers up to the face of that very same man.

"Cameron," I say softly.

"Hi, Monica."

I can see in his eyes that he is just as surprised to run into me. I give him a fake ass smile and step onto the elevator. I turn and our arms are almost touching. It's hot. I step to the left away from him.

The doors close and the tension between us feels like it is closing in. *Lord, why does it have to be ten stories before we can get off this motherfucker?*

I keep my eyes straight ahead and try to keep my face neutral even though my stomach is filled with all the emotions this man stirs inside of me. All the anger, the love, the lust, the pain, the regret . . . the hope.

I glance over at him just in time to see him quickly look away from me. I just bite back a smile—

A loud, grinding noise causes my heart to leap in my chest just before the elevator comes to a sudden stop. I fall my ass right off my heels and face forward into the steel doors.

"Whoa," Cameron calls out.

I feel his hands—those hands—grab my waist to steady me. As soon as I get my bearings I shift away from his touch and press my back to the wall of the elevator. "What the hell is going on?" I ask as I look over at him.

"I think we're stuck," he says dryly before he pushes several buttons and then opens a small door on the elevator panel.

"No shit, Sherlock." I straight mean-mug his ass as he picks up the phone behind that door in the panel and puts it to his ear.

"It's dead. I hope there wasn't a power outage—"

"Or some crazy 9/11 type of shit," I tell him as my heart beats like a motherfucker in fear.

He looks over at me with a troubled expression before he loosens his silk tie and undoes the top button. "I'm sure it's nothing that serious," he says, sounding like he doesn't much believe that shit himself.

We both reach in our briefcases. I pull out my cell phone. He pulls out his BlackBerry.

We both smile a little at the coincidence before looking away.

"I forgot I don't have a signal in the elevators." I snap *that* useless motherfucker closed and drop it back into my briefcase.

I'm not claustrophobic or nothing but being stuck in an elevator is mad crazy and I want this foolishness to end.

"Damn."

I look over just as Cameron drops his BlackBerry back into his briefcase. "No signal either," he tells me as he removes his jacket and steps over near me to bend and spread it on the floor of the elevator. "Go ahead and sit. We might as well get comfortable."

He holds out his hand to me and it might as well been a damn snake the way I look at it. *What will it feel like to him*, I wonder, just before I slip my hand onto his.

Pure electricity. Heat. Desire. Yearning.

Just like I thought.

Our eyes meet.

I feel like everything on me—including the fine hair on my

body—is sweating. And I know he feels it too. I can tell it from the look in his eyes.

I hurry to use his hand for support so that I can break the hold he has on me. As I settle on the hard ass floor, I watch as he lowers his body to the floor too and presses his back to the wall opposite me.

"So . . . how's married life treating you?" I ask him with the fakest damn smile ever.

"Don't," he said shortly, bending his legs to sit his elbows on his knees.

"What? Is it all too sacred to discuss?" I straighten my legs in front of me and pull my skirt down over my legs.

He says nothing and just reaches for his briefcase to take out a file and one of his Mont Blanc pens.

That he obviously is ignoring me bothers me. "I guess I should thank you for the transfer because I'm liking the finance department a lot."

He jots down something in the file before he cuts his eyes up to look over at me. "Better than mergers and acquisitions?"

"Yes."

He smiles and shakes his head. "Liar."

I arch an eyebrow. "What the hell is that supposed to mean?"

Cameron lifts his head and I'm looking at his handsome face. His deep set eyes and square jaw. His lips. His chin. His high cheekbones. Damn, this motherfucker is fine. "Mergers and acquisitions is about the hunt and the kill. The chase. Aggression. Finance is just a means to all of that. You, Monica Winters, are all about the chase. You go after what you want and you don't sit back and wait for it to come to you."

"True," I admit. "But I also hate to lose and no one can guarantee that everything you want will be yours."

Cameron's eyes shift away from mine.

Damn right, I'm not talking about business anymore.

"When all that bullshit went down with Dom and Rah you would drive straight from New York every night and just chill with me in my room. Bring me food. Rent me movies. Just talk to me." Emotions rose in me. "You did anything you could do to help me forget that my ass was stuck in a bed with my leg shattered in two or that one of my best friends betrayed me. I don't think I ever said thank you for that . . . for being a *really* good friend."

"I liked hanging out with you. Being around you made me feel like I was a teenager again without a care in the world." He smiles kinda bashfully. "No worries about business expectations or bills or none of that stuff. I just was a guy enjoying hanging out with a girl."

I reach over with my foot to tap it against his. "Yeah, hanging out with you was fun. It was different. No clubs. No weed. No Henny. No label dropping. No flodging. No drama. Just the realness. Just a girl hanging out with a boy and having fun."

We get real quiet . . . but in a good way. That reminiscing on good times kinda way.

"It's been a year but I feel like a different person. Things I thought were so important seem silly."

Cameron nods. "It's called growing up."

I bit my bottom lip as I kick off my shoes to free my toes. "Feels like I still have a lot of growing up to do."

"You're in your early twenties. Trust me just reaching twenty-five will be a big deal and your thirties will make you feel like you know everything. You'll see everything different."

As I wiggle my toes, I look at him with soft eyes. "Like maybe if I was older and more mature I woulda realized just how much I loved you before it was too late."

Cameron's eyes are *so* intense as he looks at me like he can see my soul. It makes me breathless as hell. My heart skips so crazily. My entire body shivers from that look.

"I never knew you loved me. I didn't want to own up that I loved you, Cameron," I admit to him softly as nothing but that undeniable chemistry stirs between us.

When he still doesn't say a word, I throw my hands up. "Listen after what happened at the church I promised I wouldn't do this with you again. I'm so sick of putting my heart out to you and then you just—"

Suddenly his lips are on mine. And his arms are wrapped around me. And his body is pressing mine to the floor. I moan from deep in my soul at the feel of his tongue stroking mine as his dick hardens against my belly and his hips grind into mine. I just feel the sweetest damn pleasure at having the man I love in my arms. Tears fill my eyes and my heart is open wide. "I love you, Cameron. I love you so much," I whisper against his mouth as he leans his head up to look down at me.

He nods slowly before he touches his lips down on my chin and admits, "I love you, too. I do. My marriage is a mess because I love you. And deep down I think she knows it, too."

Cameron gives me one more kiss that feels like it's the last one ever before he rolls off my body and climbs to his feet. He lets out this deep ass breath before he slams his fist against the wall of the elevator. "I fucked up, Monica. I fucked up."

It hurts like a motherfucker to hear that torture, that regret, in his voice.

"I care for my wife. I do. But you can only love one person at a time and I try to deny it but deep down I knew you were the one I love. I shouldn't have married her. I shouldn't hurt her . . . or you." He turns and looks down at me. "I fucked up. I thought I was over you. I really thought I could make this marriage with Serena work. *This* drama. *This* bullshit. *This* triangle shit ain't me. I fucked up."

I get up on my feet and walk over to press my hands to his face. "Cameron, what are you going to do about it?" I ask him softly. I'm happy that he still loves me but I'm sad because he seems to regret it.

The elevator jolts and the lights on the panel flicker as it begins to move downward. We move apart to gather our things and straighten our clothes.

"What are you going to do, Cameron?" I ask him again just before the elevator eases to a stop and the doors open.

"Cameron!"

We both look up at his wife, Serena, standing in the front of a crowd of people in the lobby. She makes a slight face at seeing me in the elevator with Cameron before she throws on a smile and steps forward to wrap her arms around his neck and kiss him in a way that is nothing but some bullshit ass show for me.

Cameron pulls back from the kiss with a small shift of his eyes towards me. We all step off the elevator as the maintenance man steps on.

"I came to surprise you with dinner in your office," she says.

"I was on my way home," he tells her.

"Then let's go home," she tells him.

I stop by the massive security desk and watch them leave arm in arm. Just before they walk out the automatic doors, Cameron turns and gives me one last look.

"Are you okay, ma'am?" the elderly security guard asks me.

I watch through the glass as Serena and Cameron walk away together. They look so happily-ever-after together. "No. No, I'm not okay," I answer him with the God's honest truth.

Chapter Thirty-Five

Dom

May 15

So much to fuckin' write, not enough pages to write it on. Kimani: I still haven't told her about her new granddaddy or her auntie Hiasha. I still had to deal with that shit myself. Maybe once I got used to knowin' that the last twenty-two years of my life has been a big-ass lie then I can accept his offer to come into my life. I just thank God he givin' me time to get my mind right. I ain't ready for more sisters and brothers, cousins, and aunts and shit. Not now. Corey says I should feel blessed to have this huge family that is waitin' just to meet me. He says I should know that I'm special. And that's what I love about him—and yes I love him even though I ain't admitted that to his jokey, big dick self. Our sex is mad crazy and wild and all that good shit but so is our conversation. He makes me think about things I ain't ever paid attention to and he asks me questions and listens to me. Bein' around that nigga makes me feel grown up and shit. And I like it. When I have to work hard at my two damn jobs he makes sure the time we gots together is always special. And although I don't ask for no money if I come up short, his ass is right there to help me out. I love him because he loves me just for me. No questions. No bullshits. No drama. No changes. I never thought my ass would fall in love again after Lex died but just livin' life has a way of changin' what you do and think and say. So yes, I love that motherfucker but no one knows that but me, myself, and this diary which damn sure ain't telling shit. Ha-ha.

The doc says he wants me to invite Diane's crazy ass in for a session. Although I know that crazy bitch need therapy like a motherfucker I just don't know if I ever want her in my life again. Look at the way she treated me and the way she act like pinpointin' the wrong mother-fucker to be my daddy ain't no big shit. For me to keep my ass off the next dope corner I got to stay clear of Diane and her bullshit. Fuck that. Stayin' clean so that I can raise my daughter is more important than that bullshit 'bout rebuildin' broken relationships. Just thinkin' 'bout that shit makes me mad as hell. It makes me want to fight my own mother. Man, fuck Diane!!!!!!!!

Girl Talk

Alizé, Moët, and Dom all cornered Mohammed as soon as he walked out of the storeroom in the basement. He jumped back a bit to find them all standing there waiting for him with their arms crossed over their chests.

"Hello ladies," he told them in that infectious Jamaican lilt as he shifted to the right to move past them.

The ladies all shifted to the right with him.

He rolled his clear white eyes to the ceiling as he leant against the push broom he held in his hands. "If this is about your friend again then don't bother. I done made up my mind. To hell with R. Kelly 'cause a woman ain't the only one who gets fed up."

"Mohammed, I thought your Bob Marley–lookin' ass said you believe it now that Cristal and Sahad ain't fuckin' around," Dom snapped with just a little bit of annoyance.

Mohammed cut his eyes at her. "Look here, your girl want more than I got to offer her. Hell, why you three blind mice care so much when she left your asses hangin' in the damn wind too?"

"Because we love her."

"Yeah, well I hate to sound cliché but my love shoulda kept her ass home more." He eyed each lady directly before he walked off with his dreads swinging slightly against his back.

"I should have told him that you *always* have to fight for the ones you love," Moët said.

"Or that love means being able to forgive even if you don't forget," Alizé added.

Dom reached over and squeezed Alizé's elbow. "True."

Moët thought of her love for her child and her whole soul felt warm.

Alizé's heart swelled with love and then ached with regret for Cameron.

Dom smiled a little as she thought of her Corey. "Well, I learned lately that love is a *damn* good thing."

Part Four

"It Ain't Over 'Til It's Over"

Chapter Thirty-Six

Moët

This is the biggest mistake I ever made. Okay, not *the* biggest, but it is up on the Top 10 list.

As if he can sense my frustration, Taquan reaches over to grab my hand under the dining room table. I look over and give him a wink and a smile.

"I just don't understand, Latoya, if you've read those things in those papers about that that . . . *rapper.* How can you trust your child with him?"

My grip tightens around Taquan's hand and he winces a little. "Daddy, I don't believe those things in the paper. I never thought Bones would hurt Tiffany."

My mother spoons mashed red potatoes onto her plate before passing it to my youngest sister Latrece. "How can you be sure?"

"His mother lives with him and helps out with the baby."

As soon as my mother eyes me I know I have stuck my foot in my mouth. My moms has been begging me to let Tiffany stay overnight. My answer has always been no.

When I admitted to my parents that I lied about the rape and that I was sexually involved with our minister since I was sixteen, I didn't know what to expect. Their anger and immediate condemnation of me hurt like crazy. They put their love of religion above me and it hurt like hell. It wasn't until that devil Reverend DeMark was arrested for sleeping with a sixteen-year-old from their church that they even spoke to me.

And they have yet to say they were sorry.

Even though I go through the motions, a part of me hasn't gotten over that. A girl never forgets her father damn near calling her a whore to her face.

I began to shake my leg as my anger rises again.

I know my parents wouldn't hurt her physically but my childhood was rough. Restrictive. Reclusive. It was all about church until I felt like it strangled me. So I rebelled . . . in my own way. I lived a double life to find the freedom I needed so that their faith wasn't such a noose around my neck. I rebelled right into situations I had no business being in.

I just don't want them to make Tiffany feel the way I did growing up.

"Taquan, I'd like a little chat with you if we're all done with dinner," my father says before he drops his napkin onto his plate and rises from his chair.

It's Taquan's turn to squeeze my hand.

He's the first man I ever brought home to meet my parents. My folks never met the father of their only grandchild. He was another of my secrets from last year.

I didn't want the same for Taquan. I'm proud that he's my man. He's good to me and he loves Tiffany just as if she's his own.

I wonder if he loves me too.

My brows draw together a bit. Do I love Taquan?

I watch him as he follows my father into the living room. He turns to smile at me over his strong and broad shoulders. My heart skips several beats.

He helps keep me locked to my faith. He is so easy to talk with about anything . . . everything. He makes me better, stronger, calmer. We have such amazing chemistry and even more amazing "sex" (well, our non-penetrating version of sex). I miss him when he's not near me and I am happier than Reverend DeMark peeping through a hole in the wall of a girls' locker room when we're together.

My daughter's soft cries from her portable bassinet in the living room causes me to head that way as my mother and sisters began to clear the table.

"She's always a little cranky when she wakes up," I hear Taquan say. I pause before I reach the living room and watch as both he and my father bend over the bassinet. "Latoya always just rubs her back a little and she goes back to sleep."

My mouth drops open a little as my father reaches down to rub his grandchild's small back. "It's funny, but Latoya was the same way as a baby except we would pat her back and she would go right back to sleep," my father says. "I used to just lay with her across my chest and just pat that back for her. Her mama said I was spoiling her."

The men share a soft laugh together while I am surprised. I can't imagine my father giving out any affection far less spoiling me.

"She was a beautiful baby girl and while I was doing all that spoiling I thought of just the speech I would give any little boy, or teenager, or man that came by to visit."

I watch as my father and my man look at each other with their bodies still bent over my daughter's bassinet.

"Neither I nor her mother nor God created her to be any man's plaything. She was created to be the best she can be and not the best you want her to be. She was created to grow and spread her wings and not her legs. She is special to me and she is rare because she is my child. Respect that. Respect her. And respect me when I tell you that you don't want me to lose my religion."

Taquan nods and clears his throat. "Good speech."

My dad nods his head as he looks at Taquan with clear intent. "I think so."

For the first time in a long damn time I feel like my father loves me.

Chapter Thirty-Seven

Cristal

The Hamptons!
I am standing on the balcony of my bedroom in the Ingrams' house looking down at the Who's Who at their all-white pool party. My eyes sweep the crowd and fall on Marc Ellison standing there looking fine as all get out in a white linen pants suit. The wind blows slightly and the thin linen attaches to his thighs and his dick. My eyes shift up to his face and he is looking at me. He raises his glass of champagne to me and I smile at him.

The gifts have not stopped—in fact I am wearing the white Gucci bathing suit he sent to me just yesterday. My man threw me out his house and stopped answering my phone calls. Oh, this just might be Marc's lucky damn day.

Yes, Mohammed hurt me. It still hurts. He never came back to his house that day or that night or the next day. I sat there and I waited for him to come back. I called his cell phone endlessly. I left the kind of crying "please don't go" voice mail that he could play to a crowd for laughs. He never came back.

I finally picked up my face and my things and went home but I drove back to his house late that same night. To see his beat down jeep finally parked there hurt. I wondered if he came home, saw my car still there and then just kept on moving. It took all the fight I had in me to drive back home.

It is over. Mohammed wanted it over and it is over.

I clear my throat and squint my eyes against the sun. It is a sorry attempt to push away my pain.

I will focus on living my life. I have to.

Hours later, Marc finally traps me in a corner of the cabana. I take a deep sip of my champagne as I am overwhelmed by his warm and delicious scent and his presence. He leans in closely to my neck. "God, you smell good," his words whisper against my throat. "And you wear Gucci so damn well."

I shiver a little as I turn my head slightly to take another sip of my champagne. "Yes, I do," I tell him smugly.

"But I bet you look even better out of it." He presses one kiss and then another to my neck as he brings his hands up to that deep curve of my waist. He does not cause the kind of sparks and electricity I receive from just being near Mohammed, but this warm fuzziness is nice. Shit, in the past I have slept with a lot worse.

My champagne glass slips from my hand as I bring it up to stroke the side of his face. I turn his head and press my lips to his just as the glass shatters against the cement floor of the cabana.

One of my eyes pops open as he damn near sticks his whole tongue down my throat. I ease my head back and take the lead to show this sexy millionaire just how to kiss a woman.

As he eases some of that tongue back inside his own damn head I let him press me down onto one of the plush lounge chairs. I try not to think of Mohammed and wish he was Mohammed as he kisses an overly moist trail down my neck. Lord, more and more I am feeling myself fall into bad sex. Damn. Damn. Damn.

He eases the straps of my bathing suit down exposing my breasts. I close my eyes and arch my back as I massage his broad shoulders through the thin linen of his shirt.

He rubs his fingers across my nipples and they tingle from his touch. Damn, they tingle so much they feel numb. He starts sucking and licking my nipples. I open my eyes just in time to see him use one hand to pour some white powder across my chest. "What is that?" I screech.

My question is useless as he lowers his head and snorts the powder from my body. *Is that why my damn nipples feel like that?*

"Man, get your cokehead ass off me," I yell as I push against his shoulders.

"Huh? What?" he asks as he looks down at me.

Why am I just noticing how glassy his eyes are?

"I do not do coke," I tell him as he finally rolls off me. I frown as he sits up on the edge of the lounge chair and pours more coke on the back of his hand to snort.

I grab a throw pillow from the lounge and wipe the coke powder from my chest before I ease the straps of my bathing suit back up onto my shoulders. My damn nipples are *still* numb as hell.

Marc laughs as he looks up at me. "You keep your nose up Carolyn's ass and you don't do coke? Man, what the fuck ever."

Huh? What is that? Say what? Say who?

"Carolyn gets high?" I ask him as he wipes his nose with a handkerchief he pulled from his pocket.

He looks up at me and shakes his head at me like *I* am pitiful.

In the words of Dom: "What the fuck ever."

I whip open the curtains of the cabana and step out into the pool party that is still in full effect. A servant carrying a tray of drinks grabs my arms.

"Mrs. Ingram wants to see you."

"Good, because I want to see her too. Where is she?"

"In her bedroom suite," she answers.

I breeze past her to walk into the house. I damn near run up the stairs and barge right into her suite. I stop in my tracks as my mouth drops open. What the fuck?

I close my eyes and try to erase the image of Carolyn butt naked and bent over touching her toes as some big-dick, tall, buff brother is stroking her from behind. What the fuck? Does she get off by me being in the room while some random man is sexing her?

"Oh, my, Danielle," she purrs as she reaches back with a thin and wrinkled hand to his chest (you can have all the plastic surgery you want but them hands and neck NEVER lie). He backs right out of her. My eyes get wider because I am thinking I will never see the tip of his dick. Well goddamn.

As he struts by me naked with his dick swinging above his balls like a muscled arm, I try my best to keep my eyes above his waist. *Shee-it.* Tried . . . and failed. His dick is making a damn shadow on the floor! I gasp when he makes it do damn pushups in mid-air. Up and down. Up and down. My eyes jump up to his and he has the nerve to wink at me before he grabs a towel and wraps it around his waist. I turn to watch him leave the room. Okay, I have seen some dicks in my day but that has to be *the* biggest—

I swerve around at the feel of a finger stroking my nipple.

"Carolyn, what are you doing?" I ask as I push her hand away.

"I'm getting what I paid for," she says in this voice that is slurred as she reaches again and snatches down the top of my bathing suit causing one of my breasts to pop free.

I feel disgust when she openly stares and then licks her collagen-filled lips. "What are you talking about?" I ask her as I step back and push my breast back inside my bathing suit from her view.

"Stop playing games, Danielle. I've waited long enough for that pussy." She advances on me and quicker than I can blink this bitch has her hand between my legs palming my pussy.

I grab her wrist. "Carolyn, I am not gay."

She flings her head back and laughs as she raises her hand and licks her tongue between the vee she makes with her fingers. "Neither was Kelle until I financed her dreams and licked that fat clit. That bitch used to beg me to eat her out."

Kelle? I frown as she turns and walks away from me. Kelle? My mind flashes back to the woman from the restaurant screaming at Carolyn. *So you don't know me now, you old bitch?*

"So you and Kelle were . . . were lovers?" I ask as she moves over to sit on the edge of her champagne silk covered bed and spread her legs wide to finger her pussy.

"Up until the day I saw you at the office. I knew as soon as I laid eyes on you that I wanted you and I always get what I want." Carolyn rises from her bed, strutting her naked ass over to her closet. "And I get what I want because I give people what they want. Like fancy clothes, my friendship and the friendship of my wealthy and famous friends, their own business."

That makes me pause. This bitch that I been hanging around is a wealthy lesbo cougar. Oh no, hell no. "So sometimes you feel like dicks and nuts, sometimes you don't?" I snap sarcastically.

She laughs as she walks back out of her closet holding a wad of bills. I watch as she carelessly flings the money up into the air above the bed just before she climbs onto the middle of it. The money rains down on her body. "You feel like eating my pussy now, don't you?"

"Carolyn, I'm sorry but you got the motherfuckin' game twisted." Oh, that hood shit always come through my ass when I'm pissed.

She climbs off the bed and walks over to me. Her hands grope my breasts as she pushes me back against the wall and tries to press her lips to my mouth. "I can make you feel so good," she whispers.

When I feel Carolyn's hands shifting my bathing suit to the side, I am repulsed. And when she attempts to slip her fingers inside of me I am fed the fuck up.

I push her off me to get just enough space to slap the hell out of that bitch and send her spinning across the room. I turn to walk out the room and pause at some random white bitch sucking off Big Dick Willie while Marc sits by snorting coke and jacking his own dick.

Marc looks up at me with glassy eyes.

I look at them all in disgust.

I walk out of that room and down that hall to my room. Quick as I can I throw as much of my shit as I can into my overnight case and pull a sweat suit over my bathing suit.

There is a knock on my door. "Danielle, I'm so sorry. Let me in, sweetheart."

Crazy ass Carolyn. *Wait on it bitch.*

I walk onto my balcony and the party is still in full effect. *Well, party on.* As I walk down the outdoor wrought iron stairs leading to the lower level of the mansion, I flip my cell phone open. It's time for me to get a one-way ride out of this jacked-up-ass world.

Chapter Thirty-Eight

Alizé

The last place I want to be is Braun, Weber. My ass is tired from having to jet out to the Hamptons and pick Cristal's wannabe bougie ass up from some corner. Seem like she caught another glimpse of the lifestyles of the rich and famous that sent her scurrying her ass back to the real world with a quickness. Drugs, ménages à trois, and an aging lesbian was more than she could handle. Thank God. For real I thought that girl was tripping so hard on being something that she ain't that she might just give Carolyn a good pussy licking. For real.

So, after listening to *that* crazy shit all night, I go home early this morning to get clothes only to find that my mama's tenderoni spent the night. I'm headed in the bathroom for a shower and they were headed out after doing only God knows what in there. Of course, I had to scrub the tub with bleach before I could take a shower. I'm saying.

And now I might have to run into Cameron after he admits that he loves me Friday but then goes home with his wife.

I drop my pen and rub my hands through my hair as I lean back in my chair in my little cubicle. My cell phone vibrates and I lean forward to pick it up from my desk. I roll my eyes at Dr. Locke's number.

Okay. I went running to Dr. Locke Friday night . . . and Saturday afternoon for a fuckfest to get my mind off my drama. By Saturday night I realized that riding and sucking and jacking and draining a big hard dick didn't stop my heart from hurting. Plus, that fool asked me to pour hot candle wax on his nipples while I ride him. What the fuck?

I send the call to my voice mail and drop the phone back onto my desk. Dr. Locke is a freak and he needs to get his ass on somebody's couch and find out why he get a kick out of being slapped and all kind of shit during sex. His ass is one therapist who needs therapy. For real.

I have that weird feeling that someone is watching me and I swivel around in my chair and my eyes fall on the elevator. Cameron is standing in the rear of the elevator with his eyes locked on me as people get off. I openly stare back at him just as the doors begin to close.

I jump up from my desk so suddenly that my chair rolls back and hits my desk. I get over to the elevator as quick as my Manolos can get me to it. I push the button like it stole something from me and the doors slowly go in reverse and open. Cameron looks up at me in nothing but surprise as I step on and stand in front of him on the empty elevator with my hands on my hips.

"Not now, Monica," Cameron says, reaching past me to hit the button to open the doors.

I twist just enough to put my hand on his even as I look him in the eye. "Now," I insist.

The doors close behind us.

"Serena is filing for divorce."

I'm shocked and it shows.

He drops his head and wipes his eyes with his fingers. "She grilled me about you and me being in the elevator and what exactly is going on between us. It was ugly and I really don't want to talk about it right now, Monica."

"You told her you loved me?" I ask him in this soft and husky voice that doesn't even sound like me.

He shifted his eyes away from mine and then shifted them back. "Yes."

I hit the button to stop the elevator and step forward to press my hands against his face and my body against the length of his.

"What are you doing, Monica?" he asks in this voice that sounds tired and a little aggravated.

"Finishing what we started in this same elevator Friday."

"No. I'm still married and if this gets out I can lose my job and you will get the reputation for being willing to sleep your way to the—"

I press my lips against his as my heart pounds and the butterflies in my stomach flutter away. "I love you, Cameron," I whisper to him in between soft kisses to his delicious mouth. I feel his heart beating just as crazy as mine and I know that he can't resist me. Us. This.

His hands grab my waist and I feel his briefcase against my ass as he jerks me closer while his tongue slowly enters my mouth to touch down on my own. We both moan deeply and release a shaky breath as our mouths part slightly. I look up into his eyes and he looks down into mine as we just stand there breathing in each other's essence. I have never felt such a connection with a man before. Oh, Cameron has me. He has me to do with as he pleases.

"I never wanted to hurt anyone but I love you. I love you so much," he whispers against my mouth.

I feel such a rush of energy and emotions and edification.

This thing between Cameron and me is bigger than both of us.

In heated seconds our hands are unbuttoning, unzipping, pulling, and tugging until my black lace thongs are on the floor and my skirt is up above my waist. His boxers and trousers are down around his ankles.

We kiss each other deeply as he turns me and presses my back against the wall. I spread my knees wide as he guides my pussy down onto every thick and delicious inch of his dick. I break the kiss and gasp for air and control as I feel complete with him buried deep inside of me.

"Damn," he swears as he presses his mouth to my neck.

We shiver together and hold each other tight as hell as he finally begins to shift his hips, pushing his dick in and out of me like we were the only people on our own damn planet. It feels like we are floating in air. Raw energy courses over our bodies and our souls shiver from the passion, the fire, the love that we share.

I arch my back and clutch him so tightly as my body spasms with each release of my cum. "Yes, Cameron. Oh God, yes," I cry out as tears fill my eyes. He is making love to my body and my soul. He touches spots inside of me that no man has ever stroked—intimate parts of me that is beyond sex. He fulfills me. He completes me.

Sweet Jesus.

The tears course down my cheeks freely and as I feel his body stiffen and then shiver as his dick literally swells with each shot of delicious cum against my walls. And with each spasm against my ridged walls I cry out with no shame in my game. Our hearts both pound wild as hell.

I bring my hands up to caress his cheeks as he kisses my lips. Our eyes lock and I feel as if our souls have kissed too.

This connection between us is real. For the first time ever I know what making love is really all about.

Chapter Thirty-Nine

Dom

Me and Kimani are sittin' in the living room watching videos as I write in my journal when Alizé strolls her ass up in the apartment lookin' like she 'bout ready to do the fuckin' runnin' man or some shit.

Kimani looks over her shoulder from her spot on the floor. "Hi, Auntie Ze," she calls out before turnin' back to the television.

"Hi, KiKi." Alizé drops down onto the sofa already out of her intern clothes and dressed in an off-the-shoulder pink and gold Baby Phat shirt and a jean skirt. I used to think she wasn't no better than Moët with her split personality bullshit. She could be Monica the preppy student or Alizé the ghetto-fab chick whenever she got ready. Now I realize the suits, briefcase, and shit is just her image to get ahead. The real Ze is sittin' right in front of me poppin' gum and swingin' her crossed leg.

My eyes dart down to the long and pale scar on her thigh. I still feel like that pain Rah inflicted on her was all my fault. Sometimes I hate the person I used to be.

"Where's everybody?" she asks as she sends off a round of gum poppin' that sounds like fireworks on the fuckin' Fourth of July.

"Cristal is somewhere in the building lookin' for Mohammed and Mo said she's gonna be late gettin' off work."

I don't miss the look of regret all up on her face. I don't think it's ever been just me and her since that day at the courthouse. I know she has some good news she wants to share but I'm not feelin' her hurtin' my damn feelings 'cause she don't trust my ass no more.

"My dad—, my father—, Willie and I are talkin' a lot lately. He wants me to meet the rest of his family," I tell her, my attempt to bridge this fucked up gap between us.

Alizé kicks off her gold sandals and looks over at me before she nods in understandin'. "I hope everything is good for you, Dom. You deserve some good times in your life."

That makes my ass smile on the inside. "So do you."

She tilts her head to the side like a goddamn owl and her eyes squint at me before she licks her lips and says, "Cameron was sent to Japan at the last minute and he wants us to hold off until he gets back. He loves me and all that jazz but I am so afraid that him and his wife will get back together or he won't let us be together if I take the summer internship there. He says he'll call but I have no idea where all of this is going. So I guess we're together . . . but we're not."

There is no denyin' that this bitch is in love. "If I can give you advice . . . you really should cut off Dr. Love."

She looks surprised.

"I overheard you telling Moët about him."

Alizé picks up her purse and looks down in it. I can tell her ass is tryin' to figure whether to be mad or not that I know her business even though she didn't want me to.

"After lookin' at how Cristal completely fucked up a good thing with Mr. Lover Lover, I just don't want another one of us to fuck up."

Alizé pulls out her MAC lip-gloss as she looks over at me. "Well, *bitch*, since you all up in the mix any damn way. I already decided that Doc's supply of goodies have been shut down. After what me and Cameron shared today in that elevator another man is going to find it very hard to top it. Trust," she says dreamily before she coats her lips with clear gloss.

"The elevator! You nasty bitch you," I tell her.

"And you know that." She winks at me and does this fake shiver that make my ass laugh.

And it feels so damn good to laugh, gossip, and just shoot the shit with my friend again.

I moan in pleasure as Corey presses a kiss to my lower back and then each of my butt cheeks. I wiggle it playfully for him and then giggle like a damn little girl when he bites down onto one ass cheek.

"I have a surprise for your sexy chocolate ass."

I lean up and look down over my shoulder at him. "I don't do rim shots."

He laughs and slaps my ass before he rolls out of bed. I turn over and the sheet drops while I watch that little sexy motherfucker strut over to the closet. He pulls out this big gift-wrapped box. "My birthday ain't for months," I tell him as he walks over to the bed.

He don't say shit and just sits the box in front of me before he drops back down onto the bed.

I open the box like my ass is five and it's Christmas. I'm shocked as hell to see a laptop computer. I look up at him and this little motherfucker is smilin' and showin' all his teeth and shit. "Damn, you got me a computer?"

"It's from a pawn shop but it works real good and when you write that first book you better dedicate it to me."

Okay, so this the shit. I always fucked with dudes that had mad cash flow. Dope dealers. Hood boys. Duffel bag boys. I have been taken on trips to the Caribbean, taken on shopping sprees most bitches would die for, I have enough ghetto gold jewelry to start my own store, and I've gotten wads of cash big enough to choke a fuckin' pit bull. I have been spoiled by these niggas.

As I rub my hands across the computer and open the lid I know that this is the best gift any motherfucker has ever given me.

See why I love this nigga for real?

Corey lays down on the bed and pulls my head over to rest on his chest. We don't fuck or nothing. We just lay there and hold each other and it's the best time we ever had in bed.

For real.

Chapter Forty

Moët

I have a million things I could be doing. There are files on my desk to be completed. Cases to be investigated. Calling my attorney back. Checking on Cristal and making sure she doesn't have a mental meltdown. Calling my parents to check on Tiffany.

All of it has to wait. I couldn't move from beside this child's bedside even if it meant saving my own life.

Parents are supposed to do whatever, whenever for their child. We are the first line of defense against them being hurt, exploited, used, or abused. We are their protectors.

But what is a child supposed to do when it's their own parents doing the using and abusing?

Tears raced down my face as I look at the eight-year-old boy whose life has forever been changed because his mother is a no-good bitch who would pour hot grease down on him. He has third degree burns on sixty percent of his small frame. They don't know if he will make it through the night.

I know I am here in a profession but right now this is so personal for me. I am a social worker. I am a protector. I am a mother.

Any guilt I feel over fighting for my daughter always leaves me when I come face to face with situations like this. As a mother and a protector, I have done and will do anything for my child. God and everyone will just have to forgive me.

And I do feel guilty. I wanted to take the high road but Bones knocked the game into the gutter and to win I had to get down in the gutter with him.

I don't know how long I sat there or how many different prayers I sent up to the heavens. For this motherless child. For my child. For Bones. For myself.

Hours later, as I left the hospital, I finally checked my voice mail messages. The one from my attorney makes me hop in my car and speed home.

It's over. I thank the Lord for that.

I feel my entire body slump with relief as my attorney tells me via speakerphone that Bones has agreed to joint custody. Tears fill my eyes as everyone in the living room begins to clap.

Someone presses Tiffany into my arms and I hold her so tight and bury my face into her warm neck. "Thank you, Jesus," I whisper against her cheeks as I cry with no shame.

"Don't cry, Mo," one of the girls tells me as they hug Tiffany and me close. It's Alizé. I can tell from her perfume.

They're all here. Everyone that means something to me beat a fast trail to the apartment once I gave them the heads up that my attorney was meeting with Bone's attorney today. My parents. My sisters. Alizé. Dom. Cristal. Taquan. Even my godchild Kimani is waiting around with us for the news. And my baby girl, Tiffany.

Taquan bends down beside me. I feel his arm around my shoulders and his lips on my cheek. "We thank you Heavenly Father," he says aloud.

"I would thank Him even more if she didn't have to share custody at all with a crackhead," my father throws in for good measure. Like I haven't heard that enough.

I just hold my child because right now that's all that matters to me.

"That *is* something to think about, Mo," Alizé adds. "I heard on the news that he might get dropped from Platinum Records."

"Oh, the streets is talkin' 'bout him. Y'all really think he a gay sex freak who smoke crack?"

Everyone laughs at Dom's words but I shake my head to clear it of their conversation. Their gossip. Even my parents are putting in their two cents. I don't want to think about those tabloid papers or the rumors in them. Or what those rumors are doing to Bones. I just want to enjoy the end of this custody battle. That's all I can focus on right now or else I might not be able to stand myself.

Girl Talk

The four friends were all in Cristal's bedroom in the apartment. They said nothing to each other. Cristal sighed as she shifted her body deeper under her covers on the bed.

Alizé nervously sucked her lollipop as she flipped through the latest *Essence* magazine while she sat cross-legged on the end of the bed.

Dom bit her bottom lip in determination as she sat typing away on her laptop computer in between blowing cigarette smoke out the open window.

Moët's eyes were troubled before she closed them and put her hands to her chin in prayer.

No words were spoken but everyone knew that each had their own battles to win. Each was deep in their own thoughts and their own worlds. Still, it was important for them to just be together.

Chapter Forty-One

Cristal

When I was a little girl there were two things I used to want so badly: love and money. They were the two things I lacked for the most. They are the two things that run my life. Last year I gave up the money for love and now I have lost love blindly chasing money.

Am I so fucked up that my adult life is going to stay this crazy ass teeter-totter between one or the other?

I can see from the look in my friends' eyes that they pity me. I do not blame them. They always wished they had a good brotha like Mohammed. Trust me, I have not missed that jacked-up irony that now they all are in love with good guys and I am alone.

It hurts more than ever that I threw him away. It hurts like hell.

I wish I could press rewind on all this high society bullshit with Carolyn. I get embarrassed every time I think of what everyone thought of me hanging out with her. That I was her paramour. Her concubine. Her bitch.

I feel so damn stupid.

"Carolyn, you look beautiful . . . as *always*."

My heart stops. I look up at Moët's attorney, Helen, standing at the reception desk as she looks through her messages. I shift my eyes over and have to bite my bottom lip to keep from cussing Carolyn as she walks over to us. The dyking bitch looks as fabulous as ever in a linen sundress that I know is Gucci. I shift my eyes again to the young curvaceous woman at her side. I have to do a double take to make sure my eyes are not lying to me.

Is that that woman Kelle? Kelle. Kelle!

I almost thrown my damn pen in exasperation. After that big a scene she made of herself at the restaurant, this silly bitch is right back digging her lips in Carolyn's ass?

These lesbian bitches are crazy.

I am not worried about losing my job. Carolyn is a smart woman and as soon as she throws salt in my work game I will go straight to Mr. Ingram and spill on every freaky-deaky little detail I know on her scandalous ass. She lucky I did not call the police on her sexually-assaulting ass. Can you imagine the scandal? Not Carolyn. I just was not having it.

Neither one of them speaks to me, but I do not miss the way Carolyn's hand lingers on Kelle's lower back as she guides her through the door to the inner offices behind Helen.

Well, better Kelle's pussy than mine.

I pick up the phone and call Alizé at her internship. "Let's all meet for dinner," I say as soon as she picks up.

"Girl you must be psychic. I was just about to call your ass anyway."

I frown in concern. "What's wrong?"

"I have to pick between Cameron and the internship at Braun, Weber."

My frown deepens. "Ooh."

"Ooh is right."

"But I thought the internship is over in a couple of weeks anyway," I tell her as I pick up a pen and scribble Mohammed's name.

"Yes, but I was invited back for the summer and this internship is important for my career. Shit."

"And Cameron?"

"He's still in Japan."

I do an eye roll. "I meant how do you feel about him," I stress patiently.

"He's important for me," she says without hesitation. "But I have doubts about his marriage really being over. I would hate to hurt my career for that."

"Then I guess you have a choice to make, my friend." I take a lot of pleasure in drawing a huge dagger through Mohammed's name.

"See, it's time like these that I miss dancing."

"You could go back to teaching," I offer as I take the sheet I scribbled on and tore it into a million pieces.

Alizé sighs into the phone. "I don't have time to teach and besides it hurts like hell being in the dance studio and knowing I can't get down like I used to."

"Well, hopefully Rah is somebody name Bubba's bitch by now," I joke, just to hear her laugh.

"Ooh, baby, I hope they make it do what it do."

We laugh like crazy.

Someone clears their throat and I look over my shoulder at Carolyn standing there looking down at me. Suddenly the vee neck of my silk dress feels too low as she eyes me like a glass of ice water on a hot day. I shiver in repulsion at the memory of how her hands felt on my body.

"Ze? Dyke alert. Let me call you right back."

Carolyn's face gets even tighter. I have to make myself not laugh. "Yes?" I say with plenty of attitude.

"Just double checking that we have an understanding that whatever happened between us stays between us," she says in that haughty tone of hers.

"Oh, trust me. Whatever happened *between* us is *behind* us."

"So your job is safe."

"And so is your marriage," I fling right back at her. Oh, I still have plenty of hood in me no matter how much I try to hide it.

The door to the inner office opens and Kelle walks through with a mean face at seeing Carolyn talking to me. She stands beside Carolyn but her eyes are on me as she says, "I played in my pussy while I was in the bathroom."

Kelle quickly runs her finger across Carolyn's mouth and Mrs. High Society's tongue darts out to taste the other woman's juices from her lips. They both eye me like my feelings should be hurt. Please. These bitches are dumb as hell.

"This is a dyke-free zone, ladies. Keep it moving please," I tell them with satisfaction as I pick up the phone and ease my finger close to the button labeled Mr. Ingram.

Carolyn catches the move and shoves her clutch under her arm before she gives me one last longing look and turns to leave. Her little flunky is right behind her like a dog on a leash. Or would it be a pussycat on a leash? Whatever.

Maybe I am crazy for wanting to go to Mohammed's favorite restaurant. Just because we are over does not mean he has a lock on good food. And The Caribbean has the best food this side of two stars. Besides, after all my drama with high society I am determined to get back in touch with the good things about Newark. I need to learn to be happy about who I am and where I am from.

I park my car inside the fenced-in lot. I see Dom's Lexus and the Camry Ze drives parked side by side. I was so caught up in chasing dreams that I missed most of their mending of the friendship. Regardless I'm just glad that the four of us can hang out again.

Hell, I am happy as hell that they are such good friends that they forgave me for kicking them to the curb to sniff under Carolyn's ass. That is what friends—best friends—are all about.

I slide my shades on to block the summer sun as I walk out of the parking lot to the front of the colorfully painted brick building. I stop in my path as Alizé, Dom, and Cristal all come out of the restaurant at once. I smile at them. "I know I am running late—"

Ze and Mo wrap their arms around mine and literally turn me around. "Girl, it's so crowded in that motherfucker," Dom says as they try to make my body move forward . . . *away* from the restaurant.

I lock my legs and plant my feet to the sidewalk just as the sun begins to set in the sky. "Hey, I am starving and I have been thinking about curry—"

"Let's just go, Cristal," Moët says with emphasis.

My eyes shift to each of their faces. I do not like what I see. "What's wrong?" I ask.

At their silence, I snatch my arms from them and turn to look through the front glass window of the restaurant. The sun glints off of it and I cannot see through it clearly. Still, I know before I even walk closer and peer in with my hand over my eyes what I am going to see.

It does not stop me.

Sure enough, there in the back snuggled in a booth together is Mohammed and that goddamn Evette. I feel like Peeping Tom as she leans over to wipe something from his mouth with her thumb. It is an intimate gesture. That of a woman looking out for her man.

"Come on, Cris, let's just go," Moët says again.

This time I let my friends pull me away.

Chapter Forty-Two

Alizé

"Cameron, this is me. I was just missing you and wanted to hear your voice. I forgot about the time mix-up. I wish I was there with you. Holding you. Kissing you. Loving on you."

I bite my lip a little as my emotions fill me up as I talk softly into my cell phone. "Sometimes I think you scootie-booted right out of town not to deal with me . . . and you. Us."

I pull my mom's old Camry into the driveway. "I know we want to wait until the divorce is final and I decide about the internship but I . . . I—"

The rest of my words catch in my throat as I climb out the car and meanmug Dr. Locke's SUV parked in front of the house. Man, what the fuck is *this* shit all about?

He's been blowing up my cell and I've been steady sending his ass to voice mail.

"Cameron, baby, we'll talk more when you call me later. Bye." I snap the phone close so hard that I mighta broke that bitch.

I walk into the house and drop my keys and briefcase onto the wooden kitchen table. I hear voices in the living room as I kick off my heels.

"Elaine, I'm glad that I was able to help you in any way," Dr. Locke says.

"I can tell Monica thinks a lot of the reason she sees a therapist is because of my relationship with her father," my mom says.

I walk closer to the doorway and pause.

"Of course I can't discuss the specifics of Monica's therapy with you—"

I roll my eyes. What the fuck he gone tell her? Lately the specifics of my therapy been a steady merry-go-round on his dick? Negro puh-leeze.

"I do think there are some issues concerning your divorce that you need to deal with."

And what the fuck you need to deal with?

"Monica thinks that's the reason my new boyfriend is so much younger than me."

"And what do you think?"

I lean in closer at the silence.

"I think that it was time for me to feel wanted. I'm a woman—a good damn woman—and this man that I love—who knows I love him—had overlooked me for years and now he's marrying someone else."

"Is the younger man and the new image another cry for attention from your ex? And if it is, when will it stop?"

Okay, I know this motherfucker in there quizzing my mama is a damn quack, but I want to know the answers to this question.

She remains silent.

I guess me and Mama done had enough.

I walk into the living room and they both look up at me. "Hi, Mama. Dr. Locke, can I speak to you outside for a second?" I ask, sounding phony as hell.

"Are you okay? Dr. Locke said you've been missing your therapy appointments so he came to check up on you."

I lock my eyes with his as I paste a smile on my face. "And that was so . . . nice of him. Dr. Locke?" I wave my hand towards the front door.

He rises to his feet and straightens his creases before he turns and offers his hand to my mother. "It's been a pleasure, Mrs. Winters. Maybe I can refer you to one of my colleagues for further—"

"Thanks but no thanks, Doc," I tell him as I grab his elbow and steer his ass right towards the door.

As soon as we step onto the front porch I whirl on him like the Tasmanian Devil. "What the fuck are you doing at my house?" I spit at him.

He removes his glasses and calmly as hell begins to clean them with a handkerchief as he leans against the railing. "Why aren't you answering my calls, Monica?"

"Because you and I are over."

He pauses in cleaning his glasses to look over at me. "No," he says simply.

I throw my hands on my damn hips and look at him like he has three heads coming out his ass. "You better get the hell out of my face, Dr. Locke."

He pushes off the railing and stands in my face to peer down at me. "Don't do this, Monica. Don't do this to me."

I step back from him. "Dr. Locke, *it's over*," I stress to him. "The therapy session. The sex. Everything. All of it. It's over."

He grabs my wrist. "It's not over until *I* say it's over."

I snatch my hand away and slap the shit out of him. It echoes into the night. He smiles and licks his lips as he peers into my eyes. "You know I love when you smack me. Do it again."

I shove him away from me and turn to dash into the house. I stand by the living room window peeking out the side of the curtain until he finally jogs down the porch and climbs into his ride to drive off.

I'm not gone lie. That shit that just went down has me shaky as hell. "Is he gone?"

I turn and give my moms a smile. "Yes. *Thank* God."

"He's one nice-looking man," she says, as she smiles and fans herself. "Well, you want me to leave my little thug alone. How about hooking your mama up with Hunter?"

I walk past her shaking my head. "Jump from the frying pan straight into the fire."

I feel her hand on my arm and I stop and turn to face her. "What's wrong with him?" she asks.

"What's wrong with him?" I ask sarcastically, even though I know I'm taking my anger for him out on my mother. I check myself and count to ten. "He's freaking me out and that's why I stopped going to him. He had no right to come here and if he comes back here don't let him in. I'm serious, Ma."

Maybe I should have walked in the truth and said: "Nothing except I've been screwing him and now he's acting like a mini-stalker because I told him it was over."

I release a heavy breath that is filled with all my drama. I can tell from the look on my mother's face that she knows there is more to the story but she doesn't want to ask. Still, I'm not ready to talk about it all. Dom. Cameron. Dr. Stalker. None of it.

But when she opens her arms and gives me that Mama smile like only she can I am more than happy to step into her embrace. I swear that I'm grown and independent and all that good shit, but it feels so good to just be in my mother's arms again.

Why did I ever want to grow up?

Chapter Forty-Three

Dom

"*This Dom. Get at me.*"

Beep.

"*How in the hell you gone call and give me the name and address to your drug counselor? Your ass the one been hooked on fuckin' dope. And hell no I don't want to meet with him. But what you can do is drop the bullshit and bring my grandbaby to see me. You're wrong, Dom, and you know it.*"

Beep.

"*Hey baby, I missed you at work. Kimani is being real good. You know I had to check up on her. Uhm, I hope you feel better. You must be sleeping. You better not be laid up with another dude about nine deep up in my pussy. Nah, I'm just playing. Anyway if you want I'll bring Kiki home and we can all go out tonight. Call me when you get up.*"

Beep.

"*You know grandparents' have rights too. I keep threatening to sue your shot-out ass and I will too.*"

Beep.

"*Keesha, I'm so happy you and Kimani are coming over for the cookout tomorrow. Everyone can't wait to meet you and I can't wait to spend some more time with you. Call me.*"

Beep . . . beep . . . beep.

I drop my cell phone onto the bed as I snuggle down deeper. I just want to spend some time by my damn lonesome because tomorrow my life won't ever be the same again. New people. New places. New things. I can't explain it but I just wanted this day to be about me. Fuck it.

Sure we talk on the phone a little but goin' over to his damn house is different.

What if I don't like Willie?

What if his family—*my* family—don't like me?

He has a wife and kids and they might see me as nothin' but trouble. A fuckin' intrusion. Some bastard kid from the projects that's a reminder of a time they wish never fuckin' happened.

I ain't gone lie. My ass is nervous as hell.

A part of me thinks I need to get myself together before I bring more people and possibly more damn drama into my life.

My eyes shift over to my laptop sittin' on the edge of the dresser. Corey brought it for me so that I can write my story, a story, any story. But the words won't come. I don't know a motherfuckin' thing about where to start a book. So now I just type my journal entries on the computer instead of write them by hand.

Corey asks me damn near everyday how the book is comin' and I straight lie to him and say everythin' is straight. Humph, 'bout as straight as Michael Jackson's ass.

My eyes shift over to the stack of books on the floor by my bed. Why the fuck do I think that can be me with my name across the cover of some damn book? Then again, why the fuck am I scared it can't be? I read a lot these days and I know what I like and what I don't fuckin' like. And maybe an online creative writin' class might teach me all the shit I need to know.

I roll off the bed and walk over to snatch up my computer. I am just about to hop my ass on the internet to check out some creative writin' courses when my cell phone rings again. I turn and snatch it up. It's Diane again.

I send her ass right to voice mail.

As soon as I drop the phone it sounds off letting me know I have a text message. I scoop the phone up from the bed again. It's from Corey.

Did you pick Kimani up from school?
She's not here.

Say what, say fuckin' who?

My heart is beatin' like a motherfucker as I dial the daycare cen-ter. "This is Keesha. Where the fuck is my daughter?" I shoot at they ass as soon as someone picks up the damn line. I don't give a goddamn if they fire my ass and I have to go get my black ass on the pole in another strip club, I want some answers with a quickness.

"She was signed out a few minutes ago by your mother."

See, this some real bullshit.

"How the fuck y'all gone let my mother sign her out—"

"You don't have to cuss and carry on, Keesha. Her name is on the list of people allowed to pick her up. The list *you* signed."

I hang up right in her face. The phone vibrates to let me know I have a voice mail message. Diane's no-good ass called me right be-fore Corey's text message so she probably left a message. My ass is shakin' and pacin', pacin' and fuckin' shakin' while I dial my voice mail.

"Hi Dom. Since you won't let me see my grandbaby I decided to scoop her right on up for a grandma-granddaughter afternoon. And she is just as happy to see me . . . whether you hate it or love it."

There's a rustlin' noise on the phone.

"Mama, Diane picked me up from school."

My daughter is excited as hell and don't have a clue that I really want to bury my foot in Diane's ass. "Okay, KiKi, let me talk to Grandma."

"Who?" she asks, soundin' like a damn owl.

"Diane."

The line rustles again.

"I don't have much else to say 'cept I'll have *my* grandchild home soon."

"Diane!" I yell into the phone as I grab my purse and my keys. "I'm comin' to get my daughter."

Diane laughs. "Coming where, smart ass? I ain't home."

It hits me big time that this is some real sad shit that my own damn mama done kidnap my fuckin' child. Why the fuck God send me to this bitch?

"You know what, Diane. I'm so sick of this shit." I'm tired of the fight and I hear it in my voice. "I asked you to come to therapy if you really wanted to see me and Kimani and instead you go snatch my child from school without my permission. Man, what the fuck, Diane? Damn."

"Who are you to put fuckin' stipulations on me to see *my* grand-baby?" she snaps.

I stop at the door and drop my keys and purse to the floor as I turn and press my back to the wall by the door. I can't do shit but slide down to the floor. I sigh and it filled the fuck up with all my sadness and regret. "Your daughter. I'm your daughter, Ma. I'm your fuckin' child."

I close my cell phone and fling that son-of-a-bitch across the room to crash against the wall.

Chapter Forty-Four

Moët

"Hold me, Taquan. Touch me."

I press his hands against one of my breasts as I glide the vibrator up and down my clit. The feel of his body next to me while I masturbate excites me like crazy. And I know he loves for me to watch him and just put my hand on his nipples or his buttocks as he jacks his dick like it's going out of style.

This is our intimacy. Our thing. That sexy and irresistible gray area between fornication and abstinence.

The more we do it, the more it feels wrong. Not unpleasant, just wrong as hell.

I feel his tongue on my nipples wetly and my eyes shoot open in surprise. This is a first. And Lord, oh Lord . . . it feels sooooo good.

"Taquan," I moan as I take the next step and reach down between us to massage the hard and long length of him.

I feel his jaw clench and the pressure of his mouth around my nipple deepens causing my clit to swell up so much that it feels numb. I shiver as his dick throbs in my hand. I tighten my grip and jack him until I feel wetness on his tip.

This is a zone we have never played in before. But we should have known this was coming. Our bodies are closer to each other every time we do this dance. We are testing the limits more and more and it makes me want him more and more. The buzzing of the vibrator is shifting further away as the real deal rubs against my leg like a snake.

I bite my lip as he shifts his nude body between my open legs. Both of his strong hands grab my breasts and pushes them up high so that he can suck both nipples hotly. I raise my leg to massage my thigh against his hard buttocks as my hands squeeze his broad shoulders.

"Yes, Taquan, suck my titties. Suck my damn titties," I holler out hoarsely as I shift my hands up to press his head closer to my chest.

His tongue flickers against my nipples. His dick presses against my thigh as he grinds his hips in a circular motion. My heart beats like crazy. My pussy is wet and throbbing. Aching and yearning.

Everything is going out the window in this gray zone we've made. I'm cussing. I'm thinking of sinning. I want to be fucked for real and if we don't stop this I will not take no for an answer.

"Taquan, we can't—"

He lifts up. "Turn over," he orders me in this husky voice.

Even as I try to fight it, I roll right over until my aching breasts are pressed into his bed. One of his hands squeezes between me and the bed to press against my pus—. *My hot spot.* I gasp as he presses the length of his . . . hardness straight up the crack in my buttocks to cup him snugly. The heat of his body is pressing me down into the bed as he plants kisses on my shoulders, grinds his . . . hardness against my . . . buttocks, and uses strong fingers to vibrate my . . . button. I squeeze my eyes shut and damn near bite the stuffing out the pillow as he continues to rock his hips, gliding his . . . his . . . Oh God . . . his dick, okay, he is gliding his nice, long, hard dick up and down between my ass cheeks cupping him like a hot dog bun.

"Damn that pussy wet," he whispers against my neck as he slips a finger inside me.

His language shocks and excites me all at once.

I start working my hips until I find his rhythm and each circle brings his fingers deeper against my clit until I am trembling from deep inside my pussy walls. He squeezes his other hand beneath me to tease my hard nipples . . . and I am lost. There is no turning back now. There is nothing for me to do but ride the delicious waves.

"I'm cummmmmin'," I moan into the pillow as my pussy walls spasm and something like fireworks seems to explode inside me until I am just floating like I'm falling through air.

"Me too, baby, me too. Get this nut," he moans in my ears as his body stiffens just before I feel his dick jerk between my ass as his cum fills that small gap between his stomach and the deep curve at the top of my ass.

"Hmmm," I moan in pleasure as I bring my hand up to suck my fingers.

He continues to play in my pussy and work his hips until the last of his nut squirts from his dick onto my wet ass. "Shit," Taquan swears before his body relaxes on me.

My eyes shoot open at his language and I close my eyes as remorse fills me. "God forgive me," I pray silently. "I have corrupted this man."

I have no right being here but something calls me to this place. I was laying in bed beside Taquan and I felt conflicted about where I led our relationship. The only thing that eased my mind was the thought of coming here.

So here I am.

I drop Taquan's key (which I "borrowed" while he slept) in my pocket as I walk into the small inner church. All the lights are off except for the one above the altar. Looking at it makes me want to sing "Amen."

I stand behind the back pew and I feel such reverence as I remember the day that the Lord finally forgave me—or taught me to forgive myself—for all my sins. Right here in this same sanctuary.

I honestly never wanted to be that person again. And no I haven't had abortions and I haven't disobeyed my parents. I haven't cut my ties with the Lord.

I have lied.

I am seducing a man to give up the very virginity he covets because he loves the Lord.

I have been manipulative.

I am sick of myself . . . again.

There is no choir tonight to sing me to my uplifting but I feel something more powerful, and that is His presence. He is here for me. He has never left me. And although I know one of my sins was for a greater good, I also know that they were detours on this path that I must take.

I'm not saved, but I was trying and now I have even stopped doing that.

"Forgive me, Lord," I whisper as I bring my hands up to steeple beneath my chin as I walk slowly to the altar.

"I should have put my faith in You that everything would be just the way You have planned for me. But I let fear and lack of faith lead me to do things I know were wrong, because I was afraid of losing her. I was afraid that he would take my baby from me. Oh, Lord, forgive me," I whisper with conviction as tears fill my eyes and tighten my throat.

"I've been fighting this feeling. I've been telling myself it's not time. But I know that my life will be nothing without You. I am nothing without You."

I fall to my knees at the praying bench as the tears blur my vision. "I thank You for sending Taquan to me and I beg You to forgive me for tempting him, Lord. For trying to steer him away from You. I don't know why I keep dancing with the devil but I beg You to please keep me with You. Don't let the devil win. Help me fight him. Help me do right. Help me be a better person. Embrace me, Lord, as I embrace You. Don't let me go. Forgive me, Lord. Forgive me. Please."

I drop my head to the bench and give in to the tears and the emotions that surround me as I relinquish the fight and surrender gracefully to His will.

Chapter Forty-Five

Cristal

You never think about your man working where you work or where you live . . . until he becomes your ex-boyfriend. I walk into the lobby of The Top and my eyes fall right on Mohammed. It has been a week since I saw him and his new love chilling at The Caribbean. Love, regret, anger, and jealousy have me nauseous as I tilt my chin up.

I know I look good in my turquoise strapless silk dress and white platform peep-toe shoes. I strut with my best overtly sexy walk. I just want him to know that Evette could not compete on her *best* damn day.

So we do not speak. We pretend like we never shared time in each other's lives. He is mad at me and I am pissed at him about Evette but we really shared an amazing connection. Some other level shit that people dream about it. Now we act like we do not even know each other.

I step onto the elevator and come face to face with Winthrop Blanchard III, sexy white man and my ex (sorta) making out with a tall, curly-haired look-alike of Eddie Murphy's ex-wife. They must have rode the elevator up from the underground parking garage.

I give them both a polite smile and turn to roll my eyes as the elevator doors close. I dated him very briefly. He was only good to me for eating pussy and buying me nice pieces of jewelry that I cashed in to help pay my bills. One racial slur from his ass and I tossed him (but not the gifts) out the door.

"Hello, *Danielle*."

I do not miss the way he stresses my name. I look over my shoulder briefly at them and frown at the way her blue-green eyes are checking me out from head to toe. I swallow back my greetings. Does this six-foot freckled-face, blue-eyed black woman think I want her man? I just turn away from them both and fix my eyes on the silver elevator door.

"This is my *new* girlfriend, Kai," Winthrop says with satisfaction in his voice.

I look over my shoulder and lock eyes with Winthrop. "Best of both worlds, huh?" I ask, alluding to her obvious mixed heritage.

I take pleasure in the way his neck reddens. I turn back.

My brows rise as I hear smacking noises and little moans from behind me. "I would say get rooms but since you are almost home why not wait until you're behind closed doors."

When the elevators stop at my floor, I am grateful. I think I hear the rustle of clothing and I do not want to catch a visual. Winthrop and his new bitch are already forgotten as I walk into the apartment. Only the lights from the kitchen and the bar are on and it gives the spacious apartment a really nice and mellow feel.

I love my friends and the kids but I am so glad that I have the apartment to myself for once. It reminds me of those long forgotten days when I would just chill at home with a glass of wine all by my lonesome.

I have just kicked off my shoes to just snuggle down deeper into a corner of the couch when the front door bursts open. My whole family (and they are my family) walks in with laughter and way too much happiness.

"Hi, Auntie Cristal." I sit up as Kimani climbs onto the couch and gives a big, wet, and sticky kiss on my cheek. It is probably the *only* time I do not care if my MAC makeup is messed up. The kisses of a godchild are way better than a perfectly made-up face.

"Guess what?" Mo asks as she sits down and lifts Tiffany from the car seat.

Alizé peels off her blazer and flings it over her shoulder as she makes a beeline for the bathroom. "Y'all fill her in. I gots to pee," she says, already hitching her skirt up over her waist.

"We just talked to Mohammed and he swears he is just friends with Evette," Mo tells me.

I sit forward and reach my hands out for my other godchild. As soon as she is in my arms I bury my face in her neck and just inhale the smell of innocence and sweetness.

"Trust me, I asked. No fucking. No fuck buddies. Nothing," Dom tries to assure me. I guess she took my silence for hesitation and doubt.

Alizé hollers out from the bathroom and we all look that way, look at each other, and then look that way again.

"Ze, you alright?" I holler out to her.

"I'm . . . I'm good," she hollers back.

"So . . . we just saw Mohammed in the lobby and we talked to him about everything—"

I cut my eyes at Moët. "Oh, y'all did?"

"We sure did."

I cut my eyes over at Dom.

"Do you want him back or not?" she asks boldly.

I nuzzle my face against Tiffany's smooth brown cheek. My head is tilted to the side as I smile down into her face as she smiles back at me. "Yes, I want him back," I admit, before I lower my head to kiss her cheek.

"Well good, y'all want the same thing then."

My eyes shoot up to Dom and my eyes are filled with questions.

Dom lights up a cigarette as she kicks off her Air Force 1s. "Dinner. Tomorrow night. He will pick you up at seven o'clock. He has been set straight to take you *anywhere* but The Caribbean."

Another chance for Mohammed and me?

I press my face back into the sweet crook of Tiffany's neck to hide my big and goofy smile. If we can talk things over and make things better, I swear I will never take him for granted again. I love him too much and I have no way of knowing if there will be a third chance for us.

Girl Talk

Cristal eyed each of her friends as they all sat around the living room in their pajamas. "It's time to get back to the way we all used to be," she begins. "Everyone is putting on a good front but I can tell there are some heavy things going on with each and every one of you. Things you're not sharing."

Dom blows smoke rings through her pursed lips.

Alizé frowns a bit before she digs in her purse for a BlowPop.

Moët reaches up to touch the diamond cross pendant around her neck.

"I thank you for stepping in with me and Mohammed but it is time that we shoulder more than just *my* burdens. I know I pulled away from our friendship and I am grateful that when it is all said and done you three bitches are right here riding or dying with me. Trust that. Believe that. But right now? Right here? It is time for the realness."

Dom flicked the ashes from her cigarette into the ashtray on her lap. "There's a lot going on that I just keep to myself but the biggest thing for me was going back into drug counseling because I . . . uhm . . . I almost relapsed. That shit about my father and this constant bullshit with Diane. I'm proud of me for throwing that dope out the window that day. It was the scariest and the bravest shit I ever done. Ever."

Dom locks eyes with each of her friends and in their depths she sees and feels their love and belief in her.

Alizé feels their eyes on her and she shrugs. "Me and Moms are doing much better—"

Cristal shook her head and held up her hand. "No, no, no. We all know about that. Tell us something we do not know."

"Okay." She picks up her glass of Alizé (of course) and takes a little breath. "I'm glad that Cameron has been out of town on business . . . I found out last week that Dr. Locke gave me trich."

"Eew," the ladies all said in unison.

Alizé made a sarcastic looking face. "Oh *eew* is right. Trust. My pussy ain't never itch so much in all my damn life."

Three sets of eyes drop down to her crotch. "Hey," Alizé says loudly as she snaps her legs shut before she laughs. The girls begin to laugh too and Alizé holds up her hand to silence them. "Trust me, we all laughing but ain't a damn thing funny."

They all sipped from their drinks as they cast their eyes at Moët. She smiles at them. "I got saved," she admits simply and then drops her eyes from theirs. "So I did want to ask that we drop the Moët thing. I mean I really can't be saved and have people calling me by my champagne. You know?"

Dom, Cris, and Alizé share quick looks. "Are you still going to be our friend?" Alizé asks.

Moët looked at each of them in disbelief. "We all have been through so much together. I mean there are things in my life I couldn't have gotten through without y'all. So yes, I am still your friend. I am still Moët . . . just better. New and improved. But I know that I couldn't find three better friends in the world and I'm not going to pull that holy conversion mess like my parents. You are my friends and I love y'all just the way you are. And you can believe that."

"To friendship," Cristal said warmly as she held her glass up.

Dom, Alizé, and Moët gladly did the same.

Chapter Forty-Six

Alizé

Two hundred phone calls.
Even more crazy-ass voice mail messages.
A dozen drive-bys at my last count.
Five dozen bouquets of roses.
Twice getting caught sitting outside my house all night.
One case of trich.
Oh, a bitch like me done had enough.

Cameron would be home this week and it is time for me to get this bullshit with Dr. Locke as cleared up as my nasty ass case of the trich.

The very last thing I need is Cameron and I being on a date and I look and see Dr. Locke's fruitcake ass sitting there peering at us while he jacks off. Trust me, I think this freak would do it.

So a bitch like me is on the grind. And if this doesn't work I'm going to have to call the po-po on his ass. For real.

I can't take the phone calls at three in the morning just to breathe on the phone or to tell me my pussy is good.

I can't take walking off campus or out of a store or out of Braun, Weber to see his ass sitting in his car waiting for me.

I can't take living my life and looking up and he is there. Watching me from a distance or coming up to me to beg me to take him back.

I am sick of the flowers.

I am sick of the sex toys he has delivered.

I am sick of his motherfucking ass.

It's time to flip the script.

I get out of my car and walk around to stand on the sidewalk in front of the two-level colonial house. Nice picture of a happy home. Dr. Locke's freakiness might just be his downfall.

I walk up the stairs big and bold and ring the doorbell. I'm feeling nervous as the door opens until I look up into Dr. Locke's shocked face. I give him that "How you like me now" look as he steps back to close the door. That would have been fine if I didn't throw my hip against the door to bumrush it back open.

"Who is it, Hunter?"

I recognize his wife's nice pleasant voice. Wonder how pleasant it would be if she knew what his freak nasty ass was up to. "Yes, Hunter, who is it?" I said in a mocking voice.

His whole face changes and he look like he is 'bout ready to shit himself.

"Not fun opening your door and having your life intruded on . . . is it?" I snap to him in a low voice. "How would you like it if I sat outside your fucking house all night long or called your house all night and hung up? I've had it with your bullshit. I gave you some ass and I don't want to give you no more . . . so leave me the fuck alone or I will wreck this shit you call a happy home for real."

"You had no right coming to my home," he whispers to me harshly as he reaches out to grab my wrist.

"Oh, it was okay for me to come to your house when you wanted to fuck me in your wife's bed, though, right?"

He drops my wrist with a quickness.

"Should I call her to the door and tell her what color her sheets are, Dr. Locke? Or describe that flat mole on your dick? Or the way you squeal like a fucking pig when you're cumming? Or the way you like your ass licked after I suck your dick? Or should I tell her how your dumb ass gave me a fucking STD? You took trich to a whole 'nother level, *trick*."

He looks offended. This crazy motherfucker got the nerve to look offended. He takes his hand and put it square in my chest to push me back. "Stay the fuck away from my house and my family."

"*If* you stay the fuck away from me," I throw back.

He slams the door and I am more than happy to feel the wind on my face as it closes.

Chapter Forty-Seven

Dom

May 2007

I'm back writin' in my journal by hand since I have finally started using the computer for starting my first book! Damn right. Fuck Nike. I'm gonna be like TI and "Do it, do it, do it." And there is no dope, no weed, or no liquor like gettin' my ass lost in the crazy world of Club XXXCite. Who knows the world of stripper better than a bitch like me fresh off the pole? And the lead character Lick Mee is wild. Not I ain't trying to say anybody will ever buy this motherfucker and publish it. But I'm gone finish it. Fuck it. I'm having fun regardless. And not just with my writin'. My life don't feel as heavy as it used to. It ain't as fuckin' dark and depressing as it used to be. I ain't the best I will be but I'm better. Having Willie—my daddy—in my life is different. He calls just to check up on me and Kimani. He asks me if we need anything and even though my ass is still strugglin' like a bitch I ain't took one red cent from him. Now that I'm gettin' to know him I don't want shit but to make up for lost time. And Kimani loves having a new granddaddy and an auntie that's the same age as her. Her and Hiasha are really inseparable now. Kimani is tickled fuckin' pink to have a new family. They've even asked if she could spend the night but the funny thing is that last year I would gladly dropped her ass off with a smile and a wave. Now? I'm feelin' like I don't know them well enough for all that . . . yet. I guess time does change a lot of things.

The sounds of Mary J Blige loudly echoed from inside my white leather hobo bag. Several eyes in the waitin' room look my way. I stick my pen inside my journal and reach over to grab my cell phone. It's Corey. A smile big as the Kool-Aid guy's spread across my face.

"Hey you," I say, as I snatch up my bag and rise to strut my ass outside.

"Hey," he says in that voice that makes my fuckin' insides warm. "I was thinking about my little chocolate baby."

I laugh just the way he wants me to. "Boy, you swear you Martin Lawrence or some shit."

"And you love it," he says.

"Yes. Yes, I do," I admit softly as I watch the New Jersey Transit bus pull to the curb across the street.

"Damn, baby girl, you sound serious as hell. Don't get me sad and you don't meant it," he jokes.

I just laugh as I bite my lip to keep from tellin' him the truth. I don't know why my ass is afraid to admit to him that I love him. Maybe the doc can help me get to the bottom of *that* shit in our meeting today.

"I'll come by your apartment as soon as I get done," I tell him as I watch a drug deal goin' down on the next block.

"Hey, you doing okay with everything, right?"

Translation: Your ass ain't back snortin' up dope is it?

I watch the woman shove her hand into the pocket of her dingy jeans as she walks up the street towards me fast as hell. I can't look away from her. I see myself in her or at least what the fuck I almost become. As she gets closer to me I see her yellow eyes and her jacked-up skin. I smell all the unwashed days she been through. And I feel how badly she wants to snort.

As she walks by me and gives me a little look before she continues on like she marching to war, I feel like I should stop her and say somethin' to her. I mean damn, I'm an ex-junkie standin' in front of the rehab clinic when she walks by me.

She turns and looks back at me.

Say somethin'.

But I don't and just then she turns the corner and she's gone.

I ain't Mo but I'll be damned if that didn't feel like somethin' the Great One wanted to go down.

I turn and jog to the corner but she's gone. I do see an old beat-up car pullin' away. Maybe she's in there. Damn.

I hug my damn self with my arms and walk back to the clinic.

"Dom."

I look up and every fuckin' thing seems to freeze as I see Diane standin' her ass in front of the clinic. I ain't spoke to her since the day she signed Kimani out of school without my permission. Once I hung up on her, she actually brought Kimani straight to me. That shocked the hell out of me but it didn't stop me from slamming the front door in her face. I ain't heard from her since.

"What you doin' here, Diane?"

She reaches in her Gucci bag and pulls out her soft pack of Newports. "I'm tryin'," she says as she shakes a cigarette loose and offers me the pack. "You wanted me to be here and I'm here."

I take the cigarette and just hold it between my fingers. "Do you want to be here, Diane?" I ask her, tryin' to sound hard towards her. I failed.

She lights her cigarette, inhales, and blows out a stream of smoke as she shifts her eyes away from me. "I'm here, ain't I," she says, before she looks me right in the eye.

See, this the shit. This woman standin' before me has hurt me and she has done me so wrong but she is my mother. I can call her Diane all I want but she is still my mother. I wanna think so bad that she did the best she could with what she knew.

I want to forgive her. I want to love her. I want to try.

I drop the cigarette and put it out with the toe of my shoe before I walk over and open the door to the clinic. She drops her cigarette too and walks over to step inside.

She's here and even if we can't work through our bullshit, it means so fuckin' much to me that she even came and that's for real.

Chapter Forty-Eight

Moët

I didn't have the heart to tell them the truth.

At the pajama party we sat up all night and talked. We revealed some secrets. We reminisced on the past. We talked about our hopes for the future.

We reconnected and it felt good.

But that whole night I thought of one last secret that I have.

"Latoya."

Taquan's warm hands settle on my shoulders and turn me to face him. I tilt my face up for the kiss I know he is about to give me. Slow and easy never felt so good. We never felt so good.

I bring my hands up to his chest and the diamond solitaire on my left ring finger twinkles in my eyes. "I still can't believe we're engaged," I admit softly against his lips.

He smiles as he presses my body close. "I can."

I feel his dick get hard against my soft belly and I step back a bit to ease the temptation. We haven't done our little version of sex since my night at the altar. No more shades of gray on that one. "And this isn't because you're ready for the honeymoon?" I ask as I bring my hand down to enjoy the sight of my bling.

He puts his hand on my chin and tilts my head back. "This is because I love you and I want to spend the rest of my life with you. I want to fill you up with my babies and make an even bigger family for Tiffany. I want to sleep with you in my bed every night and I want to wake up with you in my arms every morning. And yes, I want to be able to make love to you . . . really make love to you for the first time and every other time after that."

"I love you, too, Taquan. I do. I love you so much," I admit as I let him pull me back close to him.

I used to think I didn't deserve happiness but now I know I do. I deserve to have a man like Taquan love and cherish me. I deserve to have a beautiful daughter like Tiffany. I deserve to have good friends and a better relationship with my family.

I deserve it all.

I'm a good person and with HIM leading my life the best is yet to come.

Taquan's phone rings and he moves away from me to go and answer it. I sit down on the couch surrounded by the soft candlelight and the sweet aroma of roses as I reach for my purse and pull out my wallet. I tilt my head to the side and sigh as I look down at the ten-thousand-dollar check from Brookham Publications—the owners and publishers of *Star Gazette*, *Gossip Central*, and *Hip-Hop News* tabloids. A very generous payment for my "inside" scoop on Bones.

I've been carrying this check for weeks and it feels like a weight around my neck. I've been trying to decide if I should burn it or cash it. My intentions were not to make money but to give me some leverage to get the joint custody of my daughter.

At the time I did what I had to do.

I've made amends for that. I've asked for forgiveness and I firmly believe that He has blessed me with it.

With one last sigh, I grab a pen, sign the check, and fill out a deposit slip. The deed is done. Nothing I do will take away those headlines so I might as well start a nice college fund for *our* daughter.

I'm saved . . . not stupid.

Chapter Forty-Nine

Alizé

I hate knowing that Cameron is over at his wife's house. He went straight there from the airport and didn't even come to me. Something about an emergency or some bullshit.

I guess with him being out of town for all this time I didn't have to deal with the wife bullshit. What if Serena changed her mind and wanted Cameron back? Would he let his obligation to her keep him in the marriage? Would he want me to be his mistress? Would he follow all the love he claims is in his heart for me and get the divorce?

I flip-flop on my bed and then reach for my phone to dial his number. It rings and then goes to voice mail.

Is she waiting with some scene of seduction for Cameron? Are they making love right now while I sat here like a dumb ass waiting for him?

God, I hate love.

I glance at the clock on the wall. He landed two hours ago and it would take him thirty minutes to get to their apartment in the city. If my estimate is right, he's been there with her for an hour and a half.

Oh God, is this what my life will become? Counting minutes, mapping destinations, estimating things to be sure he's not with her—his wife. I'm already starting to feel myself morph into my mama. And even she is finally getting on with her life. Took a younger man to knock Daddy out her head but at least she's moving the fuck on while I have stuck my dumb ass in the middle of a triangle.

If Cameron flips on me and goes back to his wife I will seriously whip his ass . . . especially since I passed on the summer internship at Braun, Weber to be with him. Right now I am really regretting that. I wonder if it's too late to call back and accept the offer.

Still, could I go through another semester of watching Cameron married to another woman? So maybe Braun, Weber is off limits whether Cameron and I make it or not.

So maybe my dumb ass is putting my ass before my brains. MBA, remember, M-B-A.

I roll off the bed and walk over to the window. I frown at the sight of a black Caddy rolling down the street pass the house. My heart stops and then comes back beating full force. Oh, hell no!

Is that Dr. Locke?

I jerk open the window and stick my head out to peer at the tag. JKL 234. It's not him and I should have known that because I haven't seen or heard from that crazy bastard since my little drop-in at his house. Still . . . sometimes I still feel like somebody's watching me.

My cell phone rings and I slam my head against the window as I jerk back inside. I barely have time to rub the bruise as I race across the room. It's Cameron. It's Cameron!

Breathe, bitch. Breathe.

"Hello." I'm so glad I don't sound desperate as hell.

"Come downstairs."

I hate the relief I feel to know he is here and not there . . . with her. I dash out the room and I'm so anxious to get down there to him that I skip my little pause at the top of the stairs. I'm halfway down before I realize that my ass is *running* down the stairs.

I check myself and walk down the rest of the way as I smooth my hands over my skinny jeans. As soon as I step out onto the porch my mouth drops open to see a stretch limo parked out front. As I walk down the stairs a chauffeur hops out and walks around it to open the door for me.

I'm disappointed Cameron didn't come himself.

I smile up at the tall and bald chauffeur before I climb in.

"Hello, Monica."

I look up and smile at the sight of Cameron sitting there looking at me like I am the last morsel of food on earth and he is STARV-ING. I fling myself into that limo and land lying across his lap. God, he looks good and smells good and feels good.

He tilts his head to the side to look down at me with those eyes I love. "Damn, I missed you," he says in this deep voice.

My eyes drop to his lips as he lowers his head to kiss me but then my eyes shift to the hand on my hip and the sight of his wedding ring is enough to make me roll right off his lap.

He looks up with his lips still slightly puckered.

I climb right up onto the seat opposite him. "Listen, I've done some shit. But this thing between me and you is way bigger than any of that. Maybe another man, another time I wouldn't care . . . but with you I cannot play the mistress role. Not with you."

"I've never asked you to," he inserts.

"Then if you say you guys have decided it's over then why did you carry your ass over there today?" My eyes shift to his hand. "Why in the hell are you still wearing that ring? Cameron, are you trying to play me?"

His eyes harden as he leans back in his seat and looks at me. "You have been throwing yourself at me and then you have the nerve to ask me if I'm playing you? Come on, Monica, be for real."

"I am."

We sit there and just stare at each other as we sit in this limo that looks out of place for my neck of the hood.

"Monica, do you think I'm lying about my divorce? Do you think I want to keep you *and* Serena?"

"No, no, no. I don't think you're that kind of person. I don't. I'm just scared because I have never loved anyone like I love you."

He reaches down and picks up his briefcase. I watch as he opens it and pulls out legal documents to hand to me. "Serena didn't call me over to the apartment. I went by there to give her these."

I take them from him and I nod as I recognize they are divorce papers.

"I had my attorney draw them up while I was in Japan," he says.

I feel the intensity of his eyes on me as I focus on the papers without even seeing the words. "They're not signed."

Cameron releases a heavy breath as he wipes his mouth with his hands. "I went by there first to get them signed. To start the process so that you're not my mistress or we're not having an affair."

"And she wouldn't sign them." My voice sounds as dull and void of emotion as my soul right now. I look up and lock my eyes with his.

"No, she wouldn't," he admitted, never once breaking our stare.

"So what does this mean?" I ask as I fling the damn papers across the limo to land on the seat beside him.

"It means that the divorce will not be easy but it will happen and not just because I want and love you but because I don't love her. It's not fair to lead her on anymore. I don't want to hurt her anymore either."

"*So* . . . what does this mean?" I can't do the married man shit . . . not with Cameron. I just can't.

"It means that you and I either wait for the divorce if that makes you feel more comfortable or you let me file these papers and get the divorce going—contested or not—and we're together. I'm staying at a hotel until I get my own apartment. She knows about you and there's no hiding or sneaking and ducking. It's you and me. It's not the best situation. I know this but I love you and I know you love me."

"Does she love you?"

He shrugs. "I don't know. I don't think so. I mean you're not the only issue in our marriage. I don't think we really knew each other and once we did I don't think either one of us was quite caught up in what we saw."

"So why is she refusing the divorce when she asked for it?"

"Honestly?"

"Always."

"Pride."

I look at him as I struggle with my feelings. How badly do I want him? Is it worth the risk?

Even as he reaches across to grab my hands and pull me to him, I have so many reservations. I love him and I need him but what if this all blows up in my face? What if he flips and decides he wants his wife back and then I'm ass out? Do I want to fight another woman for *her* husband?

Damn, this sound like some real cliché bullshit.

"It's up to you, Monica. Are you going with me or staying?" he asks as his hands shift up to stroke my face as he places these sweet kisses on my lips.

"I'm going," I whisper against his mouth.

He signals the driver and I feel the limo pull off. "I love you and everything is going to work out fine. Trust me."

I love Cameron and I have to believe in him.

For now.

Chapter Fifty

Cristal

The last lesson I learned was not to depend on a man to provide you with things and I think I learned the lesson well, but in life you grow, you continue to live and you continue to learn. I am learning that I cannot depend on a man for my happiness either. Ultimately all the things I want and need in life are up to me. For me. By me.

I love Mohammed but now I know that despite my show of confidence or conceit I do not love myself enough. But thank God I am young and it is never too late to start the process.

No more dreams about wealthy parents coming to save me. No more hopes for a wealthy friend to show me a life I can only dream of. No more looking for someone else to give me the money to finance my dreams. No more looking to a man to make me feel special—which gives him the power to make me feel less than special.

Mohammed.

I sigh as I stand at my bedroom window and look down at him crossing the courtyard. He looks up suddenly, unexpectedly, and his eyes are on me in the window.

I miss him in my life but I know for now that I made the right choice. At least I hope I did.

I never went to our "reconciliation" date that night. I remember standing at the entrance of the restaurant dressed to impress and finesse with my eyes locked on him . . . but I felt reluctant to go to him. In that moment, I knew that things had changed.

See, deep down I felt like Mohammed should have trusted me to tell the truth about Sahad . . . the same way I trusted him that he told me the truth about Evette. Deep down even as I yearned for him that thought nagged at me. Ate at me. Did I want him so badly . . . so desperately . . . that I was willing to overlook him playing holier-than-thou with me? And then that one thought made me do some evaluating on myself.

I did not like what I saw. Things had to change. *Everything* had to change and change can only come with time. I knew that even as I dressed for the date and drove to the restaurant. And I knew it as my feet just wouldn't carry me forward to join him.

I love Mohammed but I need to learn to love me. I have read enough of those magazines to know I will never be happy until I do. I had Sahad and the money and it was not enough. Then I had Mohammed and the love and I still felt empty. I will always put money first because to me money and status make me feel important. That is sad.

Leaving the restaurant was not easy, but soon each step made me feel a little lighter.

For a few moments we just stand there looking at each other before he waves and then drops his head to continue on his way.

Life is a confusing bitch.

I wonder if I—or any of my friends—will get this adult thing down. When will the choices we make and the roads we take get any easier? I will be damned if I do not climb over one big-ass hill just to find out there is another waiting for me to climb.

Dom's reunion with her father has inspired me to find my own parents. I know my story may not have such a happy ending as hers but on this path to self-discovery I need to know it all—the good and the hellish bad. Maybe if I get rid of that dream about my parents I could move the fuck on.

All the magazines I read say life is so much clearer in your thirties, wiser in your forties, and damn near divine in your fifties. After looking at Alizé's mom flip out over her husband and Carolyn on the prowl for pussy, I do not know how right "they" are. Still, I am ready to start the journey to find out just who I am.

I turn away from the window and walk over to the end of my bed to my bright red Birkin bag (one of the few relics from my past with Sahad that he did not repossess). I reach in and pull out my address book. As I open it and flip through the pages everything in it and about it makes me feel weighed down again. It is an example of my fight of love versus money. I never once used it when I was with Mohammed but I did not have the clit to throw it away either.

I close it and tap it against my hand as I strut into my adjoining bath. I grab the chrome garbage pail and sit down on the padded toilet seat. Slowly I begin to tear the pages from the book. They flutter down into the can like wings.

Maybe I never destroyed it before because I thought I was giving it all up for Mohammed and then if he fucked up I had no way to rewind and start again. Well, now I am doing it for me. This is— was—nothing but a book of lying, using, and manipulating people.

I reach for the chrome lighter I use for my scented candles and lit the tip of the last page. I feel the heat against my face a little as the fire spreads. Wherever it touches becomes black ashes.

I drop the lit paper into the can and sit there with my face in my hands as it burns. All of it. The pictures. The contact info. The stars and dollar signs rating their sex and their money. The nicknames I would give them and then jot down in case I forgot because they were too many to remember.

All of it.

As it begins to die down I fill a glass with water and pour it into the can. The last of the fire sizzles before it is dashed out.

That address book was just more evidence that my ass is fucked-up big time.

I leave the bathroom and make my way back over to my bedroom window. Mohammed stops just before he climbs into his jeep to look up at me. He smiles a little and even from a distance I am touched by him. I know that all I have to do is bend a finger and he will leave that jeep and come to me here. Be near me. Inside me. Loving me. Making love to me.

But I just smile and wave to him.

Maybe one day when I get myself together.

Maybe.

Girl Talk

The four friends all lounged poolside, comfortable as the summer sun beat down on their bodies toasting their various shades of brown skin to a deeper shade. Renting a suite at their favorite New York hotel for the weekend had been the right decision.

Although Cristal was the only one *sans* a date, she felt good just being around her friends and their happiness. She found it amazing just how reflective she could be without a man to distract her. She pulled her body to an upright position in her strapless white Gucci bathing suit and wire-framed shades. "Ladies, where do you think you'll be in another five years?" she asked as she pushed her shades atop her head.

Moët smiled almost as brightly as the sun in her modest pink one-piece with a matching skirt. She looked over at Taquan as he talked with Cameron and Corey at the other end of the pool. "I will still be happily married as Mrs. Taquan Sanders, a supervisor at DYFS, with one more child."

"Serving the Lord?" Dom joked as she turned over to lay on her stomach in her skimpy gold bikini that was more string than anything.

"Amen," Moët said with a wink before she reached over to playfully swat Dom's curved behind. "What's your future, chick?"

Dom leaned up to look over at her friends with mischief in her eyes. "More money. More money. More money."

"What about love, smart ass?" Cristal asks, nodding her head over at Corey.

Dom dropped her head, hiding a blush and a smile. "I gots plenty of that. It's money my ass is drawing a blank on."

"Well, I will be the CEO of one of the country's top firms and married to the CEO of another," Alizé boasted, as she reached down to pick up her glass of lemonade. "Cameron and I will be the ultimate black power couple dominating corporate America."

She turned her head and watched Cameron over the rim of her glass. The doubt in her eyes was reflected in the depths of the liquid.

"What about you Miss Cristal?" Moët asked as she twisted her engagement ring on her finger.

"I know I asked the question but I do not know the answer. I do know things can only get better so whatever life has in store for me I am ready for it. I am looking forward to it." She smiled at her girls as she reached down to pick up her glass of sparkling water. "A toast."

Dom and Moët grabbed their glasses as well just as the men swam to the end of the pool where they sat.

"Hey, we want some of that," Corey said as he climbed out of the water with ease to sit beside Dom.

Cameron and Taquan moved over by their women as well. The men all picked up their drinks as well.

Cristal shook off how deeply she missed Mohammed in that moment. "To the future."

"To the future," they all said in unison.

SHOW AND TELL

NIOBIA BRYANT

ABOUT THIS GUIDE

The questions and discussion topics that follow are
intended to enhance your group's reading of
this book.

Discussion Questions

1) Which of the ladies was your most and least favorite? Have your opinions changed since the last book? And why?

2) Sometimes, it is hard to overcome the past. Do you feel Cristal's past was the reason she was determined to be more than she was? Do you believe Cristal was ambitious or just greedy?

3) Do you think Cristal will ever truly find a love that she thinks is worth fighting for?

4) Does Alizé's relationship with Dr. Locke make you mistrust therapy? If you did discover that your therapist had an extramarital affair, would that make you mistrust his professional advice?

5) Was Alizé wrong to pursue Cameron the way that she did after she turned down his offer of love in the last book? Would you have done the same thing if you were in her situation?

6) Do you blame Bones for fighting for full custody after Moët falsely accused him of rape in the last book? If the custody battle had gone to court do you think Moët or Bones would have won?

7) How do you feel about male virgins or men who abstain from sex before marriage? Would you be able to be in a relationship that did not have a sexual component?

8) Because of Moët's desire to win custody of her child she considered taking a bribe from a wealthy man to not report his

abuse towards his children? Would you even consider doing such a thing?

9) Do you believe that Alizé should have forgiven Dom? Did Dom do enough to prove she was truly sorry for her actions? Again, do we forgive friends too easily for the sake of "friendship"?

10) Dom discovered that it was in fact Diane who kept Dom's father away from her? Do you think a woman can be vindictive enough to destroy a father/child relationship because she is angry at the father?

11) Battling a drug addiction is a lifelong process. Do you believe Dom has the tools in place to stay sober? Do you think she will continue to struggle or go back to stripping? Do you understand women who decide to dance for a living?

12) Of the two books combined, which one of the girls has shown the least growth? Which one has shown the most growth?

Dear Readers,

Did the ladies show and tell like I said they would? I think so. I enjoyed catching up with these four friends and it's sad to say goodbye to them . . . for now. I started the book thinking this was it for Mo, Dom, Alizé, and Cris but once I typed the last page of the book I knew I couldn't say farewell to them forever. So one day in the future I will revisit these four crazy friends in their late twenties or early thirties and see just what their lives have become. In the meanwhile, I am working on some even crazier stories for you all. I have plenty of tales to tell.

Be good, y'all,
N.